HARDCASTLE'S BURGLAR

Recent Titles by Graham Ison from Severn House

The Hardcastle Series

HARDCASTLE'S SPY
HARDCASTLE'S ARMISTICE
HARDCASTLE'S CONSPIRACY
HARDCASTLE'S AIRMEN
HARDCASTLE'S ACTRESS
HARDCASTLE'S BURGLAR

Contemporary Police Procedurals

DIVISION
DRUMFIRE
KICKING THE AIR
LIGHT FANTASTIC
LOST OR FOUND
WHIPLASH
WHISPERING GRASS
WORKING GIRL

HARDCASTLE'S BURGLAR

A Hardcastle and Marriott
Historical Mystery

Graham Ison

This first world edition published 2008
in Great Britain and the USA by
SEVERN HOUSE PUBLISHERS LTD of
9–15 High Street, Sutton, Surrey SM1 1DF.

British Library Cataloguing in Publication Data

Ison, Graham
  Hardcastle's burglar
  1. Hardcastle, Detective Inspector (Fictitious character) -
  Fiction 2. Police - England - London - Fiction 3. World
  War, 1914-1918 - Social aspects - England - London -
  Fiction 4. Great Britain - History - George V, 1910-1936 -
  Fiction 5. Detective and mystery stories
  I. Title
  823.9'14[F]

  ISBN-13: 978-0-7278-6631-8   (cased)

All Severn House titles are printed on acid-free paper.

Typeset by Palimpsest Book Production Ltd.,
Grangemouth, Stirlingshire, Scotland.
Printed and bound in Great Britain by
MPG Books Ltd., Bodmin, Cornwall.

Glossary

ALBERT: a watch chain of the type worn by Albert, Prince Consort (1819–61).
APM: assistant provost marshal (a lieutenant colonel of the military police).

BAILEY, the: Central Criminal Court, London.
BAILIWICK: area of responsibility.
BEF: British Expeditionary Force in France and Flanders.
BOB: a shilling (now 5p).
BRADSHAW: a timetable giving routes and times of British railway services.

CARNEY: cunning, sly.
CID: Criminal Investigation Department.
COCK-AND-BULL STORY: an idle, silly or incredible story.
COMMISSIONER'S OFFICE: official title of New Scotland Yard, headquarters of the Metropolitan Police.
COPPER: a policeman.
CRIB: a house.
CROWN-AND-ANCHOR: a game played with dice marked with crowns and anchors.
CULLY: alternative to calling a man 'mate'.

DDI: Divisional Detective Inspector.
DIP: a pickpocket, or to steal from the pocket.
DOG'S DINNER, a: a mess.
DOOLALLY-TAP: of unsound mind (*ex* Hindi from the town of Deolali near Bombay).

DUMMY: a wallet.

EIGHT O'CLOCK WALK, to take the: to be hanged.

FEEL THE COLLAR, to: to make an arrest.
FENCE: a receiver of stolen property.
FENCE, to: to dispose of stolen property.
FIND THE LADY: a three-card trick, the 'lady' being a solitary queen alongside two nondescript cards, placed face down. Bets are placed on which one is the queen.
FLASH IN THE PAN: an abortive effort.
FLUFF, a bit of: a girl; an attractive young woman.
FRONT, the: theatre of WW1 operations in France and Flanders.

GOC: general officer commanding.
GUNNERS, the: a generic term to encompass the Royal Horse Artillery, the Royal Garrison Artillery and the Royal Field Artillery.
GUV *or* **GUV'NOR:** informal alternative to 'sir'.

HAP'ORTH: halfpenny-worth; taken to mean worthless.
HAVILDAR: a native sergeant in the Indian Army.

IRON: a firearm, especially a handgun.

JILDI: quickly (*ex* Hindi).

KATE short for **KATE CARNEY:** army (rhyming slang: from Kate Carney, a music hall comedienne of the late 19th early 20th century).

LINEN DRAPERS: newspapers (rhyming slang).

MANOR: a police area.
MONS, to make a: to make a mess of things, as in the disastrous Battle of Mons in 1914.

NICK: a police station or prison.
NICKED: arrested.
NOSE, a: an informant.

OLD BAILEY: Central Criminal Court, London.

PEPPER-AND-SALT TROUSERS: black trousers flecked with grey.
PLATES: feet (rhyming slang: plates of meat).
POT AND PAN, OLD: father (rhyming slang: old man).

QUEER IN THE ATTIC: of unsound mind.
QUID: £1 sterling.

ROZZER: a policeman.
RSM: regimental sergeant major (a senior warrant officer).

SAA: small arms ammunition.
SAUSAGE AND MASH: cash (rhyming slang).
SELL THE PUP, to: to attempt to deceive.
SHIFT, to do a: to run away, or escape.
SHILLING: now 5p.
SMOKE, The: London.
SOMERSET HOUSE: formerly the records office of births, deaths and marriages for England & Wales.
SPALPEEN: a rascal; a worthless fellow.
SPIN A TWIST, to: to tell an unbelievable tale.
SPONDOOLICKS: money.

TAPE(S): the chevron(s) indicating a non-commissioned officer's rank.
TOPPED: murdered or hanged.
TOPPING: a murder or hanging.
TUMBLE, a: sexual intercourse.
TWO-AND-EIGHT, in a: in a state (rhyming slang).

WIPERS: Army slang for Ypres in Belgium, scene of several fierce Great War battles.

One

'*Great Naval Battle off Jutland – Kitchener drowned – read all about it.*' Outside Westminster Underground station, a lad with an armful of newspapers was shouting the news.

Wondering what a field marshal had been doing at a sea battle, Ernest Hardcastle alighted from the tram that had brought him from Kennington Road. In his hurry to reach the pavement – the trams crossed Westminster Bridge in the centre of the road – he narrowly avoided being knocked over by an errand boy on a bicycle.

Hurriedly thrusting a halfpenny into the young newsvendor's hand, Hardcastle seized a copy of the *Daily Mirror*. It was not his favourite newspaper – he normally took the *Daily Mail* – but he was anxious to know the details.

That morning, the sixth of June, 1916, the nation had been stunned to learn that HMS *Hampshire* had struck a mine off Scapa Flow at twenty minutes to eight the previous evening, and that the Secretary of State for War, Field Marshal the Earl Kitchener, was among those who had drowned.

The famous poster of Kitchener's pointing finger, and the exhortation: 'Your Country Needs You', had recruited millions to the service battalions of the British Army in France and Flanders. It was difficult to comprehend that the man was now dead, as were so many of those he had encouraged and cajoled to join the Colours.

As for the Battle of Jutland – which proved to have nothing to do with Kitchener – the full details were only just emerging. Although acclaimed as a victory for the

Royal Navy, the losses were stark. The British had lost
7,000 men and fourteen ships, against the Germans's 3,000
casualties and eleven ships.

Still reading the detailed accounts of both incidents,
Hardcastle walked down Cannon Row to his police station.
The awesome building, and the grim, grey edifice of New
Scotland Yard opposite, had been constructed of Dartmoor
granite hewn, fittingly, by convicts.

'Good morning, sir. All correct.' The elderly policeman,
his four stripes testifying that he was a station sergeant,
stood up. 'Have you heard the news, sir?' The officer placed
the charge book on his desk.

'Yes, I have.' Assuming that the sergeant was talking
about Kitchener, Hardcastle spoke tersely; he had a feeling
that everyone at the station was going to pose this same
question. But to him there were other matters more pressing.
As the divisional detective inspector of the A or Whitehall
Division of the Metropolitan Police, he made it his practice to examine the charge book every morning. Sitting
down in the station officer's chair and putting on his glasses,
he thumbed through the pages of the large volume, seeking
information of any arrests that had been made since he had
left the station the previous evening.

Satisfied that three drunkards and two petty thieves did
not warrant his immediate attention, Hardcastle went
upstairs to his office.

Detective Sergeant Charles Marriott was waiting. 'Have
you heard the news, sir?' he asked.

'Yes,' snapped Hardcastle. Never one to waste words, he
assumed that Marriott, like the sergeant downstairs, was
talking about the loss of Kitchener. 'And you can tell the
rest of 'em in there,' he added, cocking a thumb in the
direction of the detectives' office, 'that I've read all about
Kitchener, and I've read all about Jutland, so they won't
have to keep pestering me with the same stupid bloody
question.' He could foresee a day of people enquiring
whether he had heard about the field marshal's death, and
the naval engagement in that area of the North Sea the
Germans called Skagerrak.

'Very good, sir.' Marriott rapidly surmised that his DDI was not in the best of moods this morning. But what he was about to tell him would, Marriott feared, only make matters worse.

'Anything happening?' It was a question Hardcastle asked his first-class sergeant every day on his arrival at Cannon Row. He sat down behind his desk and began to fill his pipe.

'Yes, sir. Mr Fitnam's gone sick.'

'What?' exclaimed Hardcastle, glaring at his sergeant. 'What the blue blazes has Mr Fitnam's state of health got to do with me, Marriott?' he demanded. Arthur Fitnam was the DDI in charge of the Criminal Investigation Department of V Division at Wandsworth, some five miles away from Scotland Yard.

'A sergeant from Commissioner's Office brought a message across from Mr Wensley, sir, not ten minutes ago. There's been a murder at Kingston, and Mr Wensley's directed that you investigate it.' Marriott placed a sheet of paper on the DDI's desk.

Hardcastle donned his spectacles and read through the brief note from Detective Chief Inspector Frederick Wensley, the head of the CID at Scotland Yard. It informed him that Colonel Sir Adrian Rivers had been found murdered at his home on Kingston Hill early that morning, and concluded with the instruction: 'In view of DDI Fitnam's incapacity you are hereby directed immediately to undertake the investigation.'

'God dammit!' Hardcastle was furious that Wensley always appeared to take the view that nothing of importance ever happened on A Division, and that its DDI could be spared for out-of-town jobs. But only those serving on what was known informally as the 'Royal' A Division appreciated its problems. With Buckingham Palace, St James's Palace, Parliament, Downing Street, Westminster Abbey and the government offices in Whitehall all within his area of responsibility, Hardcastle was aware that it was the most sensitive division in the whole of the 800 square miles of the Metropolitan Police District. But he said nothing of this to Marriott. It would be most improper to criticize a superior officer to a subordinate.

'Easiest way to get there, sir, is a train from Waterloo to Norbiton and then a taxi.' Marriott, knowing that Hardcastle would want to know, had already checked in Bradshaw, the comprehensive railway timetable, and had details of the route at his fingertips.

Hardcastle grunted, and glanced at his chrome hunter pocket watch before dropping it back into his waistcoat pocket. 'I suppose we'd better go and see what this is all about, then, Marriott.' And seizing his umbrella and bowler hat, he made for the door.

The Grange, Sir Adrian Rivers's imposing ivy-clad house, was in Penny Lane, a quiet turning off Kingston Hill. A gravel drive wound its way around the edge of a spacious front lawn to a flight of steps that led up to the front door. That and the windows were gothic in design, the entire façade giving the impression that it had originally been a parsonage. But a tower had been added to one side of the house at a later date, the effect of which was to lend the dwelling a lopsided aspect. To the right, and some way back from the building line, was a stable, the doors of which were open to reveal a Rolls Royce Silver Ghost.

'There's a bit of sausage and mash here, Marriott,' was Hardcastle's only comment as they mounted the steps.

'Can I help you, sir?' A policeman stepped in front of Hardcastle, barring the way.

'DDI Hardcastle of A, and I'm here to look into this here murder.'

'Very good, sir.' The PC stepped back and gave the bell pull a sharp tug.

The man who answered the door was attired in black jacket and pepper-and-salt trousers.

'Good morning, sir. May I help you?'

'Police,' said Hardcastle. 'Are you the butler?'

'Yes, sir. Beach is my name.' The butler half bowed, exuding deference.

'Good. Where's this here body?'

'*Sir Adrian* is in the main bedroom, sir.' Beach raised his eyebrows, clearly taking exception to what he perceived to be a lack of respect for his dead master.

'Lead the way, then. I haven't got all day.' Hardcastle pushed past the butler and stopped in the tiled entrance hall. There were several doors leading from it, and a winding staircase to one side. At the foot of the stairs stood another policeman.

With a sniff and a raised chin, the butler mounted the stairs and indicated a door. A third policeman was seated on a chair outside.

'What are you supposed to be doing?' demanded Hardcastle.

Sensing that he was in the presence of authority, the policeman stood up. 'Er, guarding the scene, sir.'

'Is that a fact?' commented Hardcastle sarcastically. 'Well, you won't do it sitting on your arse.' It was an unfair comment, but the DDI was still incensed that he had been saddled with a murder enquiry that was rightly the responsibility of V Division's detectives. And in the absence of the DDI, the investigation should have fallen to Fitnam's deputy, Detective Inspector Edward Robson. If a similar situation had arisen on A Division, Detective Inspector Edgar Rhodes, Hardcastle's second-in-command, could certainly have been entrusted to deal with it. What Hardcastle did not know, however, was that Robson was already investigating a serious crime on the other side of the division.

The room that Hardcastle entered was spacious. Heavy crimson velvet curtains were drawn across the windows so that it was difficult to see.

A man scrambled to his feet from an armchair. 'I take it you're Mr Hardcastle, sir. I'm Detective Sergeant Atkins from Kingston. We was told you was coming.'

'Were you the first on the scene, Atkins?'

'Not exactly, sir. I was the first CID officer to get here. After the PC on the beat had attended, that is.' Atkins paused. 'Have you heard the news about Kitchener, sir?'

'Yes, I bloody have,' snapped Hardcastle, 'and you can

pull those curtains for a start. I can't see a damned thing in here.'

Daylight revealed that the room was surprisingly Spartan, a simplicity that Hardcastle attributed to Colonel Rivers's military background. Although there was little in the way of furniture, the walls were covered almost entirely with pictures, mainly prints of racehorses. A mound beneath the eiderdown on the huge bed indicated the presence of a body.

'Who did that?' demanded Hardcastle, pointing at the sheet that had been drawn up to cover the occupant's face.

'I believe the butler did it, sir.'

'I hope you're not trying to be funny, Atkins,' said Hardcastle, fixing the Kingston sergeant with a hostile stare.

Standing by the door, Marriott smiled; unlike Atkins, he was accustomed to the DDI's bizarre sense of humour.

'Oh no, sir,' said Atkins hurriedly. 'I meant that I imagined the butler pulled the sheet up to cover Sir Adrian's face.'

'Imagined, eh? I don't like officers who go about imagining things, Atkins. Tell me what you actually know. By the way, this here's DS Marriott, my first-class.'

The sergeants acknowledged each other with a nod.

'PC 62 Draper was the first officer on the scene, sir. He'd come on early turn at six o'clock this morning, and arrived in the lane about half past. On his bicycle, sir. The butler – that's Beach, sir – was standing at the gate, looking up and down the lane. He called Draper and told him that the colonel had been shot, sir.'

'Fetch Draper up here.' With an eye for detail, Hardcastle had noted that the PC on duty at the front door wore the divisional number 62V on his collar and his helmet plate.

'I'll go down and get him, sir.'

'Don't you go, man,' snapped Hardcastle irritably. 'Send that PC who's idling outside the door. Seems to me there's bloody coppers all over the place doing bugger all. He can relieve Draper on the front door until I'm through with him. And while you're about it, tell Beach I want to see him.'

While he was waiting, Hardcastle uncovered Sir Adrian Rivers's face. A wound on the victim's forehead was commensurate with the entry of a bullet, and a puddling of blood on the pillow implied that there would be an exit wound at the back of the skull. But Hardcastle forbore from examining the body too closely. He was no expert in the finer points of determining the cause of death, and knew that he would have to await the arrival of a pathologist.

Atkins returned to the room, and, as if reading Hardcastle's mind, said, 'By the way, sir, Dr Spilsbury's been sent for.'

'Good. How long ago?'

Atkins took out his watch and glanced at it. 'About seven o'clock, sir.'

Hardcastle grunted an acknowledgement. 'Should be here soon, then.'

'Have you seen the pillow, sir?'

'Don't talk in riddles, Atkins. What are you going on about?'

'There's a pillow on the floor on the other side of the bed, sir. There's a hole in it, and powder marks. Looks as though it was used to muffle the sound of the gunshot.'

'Leave it there. I'll look at it later.'

PC Draper appeared in the doorway and coughed deferentially. 'You wanted me, sir?'

'Sergeant Atkins says that you were the first officer on the scene, Draper. Is that correct?'

'Yes, sir.'

'Tell me about it.'

Draper extracted his pocketbook and thumbed through the pages. 'I was patrolling my beat on a bicycle, sir, and approached The Grange – that's this house, sir – when I was accosted by Mr Beach, the butler. He informed me that there had been a suspicious death, namely that Sir Adrian Rivers had been found in his bed, shot, sir.'

'Was it Beach who found him?'

'I don't know, sir.'

'You don't know? Well, didn't you ask him, man?'

'Er, no, sir. I thought it was a matter for the CID to ask those questions. Anyway, I attended the bedroom – this bedroom, sir – and satisfied myself that Sir Adrian was indeed deceased.'

'How did you do that?'

'I felt for a pulse, sir, but there wasn't one. I then tele-
phoned the police station for assistance, sir.'

Hardcastle sighed and shook his head. 'You might as well
get back to the front door, lad. And when Dr Spilsbury
arrives, bring him up here.'

'Very good, sir.' Looking somewhat relieved, PC Draper
departed.

'Did *you* question anyone about who discovered Rivers's
body, Atkins?' Hardcastle was beginning to get more and
more exasperated at the apparent indolence of the V Division
officers.

'No, sir. Once we was informed that you was on your
way, I thought it better to leave it.'

'I don't know, Marriott, it seems to me that a lot more
than murder has to happen on V Division before anyone
gets too bloody excited about it.' Hardcastle was about to
add that he was surprised that Arthur Fitnam allowed such
slackness, but kept that thought to himself.

'I understand you wished to see me, sir.' The butler stood
in the doorway.

'Did you pull that sheet up over Sir Adrian's head, Beach?'

'I instructed the footman to do it, sir. Out of respect for
the dead, so to speak.'

'Well, you've interfered with a murder scene, and I won't
have it, d'you understand?'

'Yes, sir. I'm sorry, sir.'

'Good. Did you touch anything else?'

'No, sir, that's all I did.'

'Is there a Lady Rivers, Mr Beach?' asked Marriott.

'That there is, sir,' said Beach, turning to face the sergeant.
'Muriel, Lady Rivers. They was only married a couple of
years back. In 1914, I think it was. Lady Lavinia, Sir
Adrian's first wife, died of the consumption. Only a young
woman, she was. Tragic. Daughter of the Earl of Aubrey,
you know. Give the colonel a couple of sons, she did. Ewart
– he's the eldest – is a general now, and heir to the baronetcy.
And Gerard's a colonel. Both over the other side, of course.
All Surrey Rifles: the colonel and the two sons.'

'Distinguished soldier, was he, Beach?' asked Hardcastle. 'Sir Adrian, I mean.'

'I've known him for years, sir. I was his orderly, through thick and thin. Oh yes, me and the colonel was with Kitchener at the conquest of the Sudan back in '98, the battle of Omdurman. But the regiment was sent down to Mafeking in time for Bobs – that's Lord Roberts – to take part in the relief.' Beach paused. 'Month o' May, 1900, that was. The colonel'd've been fair upset to hear about Lord Kitchener, and that's a fact. I s'pose you've heard about Lord Kitchener, sir?'

Hardcastle ignored the question. 'How long were you a soldier, Beach?'

'Did me full time, sir. I 'listed as a boy bugler back in '87, and come out in 1912. Couldn't find a billet, as you might say, and so I called here to see if the colonel could help out. I mean, I wasn't looking for a job here, but the colonel said as how he was short of a butler and he took me on the strength. The Surrey Rifles is not only a regiment, but a family, as you might say. Well, I'd better get about my chores.' Beach paused, glancing at the body of his late master. 'What's going to happen about the colonel, sir?'

'There'll be an ambulance arriving shortly to take him away, Beach.'

'I'd better be getting on, then, sir. I've plenty of jobs to occupy me, though God knows what'll happen to us now. I doubt that her ladyship'll want to stay here. Anyway, I'll be about the house if you need me.'

'Don't you go rushing off just yet,' said Hardcastle. 'Where *is* Lady Rivers?'

'In her room, sir, with the doctor.'

'Doctor? What's the matter with her?'

'I'm afraid the news of Sir Adrian's death took her rather queer, sir, and she was overcome with the vapours. I deemed it best to call the doctor, sir.'

'Really?' said Hardcastle, unimpressed with Beach's description of Lady Rivers's indisposition. 'Well, I'll have to see her at some time.'

'How many staff have you got here, Mr Beach?' asked Marriott, pocketbook at the ready.

'I've only got the one footman now, sir, on account of the war. He's called Digby. The second footman joined the Grenadiers and got hisself killed in Wipers. Then there's the parlour maid, Daisy Forbes she's called. Mrs Blunden's the cook, and the coachman's name is Daniel Good.'

Hardcastle looked up in surprise. 'Unfortunate name for a coachman,' he commented. Daniel Good was the name of a notorious coachman who had been hanged over seventy years previously for murdering his pregnant common-law wife in Roehampton, some four miles away. 'Who drives that Rolls-Royce, then?'

'Daniel Good does, sir. But the colonel always called him the coachman. I don't think he thought much of them new-fangled motor cars, but her ladyship insisted on having one. Cost nigh on fourteen hundred pounds, but Sir Adrian never denied her ladyship a thing, sir.' Beach lowered his voice, as though in fear of being overheard. 'I'm afraid Sir Adrian wasn't the man he used to be, sir. His memory had gone, you see, and sometimes he talked gibberish.'

'Did the doctor ever see him about it?'

'That he did, but there was nothing that could be done, so he said.'

'Is that the doctor who's with Lady Rivers now?'

'Yes, sir.'

'In that case, I'll have a word with him before he goes,' said Hardcastle, 'but in the meantime, I'll need a room where I can interview the staff. Can you arrange that?'

'Indeed, sir. Probably the best place would be the library.'

'Good. Now then, who found Sir Adrian's body?'

'That was Digby, sir. He always brings the colonel a cup of tea at six o'clock sharp every morning. Quite took aback, sir, he was, to find the colonel lying there dead. He called me, of course, and I went out looking for a policeman. Luckily, it was Charlie Draper. He's often on this beat and usually comes in for a cup of tea round about half past six.'

'Does he indeed?' Hardcastle's tone implied criticism, even though cadging cups of tea was a practice he had

followed himself when he was a uniformed constable at
Old Street, over twenty years ago.

But Hardcastle's conversation with the butler was cut
short by raised voices outside. He threw up the window
and peered out.

'What the blue blazes is going on down there, Draper?'

The PC looked up. 'This man says he's Dr Spilsbury, sir,
but he don't have no means of identification.'

'He *is* Dr Spilsbury, you fool. Bring him up here this
instant.' Hardcastle withdrew his head, banging it in the
process. 'God dammit!' he muttered, and turned to the
Kingston sergeant. 'Don't your people read newspapers
down here in the sticks, Atkins?'

The previous June, Dr Bernard Spilsbury's photograph
had appeared in most of the newspapers. The damning
evidence he had given against George Joseph Smith in the
notorious 'Brides in the Bath' case had established Spilsbury
as one of the country's foremost forensic pathologists. During
Smith's trial at the Old Bailey, a nurse, attired in a swim-
suit, had nearly drowned when Detective Inspector Neil
demonstrated how Smith had murdered his wives by seizing
their ankles and dragging their heads underwater. The newspapers had mistakenly attributed the experiment to Spilsbury,
and it was characteristic of him that he had never denied it.

'Ah, Hardcastle, we meet again.' The tall figure of
Spilsbury strode into the room. 'What on earth are you
doing down here at Kingston? Not got enough to do in
Westminster, eh?'

'That appears to be the view of my superiors, Doctor,'
said Hardcastle drily.

'Well now, what have we here?' Spilsbury put his
Gladstone bag down on the washstand and crossed to the
bed. 'I don't think we have too many problems here,' he
said, after a few minutes' examination. 'Perhaps you'd have
the cadaver removed to St Mary's Hospital at Paddington.
I'll do my post-mortem examination there.'

'Before you go, Dr Spilsbury, I wonder if I could impose
on you to have a word with the family doctor. He's here at
the moment attending Lady Rivers. But Beach the butler

reckons that Sir Adrian was a bit queer in the head, and I think his doctor would be more forthcoming with you than he would with me, seeing as how you're both in the same trade, so to speak.'

Spilsbury smiled. 'Certainly, Hardcastle.'

Twenty minutes later, Spilsbury returned. 'The family doctor is of the view that Sir Adrian was suffering from advanced senile dementia, Hardcastle. According to him, the colonel had absolutely no idea what was going on around him. Does that help?'

'Remains to be seen, Dr Spilsbury,' rejoined Hardcastle cautiously.

'You may also wish to know that the family doctor has prescribed a sedative for Lady Rivers. She's apparently still in shock. Not surprising really.'

Beach reappeared in the doorway. 'I've got the footman Digby in the library, sir, if you wish to see him now.'

The library was a gloomy room in which there was a strong aroma of leather and furniture polish.

'You're Digby, the footman, are you?'

'Yes, sir.' John Digby, a stooped and grey-haired retainer in his fifties, had the demeanour of a man who had spent all his working life in service.

'I'm told that you discovered Sir Adrian's body, Digby.'

'Indeed I did, sir. A terrible shock it was, finding the master lying there dead.'

'Tell me about it.' With a wave of the hand, Hardcastle indicated that the footman should sit down.

'Sir Adrian always insisted on being called at six o'clock in the morning, sir. I'd take him tea, open the curtains, and then . . .'

'Just a minute. Did you open the curtains?'

'Yes, sir.'

'But they were closed when I went into the room.'

'Yes, sir. Once I told Mr Beach about the tragedy, he instructed me to close them again. Out of respect, like, sir.'

'God Almighty!' muttered Hardcastle. 'How about the windows, Digby? Were they open or shut?'

'Oh, they was open, sir. Sir Adrian always had the bottom of the windows open wide, summer and winter. I'm surprised he never caught his death of cold.'

'But they were closed when I examined the room.'

'Yes, sir. But Mr Beach—'

'Yes, all right. Beach told you to close them out of respect for the dead.'

'Yes, sir.'

'Was there a pillow across his face when you found him?'

Digby appeared puzzled by the question. 'No, sir. The colonel was just lying there with a hole in his head.'

'So, having found Sir Adrian dead, what did you do next?'

'I went down to the pantry, sir, and informed Mr Beach. He was starting to clean the silver, sir. He always does that of a Tuesday, and—'

'And Beach called the police. Is that right?'

'That's correct.'

'How close to Sir Adrian's room d'you sleep, Digby?'

'Oh, nowhere near, sir. All the staff has rooms on the top floor at the back. And one or two of them are in the tower. And Mr Good sleeps over the stable.'

'Nevertheless, did you hear anything untoward during the night?'

'What, like noises, an' that, sir?'

'Exactly like that.'

'No, sir, nothing.' Digby's face assumed a mournful expression, as though regretting that he could not help the police in their quest for his master's murderer.

'At what time did you last see Sir Adrian alive?'

'That'd be ten o'clock last evening, sir. The colonel always has a cup of cocoa at ten o'clock. Not a minute before, not a minute after.'

'There was no cocoa cup there this morning.'

'No, sir. I removed it when I took the tea this morning.'

Hardcastle raised his eyes to the ceiling but said nothing. 'That'll be all for the time being, Digby. Perhaps you'd send in the parlour maid. What's her name?'

'Daisy, sir. Daisy Forbes.'

The parlour maid was a mature woman, probably in her

mid-thirties. Nevertheless, her brief interview with Hardcastle and Marriott was punctuated by sobs, and every so often she dabbed at her eyes with a corner of her apron, but she was unable to offer any information that would assist the police in their search for Colonel Rivers's killer.

Hardcastle let out a sigh. 'We're getting nowhere, Marriott.' He took out his watch. 'I suppose we'd better see what we can do about finding something to eat,' he said.

But that problem was solved for the two detectives almost immediately.

Two

'Cook thought you gentlemen might be getting a bit peckish, sir,' said Beach, entering the library as a tearful Daisy Forbes left to go about her duties. 'She apologizes that it's only a cold meal, but there's a pint of the colonel's specially brewed beer there for you.'

'That'll do handsomely, Beach.'

'If you care to follow me, sir.' The butler led the two detectives down the back stairs to the kitchen. 'This is Mrs Blunden, the cook, sir,' he said, indicating a large, homely woman with a red face and laughing eyes.

'I'd've got you something hot, sir,' said Mrs Blunden, 'but we're all in a bit of a two an' eight this morning, with the dreadful news of the colonel being murdered like that.' She put a dish of butter on the table, and set out plates of cheese, homemade bread, pickled onions, some cold meat and chutney, and a few leaves of lettuce. 'Specially coming on top of poor Lord Kitchener being drowned. I s'pose you've heard about that, have you, sir?'

'Yes, I have, Mrs Blunden. Dreadful news.' Hardcastle was wearying of people asking if he was aware of Kitchener's death – an event that did not greatly disturb him – but on this occasion he kept his response civil. The cook had, after all, gone to the trouble of preparing lunch for him and Marriott.

'Awful business, the colonel dying in his bed like that, after all he'd been through, sir,' said Beach. He drew tankards of beer from a barrel on the far side of the kitchen, and placed them in front of the two detectives.

'I suppose so,' said Hardcastle, speaking through a mouthful of bread and cheese.

'How is Lady Rivers taking the death of her husband?' asked Marriott.

But before Beach had a chance to answer, Mrs Blunden voiced her opinion. 'Some lady, that one,' she scoffed loudly, turning from the kitchen range. There was sarcasm in her voice, and Hardcastle would not have long to wait before learning the reason for it.

'The doctor gave her ladyship something to calm her nerves, sir,' said Beach, ignoring Mrs Blunden's outburst. 'And now, if you'll excuse me, sir, I have matters to attend to.'

'There's one thing I want you to do, Beach,' said Hardcastle.

'What's that, sir?' Beach paused in the doorway.

'Have a look round and tell me whether anything's been stolen.' Hardcastle was in little doubt at this stage of his investigation that the death of Sir Adrian Rivers had occurred during a burglary.

'Very good, sir. We have an inventory of Sir Adrian's valued possessions. He was very particular about that.'

'I get the impression that you don't much care for the present Lady Rivers, Mrs Blunden,' suggested Hardcastle, once Beach had departed to begin his search.

Mrs Blunden wiped her hands on her apron and sat down at the kitchen table. 'She might be entitled to call herself a lady, Mr Hardcastle, but she don't behave like a lady. A flighty piece of goods is that one, and no better than she ought to be.'

Hardcastle took a pull at his beer and waited. He knew that women like Mrs Blunden were useful sources of information who, once started, would be very difficult to stop. And that suited his purpose.

'She's only half Sir Adrian's age, you know,' the cook continued. 'I don't know what he saw in her, 'cept she was ready to jump into his bed before you could say knife. Talk about mutton dressed as lamb. But that's a man all over. Get a pretty woman set her cap at him, and he's putty in her hands.' She uttered a derisive laugh. 'And she spent his money like it was her own. Always down here interfering, an' all. You'd never have seen Lady Lavinia in the kitchen, and that's a fact.'

'Lady Lavinia?' queried Hardcastle, wishing to confirm what Beach had told him.

'The colonel's first wife, sir. Now she *was* a lady, through and through. She always said as how below stairs was the servants' home and the family had no right coming down here. I remember years ago she caught young Master Gerard coming up from the kitchen – well, not this one – after he'd been swanking about playing cricket for Harrow against Eton. Cor! He didn't half get an earful from her ladyship.'

'When you said not *this* kitchen, Mrs Blunden, what did you mean?'

'It was during the summer holidays, sir. In them days the family always spent summer in the country, and, of course, the staff had to go too. Sir Adrian's got a place at Tolney Reach in Wiltshire. Markham Hall, it is. Been in the family for generations. He was the ninth baronet, you see, sir.' Mrs Blunden paused in thought. 'I s'pose that makes Master Ewart the new baronet,' she mused. And with a laugh, added, 'We'll have to watch our Ps and Qs from now on.'

'Where is Sir Ewart, Mrs Blunden?' A slave to protocol, Hardcastle promptly accorded Sir Adrian's eldest son the title to which he believed he must now be entitled. But in that regard, he later learned, he was in error. 'Beach said he was over the other side. I suppose he meant France.'

'Glory be, he'll have to be told, the poor dear,' said Mrs Blunden, putting a hand to her mouth. 'Yes, I think he's in France, Mr Hardcastle, but I don't know for sure.'

'I'll look after it, Mrs Blunden. I know people at the War Office who'll take care of seeing that he's informed. But you were telling me about Lady Rivers.'

Mrs Blunden lowered her voice to a conspiratorial tone and, leaning across the table, linked her reddened hands. 'I don't know for sure, Mr Hardcastle, but I'm told Sir Adrian was introduced to her at some race meeting. A great one for point-to-points and racing was Sir Adrian. Loved horses, he did. As a matter of fact, he had a string of racehorses hisself at one time. Kept stables alongside Markham Hall.'

'When did he meet her?' asked Hardcastle, still intent on checking Beach's account.

'July 1914 they was wed, down in Wiltshire at the local country church. Very quiet it was, hardly any guests outside the family. But the minute she'd got that ring on her finger, there was no holding her. I wouldn't mind betting that it was her that brought on Sir Adrian's illness.'

'What illness was that?' asked Hardcastle, affecting surprise. Even though he had heard the professional diagnosis from Dr Spilsbury, he liked to learn someone else's version.

'Not to put too fine a point on it, Mr Hardcastle, I reckon it was after her ladyship come on the scene that the master started going a bit doolally-tap. What with her lording it about the place with her syrupy "Adrian darling" this, and "Adrian darling" that. Enough to drive anyone a bit queer in the attic, that sort of talk. Sir Adrian began by forgetting things. Most unlike him that was. He'd ask something, and you'd tell him, and then five minutes later he'd ask it again, and swear you'd never told him. Practically gaga now he is, the poor dear. Or was.'

Hardcastle had dismissed the three policemen who had been posted to the house, but retained the services of Detective Sergeant Atkins.

Standing outside the house beneath Sir Adrian Rivers's bedroom, the three detectives gazed up at the colonel's window.

'A fit man could've been up that ivy like a rat up a drain-pipe, Marriott,' said Hardcastle. 'And given that the colonel always slept with the windows open, he could've been through there a bit quick.'

'You're thinking it was a burglary that went wrong, then, sir,' said Atkins.

'You got a better idea?' muttered Hardcastle. 'The sooner that Beach comes up with a list of anything that's been stolen, the sooner we can start looking for a likely dancer.'

'A dancer, sir?' queried the mystified Atkins.

'You've spent too long at a country nick, Atkins,' said

Hardcastle. 'A dancer's a cat burglar, my lad, and I reckon we've got one who shinned up there and did the deed.' He glanced at the ivy and then turned to Marriott. 'Your eyes are younger than mine. Have a look.'

Marriott studied the ivy for a moment or two. 'It's possible it's been disturbed, sir, and there's a few marks around the base, like someone might have jumped the last few feet on his way down. But there are no discernible footprints.'

'Not much to go on there, then, Marriott, but we'll find Beach and see what he's got to say.'

The butler was in the hall when the detectives returned to the house. 'Ah, I was just coming to see you, sir. I've checked against the inventory, and there's a few pieces missing.'

'Well, are you going to let me into the secret, Beach?' Hardcastle was always impatient with people who dithered.

'Sir Adrian's three sets of gold cufflinks are gone, together with his gold hunter pocket watch, and his medals, sir,' said Beach, referring to a list in his hand. 'He had a DSO, and the Sudan and Africa Medals. Oh, and the CB, sir. And that's what is called a neck order. Worn round the neck, you see, sir. All of 'em were kept in a drawer in his bedroom.'

'What do all those letters stand for?' asked Hardcastle, irritated as always by the military terminology that soldiers used.

'DSO is the Distinguished Service Order, and the CB is because he's a Companion of the Order of the Bath,' explained Beach. 'I should've mentioned that first, because it takes precedence over the DSO. And I should know; I had to polish them often enough.'

'Don't medals have the names of the recipient engraved on them?' asked Marriott casually. Having a relative in the army, he was more conversant than Hardcastle with military matters.

'Some of 'em do, sir,' said Beach. 'I can see you know about that. In the army, were you?'

'No,' said Marriot, 'but my brother-in-law's a sergeant major in the Middlesex Regiment.'

'Now you mention it,' continued Beach, 'Sir Adrian had

his medals privately engraved with his name. The DSO in particular, I seem to recall, because that one's awarded without an engraving.'

'Make 'em more difficult to fence, then,' commented Hardcastle. 'Or if they have been knocked out to some pawnbroker, easier to trace. Anything else missing?'

'Not that I can see, sir. All the colonel's paintings are still there, and so's his racing trophies.'

'What about guns?' asked Hardcastle. 'Did he keep any?'

'There's a gunroom, sir, where the colonel had his hunting rifles and shotguns, but they're all in locked cabinets. None of them's missing.'

'There's not much shooting to be had in Kingston, surely?' asked Hardcastle, with a raised eyebrow.

Beach smiled. 'Good Lord no, sir. But the colonel was always insistent that wherever he went, the guns came too. But he only ever used them when he was down at Markham Hall.'

'Even so, I'll need to have a look at them later on. In the meantime, ask Lady Rivers when she'll be prepared to see me. And that'll be sooner rather than later.' In view of Mrs Blunden's opinion of the lady of the house, Hardcastle was by no means convinced that Sir Adrian's widow had been overcome by the news of his death.

'Very good, sir,' said Beach, and was about to depart when Daisy Forbes appeared through the door from the staircase leading to the basement.

'Excuse me, Mr Beach, but there's someone at the front door.'

'How d'you know that, Daisy?' Hardcastle was mystified that the three detectives and Beach were standing not two yards from the door, but had heard nothing.

'It only rings downstairs in the kitchen, sir. Her ladyship wouldn't have no bells ringing up here. She said it disturbed her when she was in the drawing room. So the one up here was disconnected.'

'Thank you, Daisy,' said Beach, and strode across the hall to swing open the heavy door. 'There's some ambulance men out here, sir,' he said, turning to face the DDI.

'About bloody time,' muttered Hardcastle. 'Bring them in, Atkins,' he added, and began to ascend the broad staircase.

Under Hardcastle's supervision, the attendants, two burly men in uniform, lifted Sir Adrian Rivers's body on to a stretcher. After a deal of complex manoeuvring, they managed to get it down the stairs and into their vehicle.

'You go with them, Atkins.'

'Go with them, sir?' The Kingston sergeant looked up in alarm.

'It's called continuity of evidence, Atkins,' said Hardcastle, unable to keep the exasperation out of his voice. 'We wouldn't want someone saying that the body had been swapped with someone else's would we, not before we see Sir Adrian's murderer dangling on the end of a rope? And then I want you back here.'

'Very good, sir.' Atkins was unhappy that he would have to go all the way to Paddington and find his own way back to Kingston Hill. Particularly as his limited experience of murder did not encompass the need to make such a journey.

Once the body had been removed, Hardcastle embarked on a closer examination of the bedroom. He started with the pillow on which the colonel's head had been resting.

'Ah, here we are, Marriott.' Using his pocket knife, Hardcastle extracted a bullet buried in the mattress. Holding it between finger and thumb, he gazed at it. 'That's the little bugger that done for him. Looks like a forty-five to me, but we'll get Inspector Franklin to take a look at it. He'll be able to tell us for sure. And we'll need to have the pillow bagged up, and that one on the floor that looks as though it was used to deaden the sound.'

'When will you want to see the rest of the staff, sir?' asked Marriott. 'There's Good the coachman, and I understand that there's a kitchen maid called Elsie.'

'Is there?' Hardcastle looked up sharply. 'Beach never mentioned a kitchen maid, nor did Mrs Blunden.'

Beach's arrival solved the problem of whom they should see next.

'Lady Rivers is prepared to see you now, sir.'

'Very charitable of her,' said Hardcastle. 'Who's Elsie, Beach?'

'If you mean Elsie Jones, sir, she's the kitchen maid.'

'You never mentioned her earlier.'

'I didn't think it was necessary, sir, on account of her ladyship having given her a few days off. From yesterday, that'd be. Elsie's mother's been took ill apparently. Lives between here and Richmond, on the other side of Ham Common.'

'Everything's necessary in a murder enquiry, Beach,' snapped Hardcastle, 'and I don't take kindly to having things kept from me.' In the circumstances though, Elsie Jones was unlikely to have anything relevant to contribute, but Hardcastle would not accept the butler deciding what he should be told and what he should not. 'Was this Elsie walking out, Beach?'

'Not that I know of, sir.' Beach looked puzzled at the question, but he was not familiar with Hardcastle's thinking that maybe a member of the staff had an accomplice who just might have been a villain.

'Where is Lady Rivers now?' asked Hardcastle.

'In her bedroom, sir, and she's prepared to see you. I'll show you the way.'

'In her *bedroom*?' echoed Hardcastle. 'Lady Rivers is willing to be interviewed *in her bedroom*?' To him it was a scandalous suggestion, and he could not recall, in all his service, ever having interviewed a woman in her bedroom.

Beach smiled. 'Indeed, sir. Her ladyship is a very forward-looking young woman.'

'Well, I never did,' said Hardcastle, as he followed the butler upstairs. But there were further surprises in store for him.

The spacious room into which Beach showed Hardcastle was next to the late Sir Adrian's. But the furnishings here were far different from his. Whereas the colonel's room had been almost ascetic in character, Muriel Rivers's was hedonistic.

A Heriz carpet, at least 20 feet long and nearly as wide, covered most of the floor, but where it did not, the wooden surround was highly polished. The curtains were of bold floral chintz, held open by tasselled silken cords, but it was the double bed that dominated the room by its very ostentation. To Hardcastle's astonishment, the tester, the eiderdown and the pillows were all of emerald green silk. In the centre of the bed was a teddy bear with one arm and a missing eye.

'I'm in here,' said a voice from a curtained anteroom beyond the bedroom.

There was no doubt that Lady Rivers was a strikingly handsome young woman, albeit a little coarse in appearance. Her brown hair was loose and long enough to hang well below her shoulders. Attired in a white kimono embroidered with roses, she was reclining on a chaise longue, her satin-slippered feet resting on a cushion. One hand held a silk handkerchief to her mouth, while the other clutched a small ivory fan.

There were two chairs in the anteroom, and two small tables. On the wall adjacent to the window was an escritoire, and above it a Conté-pencil sketch, in black and white on a grey background, of a naked mulatto male.

The lavish *tout ensemble* seemed to confirm Mrs Blunden's view that Muriel Rivers had been profligate with her late husband's money.

'Lady Rivers, I'm Divisional Detective Inspector Hardcastle of the Whitehall Division, and this is Detective Sergeant Marriott. I'm sorry about Sir Adrian's death.' He was not very good at uttering words of condolence.

'Thank you.' Muriel Rivers shook hands with Hardcastle and Marriott. 'Do take a seat, gentlemen,' she said. 'What are you doing down here from Whitehall, then?' Although there was the hint of a cockney accent in her voice, she had made an attempt to modify it, but, as Hardcastle later noticed, her grammar occasionally slipped. She glanced at Beach, standing in the doorway of the bedroom. 'Thank you, Thomas,' she said. 'That'll be all.'

'Very good, m'lady.' Beach half smiled and closed the door behind him.

Hardcastle was surprised at the form of address that Lady

Rivers had used to the butler. He had often been in houses
where there was a large domestic staff, but never before
had he heard a butler addressed by his Christian name.

'I cannot begin to tell you what a grave tragedy this is
for me,' said Muriel Rivers, turning her attention to the two
detectives once more. She emitted a brief sob, and put the
handkerchief to her mouth, before gently dabbing at her
red-rimmed eyes. Her distress at the demise of her husband
was natural enough, and Hardcastle presumed that Beach
had, unwisely in the DDI's view, apprised her of the brutal
manner of Sir Adrian's death. The sedatives that Spilsbury
said her doctor had prescribed seemed to have had little
effect, if she had taken them.

'I was wondering, Lady Rivers, whether you heard
anything untoward during the night. It appears that someone
entered your husband's bedroom, probably by the window.
Beach tells me that some of Sir Adrian's possessions were
stolen. His medals, a watch, cufflinks, that sort of thing.'

'No, Inspector, I never heard a sound, but then I'm a
heavy sleeper.' Lady Rivers smiled wanly at the two detectives, and then, to Hardcastle's surprise, she reached across
to the small marquetry table next to her and took a cigarette from an inlaid box. Fitting it into a long holder, she
looked enquiringly at the two detectives. 'Have either of
you gentlemen got a light?' she asked.

Hardcastle struck a match and leaned across to apply the
flame to Muriel Rivers's cigarette. 'I understand that you
and Sir Adrian had not been married very long, ma'am.'

'Two years. We were married just before the war started.
We met at Epsom races and he swept me off my feet. So
gallant. A month or two later we was wed.' For a moment
or two, Lady Rivers looked immeasurably sad. She shook
her head slowly, and dabbed at her eyes once more. 'But
within a couple of months he was taken ill with this dementia
thing. Poor dear, he's not been right since. There's nothing
the doctors could do apparently, but now he's been merci-
fully released from his troubles.' She had only taken two
or three puffs of her cigarette before she removed it from
the holder and stubbed it out in the ashtray. 'Anyway, I've

got to think of the funeral now, I suppose. Harrods do a very good service, so I understand. But Thomas is a great help, and I'm sure he'll know what to do. He was Adrian's batman in the army, you know. A tower of strength is Thomas.' She cast an appraising glance at the handsome Marriott, and smiled.

'It may be some time before the coroner releases your late husband's body, Lady Rivers,' said Hardcastle.

'I daresay, but I'm sure you'll let me know when we can go ahead, Inspector.'

'Thank you for seeing us, Lady Rivers,' said Hardcastle as he and Marriott stood up. 'I think that'll be all for now, but we may have to speak to you again.'

Muriel Rivers swung her legs off the chaise longue and stood up. She walked ahead of them to the door of the bedroom, but paused at the bed to pick up the teddy bear. Clasping it to her bosom, she smiled, and said, 'I call him Nelson. Quite a suitable name for him, don't you think, Inspector?'

Three

'**M**r Beach said you wanted to speak to me, sir.' Daniel Good was a stout man in his fifties. Dressed in a high-necked, double-breasted whipcord tunic, and breeches with leather leggings, he had a cockaded cap tucked beneath his left arm.

'I'm told you're the chauffeur, but prefer to be known as the coachman, Good.'

'It wasn't my idea, sir,' said Good, apparently assuming that Hardcastle's flourishing hand was an invitation to sit down. 'It was the colonel. He can't stand anything new, you see. I was originally taken on as a coachman, and that's what he called me.'

'Have you always been a coachman, Mr Good?' asked Marriott.

'In a manner of speaking, sir,' said Good, turning to face the sergeant. 'Royal Field Artillery. Lance bombardier, lead horse, I was,' he said proudly. 'Did me time, and the colonel took me on when he retired from the army, back in the year '10 that was. Any road, when her ladyship appeared on the scene, she got rid of the horses and the carriage, and I had to learn to drive a car.'

'That'll be the Rolls Royce in the garage, I take it,' said Hardcastle.

'Yes, sir, except that the colonel always called it a motor stable. He wouldn't never have no truck with new words like garage. Very much a gent of the old school was Sir Adrian. In fact, he never once rode in the Royce, sir. He was a horseman through and through. And a racing man, to boot.'

'So it was Lady Rivers's idea to have a car, was it, Good?'

Hardcastle had already heard from Beach that that was the case.

'Indeed, sir. Very much one for keeping up with the times is her ladyship. As a matter of fact, she got me to teach her how to drive it. Likes a bit of speed, does Lady Rivers.'

'So it's *only* Lady Rivers who uses it, is it?' Hardcastle always liked to make absolutely certain of his facts, even at the cost of sounding none too bright. But that was a pose; he found it useful occasionally to let others think he was a dim policeman.

'Yes, sir. Mainly for shopping up the West End. Harrods, Harvey Nichols, Waring and Gillows, Maples, Aspreys. Her ladyship's well known in all of them stores. And quite often she'll get me to run her down to Nuthall's Restaurant in Kingston Market Place for afternoon tea with her friends. And once a week, her ladyship's off to the Kingston Empire to see one of them variety shows. She has a box specially reserved.'

'How did Sir Adrian get about, then, if he wouldn't use the car?'

'He never did, sir. T'weren't long afore he was took bad, and he never went out after that. No, I tell a lie. The family did go down to Markham Hall a couple of times this last eighteen months or so. But they went by train and was picked up by a horse and carriage at the other end. He never liked her ladyship getting shot of the carriage and horses, and he wouldn't travel in a motor car.'

'Took bad?' queried Hardcastle, once again seeking confirmation. 'You mean he was ill?' He took out his pipe, but seeing no ashtray in the library, returned it to his pocket.

Using a forefinger, Good sketched a circle at his temple, and lowered his voice. 'Seemed like he'd lost his marbles, sir, if you know what I mean.'

'When did that start?'

For a second or two, Good stared pensively at the books lining the library wall behind Hardcastle. 'Be about the time he was wed to her ladyship, sir. Or maybe a touch after. Pitiful to see, sir, so it was.'

'Where are your quarters, Mr Good?' asked Marriott,

even though he had been told that the chauffeur lived over
the garage.

'I've got a room over the stable, sir. Only ever set foot
in the house for meals. And to take instructions from her
ladyship.'

'And did you hear anything last night? Did you hear a
shot, for instance?' Hardcastle was still attempting to estab-
lish the exact time that Sir Adrian had been killed. But as
the murderer had used a pillow to muffle the sound, it was
unlikely that Good, sleeping over the garage, would have
heard a thing. Especially as Lady Rivers, sleeping next door
to her husband, professed to have heard nothing.

'No, not a thing, sir. It was a terrible shock when I come
in for breakfast this morning to hear that Sir Adrian had
been murdered. Specially on top of Lord Kitchener being
drowned.'

'I'm not hanging about in Kingston forever, Marriott,' said
Hardcastle, once Daniel Good had departed from the library.
'There's not much more to be done here right now. But it
might be a good idea to have a man posted on the premises,' he added, regretting his earlier decision to dismiss the
three uniformed constables. 'You never know, once word
of this murder gets in the newspapers there'll be all manner
of nosey parkers turning up here.'

'What about Sergeant Atkins, sir?' asked Marriott.

'What about him?'

'You told him to come back here once he'd delivered Sir
Adrian's body to St Mary's Hospital.'

'He'll work it out, Marriott. I hope. But leave a message
with Beach. Tell him to tell Atkins that I want him back
here at nine o'clock sharp tomorrow morning.'

But as Marriott was about to depart in search of Beach,
the butler appeared in the hall. Nodding briefly to the detectives, he opened the front door.

A woman in nurse's uniform stood on the step.

'Good afternoon, Mr Beach.'

'Good afternoon, Sister. I'm afraid you've come on a
fool's errand. You see, Sir Adrian . . .'

'Who's that, Beach?' asked Hardcastle, stepping across to the door.

'It's Rose Banks, sir. She's the nursing sister who comes in every day to cast her eye over the colonel.'

'I see. You'd better come in, Sister,' said Hardcastle, taking over.

'Whatever's wrong?' asked the nurse. 'Who are you?'

'I'm Divisional Detective Inspector Hardcastle of the Metropolitan Police, ma'am. I'm afraid Sir Adrian's dead.'

'Glory be!' The sister put a hand to her mouth, a distressed expression on her face. Doubtless, she was wondering whether any professional shortcoming on her part had contributed to the colonel's death.

'I'm sorry to have to tell you that Sir Adrian was murdered during the night, Sister,' explained Hardcastle.

'Holy Mary, Mother of God!' exclaimed Sister Banks and, despite her encumbering cape, managed to cross herself. 'May his soul rest in peace, the poor man.'

'Did you come in yesterday, Sister?' asked Hardcastle.

'Yes. Like Mr Beach said, I come in every day about this time, just to see that the colonel's all right. There's not much I can do for him, mind you. As far as I could tell, the poor man was physically quite fit, but he never seemed to know what day it was, or, for that matter, who I was.'

'I'll speak to her ladyship, Sister,' said Beach, 'and make sure you get paid.'

'Bless you, Mr Beach.' Sister Banks turned and walked slowly down the steps.

'A good woman, but there's not much she could ever have done in the circumstances,' said Beach, with a shake of his head.

'Are you connected to the telephone here, Beach?' asked Hardcastle.

'Of course, sir. Her ladyship insisted on having the instrument installed.'

'I was wondering why you ran out to the gate to call a policeman when Sir Adrian was found by Digby, rather than telephoning the police station.'

'I suppose I never thought of it, sir, what with the shock

of the colonel being dead. I was brought up in an age when we never had such things. Like I said, the one we've got here was only put in when her ladyship took up residence.'

'Perhaps you'd use the instrument to call me a taxi, then.' Hardcastle turned to Marriott. 'Go with Beach and when he's done calling a taxi, get on to Kingston nick and tell 'em to send a PC up here a bit *jildi*. And, on second thoughts, leave a message for Atkins not to come up here tomorrow. I don't want him making a Mons of things.'

'Very good, sir,' said Marriott, and he and Beach departed to do the DDI's bidding.

While Marriott was making his telephone call, Hardcastle remained in the hall, soaking up the atmosphere, as he liked to describe it.

'I'm not spending my time hanging about in Kingston, Marriott,' said Hardcastle again, once his sergeant had returned from the kitchen. 'We'll go back to Cannon Row. We can work as easy from there as we can from down the road, and I suspect there ain't much more we can do here anyway. Not for the time being.'

'New Scotland Yard,' said Hardcastle, as he clambered into a taxi on the rank at Waterloo. Turning to Marriott, he added, 'Tell 'em Cannon Row and half the time you'll finish up at Cannon Street in the City.'

'Yes, sir,' said Marriott wearily. The DDI had told him this on almost every occasion that they had shared a taxi back to the police station.

'First thing tomorrow morning, we'll pay a visit to the army, Marriott. Make sure that Sir Adrian's sons are notified of the colonel's murder. The military might be able to tell us a bit about Beach, too. I'm wondering why a fit man like him hasn't been recalled to the Colours. The war's been going on for nigh on two years now, and according to the linen drapers they're running a bit short of men.'

'Beach is time-expired, sir,' volunteered Marriott.

'So's the colonel,' muttered Hardcastle drily, 'and we've got to get to the bottom of why he is. In the meantime, Marriott, go across to Mr Collins's office and ask him to have one of his men examine Sir Adrian's bedroom for fingerprints.'

It had been an afterthought. Hardcastle, in common with many other detective officers, was only just beginning to recognize the value of this new science. In 1905, the Stratton brothers had been hanged for murder after the thumbprint of one of them had been found on a cashbox at the oil shop in Deptford they had robbed, and whose owners they had murdered. It was the first time that fingerprint evidence had been accepted by the courts, and a search for such clues was to become normal practice. Detective Inspector Charles Stockley Collins was one of the foremost experts in the field.

At ten o'clock the following morning, Hardcastle and Marriott set off down Whitehall. As they entered the gates at Horse Guards, the two mounted sentries raised their swords in salute. Hardcastle, accustomed to being mistaken for an army officer, hooked his umbrella over his left arm, and solemnly doffed his bowler hat in acknowledgement.

A sergeant of the Military Foot Police briefly examined the detectives' warrant cards and showed them into the assistant provost marshal's office.

'Good morning, Inspector.' Lieutenant Colonel Ralph Frobisher of the Sherwood Foresters was the APM of London District. As such, he was one of the army's most senior policemen. There was, however, a measure of caution in his greeting. He knew that whenever Hardcastle came to see him, it usually heralded some difficulty. Nothing involving the Metropolitan Police ever seemed to be easy.

'Good morning, Colonel.' Responding to Frobisher's invitation to sit down, Hardcastle took a seat. 'A delicate matter,' he said.

The APM drew a pad of paper across the desk and took out his fountain pen. 'What can I do to assist the civil police?'

Hardcastle explained about the murder of Colonel Sir Adrian Rivers. 'My problem is that his two sons need to be informed, Colonel. I've been told they are somewhere in France, or maybe Belgium, but I don't know where. Even if it's true.'

'They are officers, I presume,' said Frobisher.

'Yes,' said Hardcastle. 'I'm told the eldest one, and heir to the baronetcy, is Ewart, a general, and the younger one is called Gerard. Apparently he's a colonel.'

'A full colonel, or a lieutenant colonel, Inspector? It can make a difference, you see.'

'Colonel is all I was told.'

'Probably on the staff, then,' muttered Frobisher.

'According to Sir Adrian's butler, a man called Beach, the father and his sons were all in the Surrey Rifles, if that's any help, Colonel. I'd be interested in Beach's background, too.'

'And his regiment?'

'The same, Colonel. Surrey Rifles, so he claims.'

Frobisher made a few notes on his pad, and then looked up. 'It'll take a day or so, Inspector, but I'll let you know as soon as I have anything. You can certainly leave it to the military to advise Sir Adrian's sons of their father's death.'

When Hardcastle and Marriott returned to Cannon Row, there was a note from Dr Bernard Spilsbury. The post-mortem examination of Sir Adrian Rivers was to take place at Paddington at three o'clock that afternoon. And that left Hardcastle sufficient time to put a few other matters in hand.

'Send DS Wood in here, Marriott,' said Hardcastle.

'He's not here, sir. He and Wilmot are out on an enquiry. Alleged theft of silver from the Army and Navy Club.'

'Who is out there, then?'

'Catto, sir.'

Hardcastle groaned. 'Send him in.'

Detective Constable Henry Catto entered the DDI's office in his customary state of nervousness. 'You wanted me, sir?'

'Not really, Catto, but you'll have to do, I suppose.' Hardcastle finished filling his pipe with his favourite St Bruno tobacco and felt in his pocket for matches. 'Get yourself up to Somerset House, lad, and see what you can find out about Sir Adrian Rivers's second marriage to Muriel, Lady Rivers, in about 1914. And, while you're about it, see what you can find out about his previous marriage to Lady Lavinia Rivers.'

'Yes, sir.' Catto took out his pocketbook and licked his pencil. 'That's Sir Adrian Rivers, Lady Lavinia Rivers and Lady Muriel Rivers,' he mumbled, as he wrote down the names.

'No, it's not,' barked Hardcastle. 'Have you got cloth ears or something?'

Catto looked puzzled. 'But that's what you said, sir.'

'That is not what I said, Catto. What I said was Muriel, Lady Rivers, and Lady Lavinia Rivers. Lady Lavinia was the daughter of an earl and a lady in her own right. Muriel, Lady Rivers, is a commoner. That's why she's called Lady Rivers and not Lady Muriel Rivers. I should've thought that having been on the Whitehall Division all this time, you'd've picked up a few wrinkles about titles. By the way, Lady Lavinia Rivers is dead. Now, off you go and don't make a Mons of it.'

A somewhat bemused Catto fled the office, only half sure of what he was supposed to do at Somerset House once he got there.

Dr Spilsbury, in waistcoat, rolled shirtsleeves and long, rubber apron, was already at work on Sir Adrian Rivers's corpse when Hardcastle and Marriott arrived.

'I've almost finished, Hardcastle,' said Spilsbury, without pausing in his work. 'Let me have a bit more light over here, Donald.' His assistant lowered the overhead lamp so that it was concentrated on the cadaver on the table.

'After you left, we found a bullet buried in the mattress, Doctor,' said Hardcastle. 'Looks like a forty-five, but I've sent it for ballistic examination.'

'That accords with my findings, Hardcastle,' said Spilsbury. 'Not that there was much doubt.' He put down the scalpel and the forceps with which he had been working and crossed to a sink to wash his hands. 'I'd put the time of death at about eleven o'clock last night, perhaps an hour either way.'

'The footman says he took Sir Adrian a cup of cocoa at ten o'clock,' said Hardcastle, 'and he's certain of the time because Sir Adrian was a stickler for it arriving at ten on the dot.'

'Well, there you are then. Between just after ten and, say, midnight. That help you, does it?'

'It could do, I suppose, Doctor, but it's early days yet.'

'There's a couple of other things that might interest you, Hardcastle. Rivers had emphysema. Probably the result of smoking those damned Turkish cigarettes that soldiers seem to favour. I wouldn't have thought he'd've lasted much longer than a month or so. Whoever killed him certainly saved him a lot of pain.'

'The nurse who called every day said that he was physically fit, Doctor.'

'I doubt she'd have detected emphysema,' said Spilsbury dismissively.

'And the other thing you mentioned, Doctor?'

'There's an old bullet wound on the left shoulder, but as Rivers was a soldier, I suppose that was one of the hazards of his trade.'

Catto was waiting when Hardcastle and Marriott got back to Cannon Row.

'Well,' barked Hardcastle, 'what have you found out?'

Clutching a sheaf of papers, Catto followed the DDI into his office. 'I've got some dates, sir.'

'I should hope you have.' Hardcastle examined the detective constable closely. 'Is that the only suit you've got, Catto?'

'No, sir. I've got another one at home.'

'Any better than the one you're wearing, is it?'

'Not really, sir, no.'

'It won't do, Catto. It won't do at all. You're a detective officer of the Royal A Division. Supposing I was to send you to Buckingham Palace looking like that. What d'you think the King would say, eh? He'd be sending me a memo about you a bit *tout de suite*, and that's a fact. Marriott!'

'Yes, sir?'

'See that Catto here gets himself properly dressed in future, Marriott.'

'Yes, sir.'

'Now then Catto, what've you got to tell me?'

'Muriel, Lady Rivers, sir . . .' Catto spoke hesitantly, expecting a reproof.

'Yes, yes, get on with it.'

'She was born Muriel North on the twenty-fifth of January, 1881, sir, and she married Sir Adrian Rivers on the third of June, 1914.'

'Was married to, Catto, not married. It was a clergyman who married them.' But Hardcastle was being perverse; he rarely made the distinction himself.

'Yes, sir,' said Catto, failing to understand the DDI's pedantry.

'Got the names of her parents, have you?'

'Yes, sir. Her father is Albert North, and her mother is Marjorie North, née Gibbons. Albert North is a bookmaker, sir. At least, it said turf accountant in the register, but I reckon that makes him a bookmaker.'

'You reckon right, Catto. A bookmaker, eh? That's interesting because Sir Adrian was keen on racing. D'you remember what Mrs Blunden said about her ladyship, Marriott?'

'Yes, sir. She said that Sir Adrian met her at some race meeting.'

Hardcastle looked thoughtful for a moment or two. 'Where was she born, Catto?'

Catto shuffled through his handful of papers. 'Wandsworth, sir.'

'Wandsworth, eh? Well, that don't help much,' said Hardcastle.

'If you remember, sir,' said Marriott. 'Lady Rivers actually told us that she met Sir Adrian at Epsom races.'

'Yes, so she did,' said Hardcastle. 'There's a big racecourse at Epsom, Marriott. It's where they hold the Derby.'

'Not any more, sir,' said Marriott. 'It's full of soldiers now. The Derby's been held at Newmarket since the war started.'

Graham Ison

'Really?' said Hardcastle crossly. He did not much care for being corrected.

'The nearest open course now is at Hurst Park,' continued Marriott. 'Near Hampton Court.'

'Perhaps Albert North's got a stand there, then,' said Hardcastle. 'Remind me to have a word with the Molesey police some time.'

'I looked up Lady Lavinia Rivers, too, sir,' said Catto. 'She was born on the sixth of July, 1859, the daughter of the Earl of Aubrey. She died of consumption on the second of September 1904.'

'When was she married to Sir Adrian?' asked Hardcastle, more out of devilment than the need to know.

Catto looked crestfallen. 'Oh, I didn't think you wanted to know that, sir. You never mentioned it.'

'Didn't I? Well, never mind. It don't really matter. Off you go, Catto, and well done.'

'Thank you, sir.' Catto grinned at the rare word of praise.

'And Catto . . .'

'Sir.'

'Do something about that suit.'

Four

Detective Inspector Percy Franklin had developed such an interest in weaponry that he had eventually persuaded the authorities at New Scotland Yard to give him space to pursue this new 'science'. As a result, he had set up the first ballistics workshop in a cramped room in the basement.

'I've examined the round you took from the mattress on Sir Adrian Rivers's bed, sir,' he said to Hardcastle, 'and you were right. It's what's known as a point four-five-five calibre SAA bullet. The likelihood is that it was fired from a service revolver, most probably a Webley & Scott.'

'Is there any way of finding out which weapon, Mr Franklin?' asked Hardcastle, whose knowledge of firearms was minimal.

Franklin smiled. 'Not until you find the weapon you think might have fired that, sir.' Using a pair of large callipers, he indicated the round that was lying in a kidney-shaped enamel bowl on his workbench. 'Then I stand a good chance of telling you whether it was the one that was used.'

'There's a gunroom at the Rivers house,' said Hardcastle, half to himself. 'I'll obviously need to have a look at it. Not that I think the weapon came from there. The butler assured me that none of them was missing. Obviously, the burglar would've brought the weapon with him, and has most likely disposed of it by now.'

'I'm sorry I can't help any further, sir, but, like I said, find the gun and I should be able to tell if this round came from it. We're lucky in that it was hardly damaged by passing through the victim's skull, so the characteristic groove marks caused by the rifling won't have been affected.'

'I'm sure you're right, Mr Franklin,' said Hardcastle drily.

On the Friday morning following the murder of Sir Adrian Rivers, Hardcastle received a message from Lieutenant Colonel Frobisher to say that he had information for him.

'We've located Colonel Rivers's sons, Inspector,' said Frobisher, as Hardcastle and Marriott entered his office. 'They are, in fact, Brigadier General Ewart Rivers and Lieutenant Colonel Gerard Rivers.'

'And they've been notified of their father's death, Colonel?'

'They have indeed, and they're both on their way home. They should arrive late tonight or early tomorrow.'

'Were they told that he'd been murdered, sir?' asked Marriott.

'Yes. They're both soldiers, and there seemed no point in keeping the brutal truth from them. Fortunately, they are both serving in Fourth Army, and General Rawlinson released them immediately. General Ewart Rivers is on the staff at army headquarters, and Colonel Gerard Rivers is commanding the third battalion of the Surrey Rifles.'

'I suppose they'll be going straight to Kingston,' said Hardcastle, thinking that he would have to wait at The Grange for their arrival.

'I imagine so,' said Frobisher. 'They were told that that's where the murder occurred.' He plucked a file from his pending tray. 'I also have some information about Thomas Beach. You were quite right, Inspector, he was in the Surrey Rifles, and served his pensionable time. There seems no reason for his not being recalled to the Colours, other than his age. But more likely because he had a rather chequered service history.'

'I'm not surprised,' said Hardcastle. 'I don't much care for smooth-talking butlers. Most of 'em have ideas above their station. Was he Sir Adrian's orderly at any time?'

'He may have been, but it's not the sort of thing that would appear on his service record.' Frobisher opened the file. 'He was at one time a sergeant, but was reduced in rank for borrowing money from subordinates. He was a bit of gambler, by all accounts. I gather, reading between the lines, that the loans were extracted from private soldiers under pressure, so to speak.' The APM looked up and smiled. 'Anyhow, the result was that he was court-martialled and reduced in rank to private. And it was in that rank that he was eventually discharged in 1912.'

'Interesting,' said Hardcastle. 'Sir Adrian met his second wife, the present Lady Rivers, at a race meeting at Epsom in 1914. They were married in the June. And her father's a bookmaker. I wonder if there's any connection.'

'I don't know if any of that is any help, Inspector,' said Frobisher, closing the file and tossing it back into his pending tray.

'Nor do I, Colonel,' said Hardcastle, 'but I'll tuck it away for future reference. You never know,' he added mysteriously. 'One other question. Are service revolvers only carried by officers?'

'Generally speaking, yes, but there are one or two other categories that are issued with them. Non-commissioned officers in cavalry regiments. Oh, and some artillery drivers.'

'Like a lance bombardier who drove a lead horse in the Royal Field Artillery for example, sir?' asked Marriott.

'Exactly so,' said Frobisher. 'Why d'you ask?'

'Because,' said Hardcastle, 'that's what Sir Adrian's chauffeur was, before he became a coachman.'

Saturday started badly for Hardcastle. Arriving at Cannon Row police station just before eight o'clock, he found a report awaiting him from Detective Inspector Collins. One of Collins's sergeants had examined Sir Adrian Rivers's bedroom, but found no fingerprints that were likely to assist Hardcastle's investigation. The report went on to say that elimination prints had been taken from all the staff, and Lady Rivers – under protest, it added – but those prints were the only ones found. And each member of the house-hold had a legitimate reason for having been in the room at one time or another.

As if this were not enough to depress him, Hardcastle arrived with Marriott at Norbiton railway station at ten o'clock only to discover that there were no taxis. And it was pouring with rain.

'Is there likely to be a cab along soon?' Hardcastle asked a porter.

The porter shook his head, and afforded Hardcastle a pitiful smile. 'Bless you no, sir, not of a Saturday. You'll find 'em all down Kingston, waiting for the nobs to finish their shopping. All outside Bentall's store, they'll be, or in Market Place near the Sun Hotel and Nuthall's or thereabouts.'

'Fat lot of bloody good, that is,' muttered Hardcastle. 'How do we get up Kingston Hill to Penny Lane, then?'

'You'd be best off walking through Wolverton Avenue and taking a tram, sir,' said the porter, pointing across the road. 'That'll get you as far as the George and Dragon pub. Penny Lane's only a short stride from there.'

The two detectives raised their umbrellas, crossed Coombe Road, and made their way past Kingston Infirmary. Hardcastle complained for most of the way, and was only slightly mollified when they were fortunate enough to see a tram toiling its way up the hill as they arrived at the stop.

Finally, they reached The Grange, but with their trousers wet from the knees downwards, and their shoes soaked.

'Good morning, sir,' said Beach, throwing open the front door. 'Dreadful day, sir.'

Hardcastle grunted a response, and he and Marriott shook their umbrellas and stood them against the wall of the porch. 'Have Sir Adrian's sons arrived yet, Beach?'

'Indeed they have, sir, late last night. The gentlemen are in the drawing room, sir.' Beach turned and led the way.

The two men were attired in smartly cut khaki tunics, sandy-coloured breeches and riding boots. The man whose rank badges indicated that he was a brigadier general wore red tabs at his collar.

'Good morning, gentlemen. I'm Divisional Detective Inspector Hardcastle of the Metropolitan Police. I'm sorry about your father,' he mumbled, as usual having difficulty with words of sympathy.

'Thank you, Inspector.' The elder Rivers stroked his moustache, and introduced himself and his brother.

'You look as though you've been dragged through a wet hedge backwards,' said Gerard Rivers, with a laugh.

It was a comment that did nothing to lift Hardcastle's foul mood. 'It is rather wet out there, Colonel,' he responded coolly. 'There were no taxis at the station, and we were obliged to take a tram.'

'You'd better have a glass of whisky, then, Inspector. And you too, er . . .'

'This is my assistant, Detective Sergeant Marriott.'

'Do take a seat, gentlemen,' said Ewart Rivers, as his brother handed round the whisky, 'and tell me about the murder of our father.'

As briefly as he could, Hardcastle outlined the circumstances surrounding the death of Sir Adrian Rivers, including Inspector Franklin's opinion that the murder weapon had been a service revolver.

'And have you found this revolver, Inspector?' asked Ewart.

'Not so far, Sir Ewart.'

Ewart Rivers held up a hand. 'I'm not Sir Ewart yet,' he said. 'For some perverse reason, an heir to a baronetcy has to produce all manner of documentary evidence to the Lord Chancellor before he can assume the title. If my father had been a peer, there wouldn't have been a problem, but in the dim and distant past it seems that some imposters took it upon themselves to assume a baronetcy. Now we have to go through all this ridiculous palaver. However, that is of no import at the present time. Our concern is that you find whoever killed the governor.'

'As far as I can see, General,' said Hardcastle, amending his previous form of address, 'a burglar gained entry to your father's bedroom through an open window and stole his medals, a gold watch and some items of jewellery: cufflinks and the like.'

'I told him often about sleeping with the damned window open at the bottom,' muttered Ewart Rivers.

'This burglar must've been a pretty fit sort of chap,'

suggested Gerard Rivers. 'D'you think he shinned up the ivy, then?'

'At the moment, Colonel, I can see no other explanation. The butler assured me that all the doors were locked and bolted. He said he checks them every night before retiring.'

'Does he indeed?' snorted Ewart Rivers, but the way in which he said it implied that he had no great opinion of the butler. 'How soon d'you think our father's body will be released for burial, Inspector?'

'The inquest is due to open on Tuesday, General. If it follows the usual pattern, it will be adjourned until I'm in a position to offer further evidence. I can't see that there'd be any reason for the coroner not to release your father's body.'

'Damned red tape,' muttered the general. 'D'you know, Inspector, the BEF are burying hundreds of men every day across in Flanders. The pioneers dig a hole, the padre mumbles a few words over them, and that's that. When this bloody war is over – if it ever is – all of Belgium and half of France will be one bloody great cemetery.' He sounded very bitter.

'There's nothing I can do, I'm afraid, General,' said Hardcastle. 'I'm obliged to comply with the law.'

Ewart Rivers waved a placatory hand. 'Oh, I'm not blaming you, Inspector, but I do get the impression that the British are now divided into two groups of people. On the one hand, there's this lot at home who haven't the faintest idea what's going on across the Channel, and on the other, there are those of us who are doing the fighting, up to our necks in mud.'

But General Rivers's diatribe was interrupted by the arrival of Lady Rivers. She flounced into the drawing room, resplendent in a flame-red georgette confection, the hem of which was a good eight inches from the floor, revealing art-silk stockings and glacé kid court shoes. The neckline of the dress plunged to a level that, to Hardcastle's eye, was indecently low. All in all, it was an outfit that Mrs Hardcastle, had she seen it, would certainly have condemned as being fit only for a tart.

'Hello, boys. Welcome home.' Lady Rivers laughed gaily,

flicked open an ivory fan and gently waved it back and forth in front of her face. 'When did you arrive?'

Ewart Rivers ignored the question. 'You seem to have recovered from my father's death remarkably quickly, Muriel.' He fitted a monocle into his right eye and examined Lady Rivers's outfit critically.

'One 'as to rally round, Ewart,' said Muriel Rivers, inadvertently dropping an aspirate. 'Put a brave face on it all.'

Although the exchange had been civil, it failed to disguise the underlying animosity that was apparent between the pair. It was not lost on Hardcastle.

'And have you any news for me, Inspector?' asked Muriel Rivers, turning to Hardcastle.

'Not as yet, Lady Rivers, but these are early days.'

'I suppose so.' She crossed the room and gave the bell cord a sharp pull. When Beach appeared, she said, 'Thomas, be a darling and ask Daniel to bring the car round to the front. I'm meeting a friend at Nuthall's for morning coffee.'

'Very good, m'lady,' said Beach, glancing apprehensively at her two stepsons before retreating from the room.

'You ought not to call Beach by his Christian name, Muriel, nor Good for that matter,' said Ewart Rivers stiffly. 'You mustn't forget that they're servants. You're far too familiar with them.'

'Oh, stuff!' cried Muriel Rivers, waving her fan dismissively. 'I'm not one of your soldiers, you know, Ewart, and I'll call the servants what I like.' And with that she swept imperiously from the room.

'I wouldn't be surprised if that woman turned out to be a suffragette,' muttered Gerard, but was silenced by a stern glance from his elder brother. In Ewart's view, it was unseemly to discuss family members – even those whom they held in no high regard – in front of strangers. Particularly those of the lower orders. Like policemen.

'I've just remembered that pater had a revolver,' said Ewart thoughtfully. 'Hung on to it after he retired. I don't know if he's still got it, though.'

'D'you have any idea what sort it was, sir?' asked Marriott.

'It was a Webley & Scott Mark Four, Sergeant.' Ewart Rivers replied without hesitation. 'Takes point four-four-five SAA ball.'

'And would that be the same as the weapon issued to, say, lance bombardiers in the Royal Field Artillery, General?' asked Hardcastle, his interest suddenly aroused.

'Most likely, Inspector, but you'd have to talk to a gunner officer about that. My brother and I are infantrymen. Why d'you ask?'

'Daniel Good, the coachman-cum-chauffeur was such a man, General.'

For a few moments, Ewart Rivers gazed pensively at a portrait of a man, probably an ancestor, to whom he bore a striking resemblance. 'I somehow doubt that Good has it in him to murder my father, Inspector. He's one of the most subservient fellows I've come across.'

'In my experience, General,' said Hardcastle, 'it's them what you least suspects that often turn out to be the villain of the piece, so to speak.'

'Yes,' said Ewart Rivers, 'possibly. I've no doubt you know your own trade far better than me, Inspector.'

'You can rest assured on that point, General. And he wouldn't be the first servant to have topped his master, not by a long chalk.'

'Topped, Inspector?' Gerard Rivers raised a quizzical eyebrow.

'It's what we in the business call murder, Colonel. Or hanging, which is what'll happen to your father's murderer when I lays hands on him.'

'That's very comforting, Inspector,' said General Rivers. 'Is there anything else we can do to assist you?'

'Not at the present time, General. I'll let you know as soon as the coroner releases your father's body.'

'Thank you.'

'Will you be remaining here for a while, sir?' asked Marriott.

'Certainly until after the funeral, Sergeant,' said Gerard Rivers.

'In that case, General, we'll take our leave,' said

Hardcastle, rueing the fact that his journey had been largely a wasted one. Except for that undertone of hostility between Ewart Rivers and his stepmother, and the comment of the younger Rivers. Such family friction interested him, although he could not see its relevance in the present circumstances. Nevertheless, he tucked it away in his memory.

As Hardcastle and Marriott reached the front door, the Rolls Royce drew up, its tyres crunching on the gravel of the drive. At the same time, Lady Rivers appeared in the hall. Although it had only been fifteen minutes or so since she had left the drawing room, she had found time to change into a cream drill costume. A wide-brimmed Spanish straw hat, a handbag and a tightly rolled, black silk umbrella completed her fashionable ensemble.

'Where are you off to, Inspector?' asked Muriel Rivers, affording Beach a smile as he opened the front door. 'Thank you, Thomas.'

'To Norbiton railway station, Lady Rivers.'

'Jump in. I'll give you a lift. It's such an appalling day.'

Daniel Good stood by the rear door of the car, and ushered in Lady Rivers, followed by Hardcastle and Marriott. Hardcastle sat beside her, while Marriott sat on the jump seat opposite them.

'Were my two stepsons able to help you in any way, Inspector?' Lady Rivers leaned back against the leather upholstery. It amused Hardcastle that she occasionally referred to the two soldiers, who were of a comparable age to her, as stepsons.

'Not really, Lady Rivers, but it was necessary for me to see them. I had to explain the circumstances of their father's death, and, of course, the procedure regarding the inquest.'

'I suppose so.' Muriel Rivers spoke in an abstracted sort of way. 'Ewart don't like me, you know, Inspector,' she said suddenly.

'Really, ma'am?' Hardcastle glanced quickly at the screen separating the chauffeur from his passengers, and was pleased to see that it was raised.

'I met Ewart and Gerard at Epsom races two summers ago, at the same time that I met Adrian. And I rather think the general would have liked to marry me rather than see me marry his father. We're about the same age – perhaps a year's difference – but I'm afraid that the life of a soldier's wife wouldn't suit me. Especially now with the war. I mean to say, he could be killed at any time. But he certainly made it very obvious that he wouldn't've been opposed to taking me as his wife . . . or at least his mistress. Poor boy. A woman can always tell when a man takes a fancy to her, you know. But I could see what he was after,' she added, and winked at Marriott.

There was really no reply that Hardcastle could make in the face of the woman's bawdy candour. Here she was, recently bereaved, sitting in the back of a Rolls Royce openly discussing her private life, and hinting, none too subtly, at intimacies that should never have been raised in mixed company. At least, not by a lady. It was certainly something that neither of Sir Adrian Rivers's sons would have done.

But having met Ewart Rivers, Hardcastle could not visualize him ever having contemplated marrying Muriel. A quick tumble maybe – and she had half implied that that had been his only interest in her – but marriage, never. Despite her airs and graces, her expensive outfits, and her profligacy, there was no disguising her working-class origins.

Five

Hardcastle was in no better mood by the time he and Marriott arrived back at Cannon Row police station. It had been a frustrating day, and his enquiries had not progressed at the rate he would have desired. But then, as all his subordinates knew, he was always impatient at the slowness of an investigation.

Dashing Marriott's hopes of having a free Saturday afternoon, Hardcastle insisted on adjourning to his office and discussing the case.

Having removed his still-damp spats and shoes, the DDI spent a few minutes massaging his feet. Finally, he filled his pipe, lit it, and leaned back in his chair.

'It occurs to me,' he began, 'that there's something fishy about all this.' He waved a hand in Marriott's direction. 'Smoke if you want to, m'boy.'

'Thank you, guv'nor.' Recognizing Hardcastle's relaxed attitude, Marriott adopted the informal mode of address, and took out a packet of Gold Flake. 'In what way fishy, guv'nor?'

'Well, for a start, why was it that the footman Digby always took Sir Adrian's cocoa up to him at ten o'clock each evening?' Hardcastle posed the question casually, almost as if he were asking himself rather than his sergeant. 'Beach was supposed to have been his trusted orderly. I'd've thought that Beach would've taken it up.'

'Perhaps Sir Adrian recognized that the butler had other duties to attend to, guv'nor,' suggested Marriott, failing to see the point of his DDI's thinking. 'He is head of the domestic staff, after all.'

'I doubt he holds much sway over the cook,' muttered

Hardcastle with a chuckle. 'What was her name?' He knew
perfectly well what she was called, but it was one of his
idiosyncrasies to pretend forgetfulness.

'Mrs Blunden,' said Marriott.

'So it is. It might not be a bad idea to get the cook on
her own, you know, m'boy. I've got the feeling she might
have a bit more to tell us than she has already.'

'She certainly didn't mince her words about Lady Rivers,
guv'nor. I got the impression she didn't think much of her
ladyship.'

'Neither did General Ewart, m'boy. That was bloody
obvious. That story of Muriel's that Ewart was keen on
marrying her is spinning the twist in my book. He might
have fancied bedding her, and who'd blame him? You can't
deny she's an attractive wench, but I can't see Ewart Rivers
ever wanting to make an honest woman of her. Don't exactly
come up to snuff as a general's wife.'

'She was a bit open, the way she was talking about it,
guv'nor. My missus would never have said things like that.'

'Nor would mine,' agreed Hardcastle. 'In fact, Mrs H
would've described Muriel Rivers as being as common as
muck.' He took a moment or two to relight his pipe. 'And
then there's Daniel Good, the chauffeur. Bit too bloody
smarmy for me, that man. All that "Yes, sir, no, sir, three
bags full, sir." And according to the APM, he might've been
issued with the sort of revolver that done for Sir Adrian.
And if Sir Adrian got away with hanging on to his when
he left, Good could've done so as well.'

'What about Beach, guv'nor?' Although Marriott was
resigned to spending the afternoon talking about the Rivers
murder, he decided to move things on by asking the questions that experience told him the DDI was likely to pose.
But what interested Marriott more was that the DDI seemed
to be veering towards thinking that the mysterious burglar
might not have existed at all.

'He was a gambler,' said Hardcastle flatly, 'leastways
according to Colonel Frobisher. And I never trust gamblers.
What's more, her ladyship, whose old pot-and-pan, don't
forget, is a bookie, seems a bit too familiar with the servants,

calling them by their Christian names. I've never heard the like of it before.'

'So what's the next move, guv'nor?'

'A couple of things need doing, m'boy. We'll have another go at the staff, see if we can't get a bit more out of them. And I think we'll have a run down to Hurst Park on the off chance that Mister North's shifted his stand there from Epsom. Might be useful to hear what he's got to say about it all.'

'When d'you plan on doing that, guv'nor?' asked Marriott, fearing that a precious Sunday off might be in jeopardy.

'We'll have a go at Beach and company on Monday, m'boy. The inquest's on Tuesday, and God knows how long these local coroners go on. When they've got a juicy case like this one, they're inclined to play to the gallery, especially if the press is there. Then, all things being equal, we'll have a trip to the races on Wednesday.' Hardcastle took out his hunter and glanced at it. 'Five past four. I don't think there's anything else to be done until Monday. I'll see you then.' Winding his watch briefly, he dropped it back into his waistcoat pocket.

'Monday is Whit Monday, guv'nor,' Marriott reminded Hardcastle, hoping the DDI might change his mind.

'So it is, m'boy. Doesn't time fly. Seems like only yesterday it was Easter Monday. My respects to Mrs Marriott.'

'Thank you, guv'nor, and mine to Mrs H.' But Marriott knew that his own wife would be as displeased as Hardcastle's that the two of them would be working on a bank holiday.

It was six o'clock before Hardcastle arrived home in Kennington Road.

'Are you home for the weekend, Ernie?' asked his wife. 'And Whit Monday?'

'I hope so, Alice,' said Hardcastle, but he did not mean it, and she knew he did not. He thought it unwise to tell his wife that he had already arranged to work on the bank holiday, traditionally a day for funfairs or outings to the seaside. Not that either of those diversions appealed to the DDI; in fact, he was usually quite bad-tempered if he was forced to spend such a day out with his family. There was no denying that he was a dedicated policeman, and never happier than when he was at work, solving a difficult crime. And the murder of Sir Adrian Rivers was certainly proving to be an enigma. Despite a thorough search of the grounds around The Grange, there was no tangible evidence to indicate that a burglar had entered the house, apart from the dead body of its principal occupant.

The character of Lady Rivers, when coupled with the senile dementia of her late husband, was interesting enough, but Hardcastle knew that he had to guard against being misled into thinking it was relevant to his enquiry. He decided to put it all from his mind – if he could – and enjoy the day off he had granted himself.

'Where are the girls, Alice?'

'Kitty's gone up to Oxford Street with a friend to do some shopping,' called Alice from the kitchen, 'and Maud's in her room doing some knitting. Apparently she met a soldier last week, and . . .'

'Met a soldier?' Hardcastle spoke sharply, and lowered his newspaper. He had been catching up on the latest war news in the *Daily Mail*, but his wife's mention of his youngest daughter meeting a soldier concentrated his mind on family matters. 'What's she doing going out with a soldier?' he demanded. 'For God's sake, the girl's only sixteen years of age. And you know what these damned soldiers are like.'

'Ernest!' Alice's use of his full Christian name was reproof enough for his profane language; she only ever did so when he irritated her. 'I didn't say she was going out with a soldier, I said she'd met one. The church group she belongs to had a visit from a soldier – in fact, he was an officer – whose sole purpose for being there was to ask the girls to knit scarves, socks, and things called cap comforters. Your trouble is that you're always jumping to conclusions, Ernest. The wrong conclusions.'

Hardcastle lapsed into silence, and contemplated the

possibility that he might also be jumping to the wrong conclusion insofar as the Rivers murder was concerned.

'I want to see the gunroom, Beach,' said Hardcastle, as soon as the butler had admitted the two detectives to The Grange.

'The gunroom, sir? But as I told you on Tuesday, sir, there's nothing missing from there.'

'So you said, Beach, but part of the duties of a detective officer investigating a brutal murder is to leave no stone unturned.'

'Very good, sir.' Beach turned abruptly and led the way through the house to a room at the end of one of the corridors leading off the hall. Pulling out a keyring attached to a chain, he opened the door. 'There we are, sir,' he said, standing back so that the two police officers could enter.

There was not a great deal to be seen. A few hunting prints, the heads of one or two stags mounted on the walls, and the pelt of a tiger, complete with its fanged head, spread across the centre of the polished floor. In one corner of the room was a large mahogany desk. The only other furniture comprised two leather chesterfields, placed at right angles to the open brick fireplace, over which a military sword had its own special place in a glass-fronted case.

'Well, where are the guns, Beach?' asked Hardcastle.

'In that cupboard there, sir,' said Beach, pointing at a six-foot-high oak cabinet at one end of the room. 'Sir Adrian was very particular about security, on account of some native bearer stealing a rifle one time when the colonel was in India. Seems this here bearer went a bit doolally-tap and murdered a havildar, and then he took a potshot at the colonel when he tried to disarm him. The colonel got hit in the shoulder. I don't know what it was all about, but the bearer was hanged,' he added, as an apparent afterthought.

'Very interesting,' said Hardcastle caustically. It certainly explained the old wound that Dr Spilsbury had found on Sir Adrian's left shoulder. 'Who's got the key to this cabinet?'

'I have, sir. It was my job to keep the weapons clean and well-oiled.'

'Let's have a look inside, then.'

Beach opened the cupboard to reveal a steel cabinet within. He unlocked the doors to reveal six hunting rifles, two shotguns, and several boxes of ammunition. 'Purdeys, they are, sir,' he said, pointing to the shotguns. 'The colonel always went to Churchill's for them, and for the sporting rifles. They're Mausers, sir.'

None of the names meant much to Hardcastle. 'You seem to know a lot about firearms, Beach.'

The butler preened himself slightly. 'It was my trade, sir. Twenty-one years in the Surrey Rifles.'

'Is that it, then? No handguns?'

'No, sir, only what you see. And they haven't been touched since before the war.'

'Why's there a desk in here, Beach?' asked Hardcastle, losing interest in the gun cabinet.

'The colonel had a mind to write his memoirs, sir, and he'd sit there for hours on end sometimes, reliving the Relief of the Sudan, and the Boer Wars, and getting it all down on paper. Kept asking me questions about what I remembered. I got right fed up with it after a while. But then he seemed to go off the idea, and he told me to take it all out to the garden and burn it. Pages of it there was. Not long after that, the poor man was took ill with his memory. Before he told me to get rid of it, he'd make me read it over to him, but then he'd say he'd never written it, or he'd never been there. One time, he even accused me of making it up. Very sad it was, sir.'

'Sit down, Beach.' Hardcastle pointed at one of the chesterfields, and he and Marriott sat down on the one opposite.

'I'd rather not, sir, if it's all the same to you. If her ladyship happened to come in, she might—'

'Sit down, I said.' Hardcastle was beginning to tire of the butler's sycophantic demeanour.

'Yes, sir.' Without further demur, Beach parted the tails of his morning coat and sat down, linking his fingers in his lap.

'You and Lady Rivers seem to get on very well, Beach,' said Hardcastle.

'She's a very nice lady to work for, sir.' Beach's reply was non-committal.

'Uses your first name, I notice.'

'Yes, well, she's like that, sir. Very easygoing, is her ladyship.'

'Now then, Beach, as the butler you're in a very privileged position. You know things that no one else knows about, and you're privy to all sorts of information.'

'Well, I suppose that's true,' agreed Beach.

'So you're the very man to assist me in my enquiries.'

'I hope you won't be asking me to reveal confidences, sir.'

'Oh, but I will, Beach. You see, Sir Adrian has been murdered, and it's my job to make sure that his killer takes the eight o'clock walk. You do see that, don't you?'

'Yes indeed, sir, and if I can help you in any way, I'll be happy to do so.' Beach adopted an attitude that was even more conciliatory than usual, and began to 'wash' his hands.

'Good. Well, for a start, how does Lady Rivers get on with General Ewart Rivers?'

Clearly taken aback by the question, Beach remained in thoughtful silence for a moment. But then he said, 'Quite well, I believe, sir.'

'I understand that Lady Rivers met Sir Adrian at a race meeting in Epsom, and that the colonel's two sons were with him.'

'That's correct, sir.'

'How d'you know?'

'I was there as well, sir.'

'Oh, and what was a butler doing going to a race meeting with his betters, eh, Beach?'

Beach did not seem at all affronted by Hardcastle's implication that the butler was, therefore, of a lower order, but perhaps he recognized it as the case. 'The colonel thought it would be a nice idea to have a picnic on the Downs, sir. Daniel Good drove us all down in the carriage. Well, I wasn't in the carriage; I was on the box with Daniel. But Sir Adrian and the two young gentlemen went. My job was to serve luncheon when the time came.'

'So how did it come about that Lady Rivers met up with Sir Adrian?'

'I believe she was in the same enclosure at the races, sir, and I seem to recall that she fell into conversation with Colonel Gerard to start with.'

'Are you telling me that her ladyship's got a soft spot for men in uniform, Beach?'

'That may be so, sir.' Beach afforded himself a smile. 'But neither of Sir Adrian's sons was in uniform that day, so's she wouldn't have known they was in the army.'

'And then she got talking to Sir Adrian, I suppose.'

'So I understand, sir. I have to say I was busy putting the luncheon together, with Daniel Good's help, of course, so I wasn't privy to too much of what was going on. But I do know that one of Sir Adrian's sons invited her to partake of luncheon.'

Having succeeded in getting Beach to open up a little, Hardcastle abandoned the matter of Lady Rivers's first meeting with the late Sir Adrian, and turned to the subject of the chauffeur.

'D'you trust Daniel Good, Beach?' It was a blatantly direct question, but Hardcastle was a skilled interrogator, and there were times when such a stratagem paid dividends. If he could divide the servants, he might get to the bottom of what had actually occurred on the night of Sir Adrian's murder.

'Trust him, sir?' Beach's facial expression showed concern at the inference he had drawn from what Hardcastle had said: that Good was *not* to be trusted. 'I don't see why I shouldn't,' he said hesitantly.

'Good said that he was in the Royal Field Artillery, Mr Beach,' said Marriott. 'Is that right?'

Seemingly surprised that the question had come from Hardcastle's sergeant, Beach turned to face him. 'So I believe, sir.'

'And I suppose he would have been issued with a revolver. As the driver of a gun team, I mean.'

'That may be so, sir, but being a rifleman myself, I'm not too familiar with what goes on in the Gunners.'

'Did he ever mention that he'd retained a revolver when he was discharged from the army?' Hardcastle asked.

Beach assumed an air of perplexity. 'He's never said so, sir.'

'Well, d'you think he might've done?' persisted the DDI.

'I wouldn't know, sir. We've certainly never discussed it. But I'd think it unlikely. Apart from anything else, the army's very careful about firearms.'

'And what about the colonel? Would he have kept his service weapon?'

'No, sir, definitely not. I'm sure if he had, he'd've given it to me to clean and oil. As I said before, the colonel was very particular about the care and security of his weapons.'

Hardcastle stood up, and Beach instantly scrambled to his feet. 'Thank you for your assistance, Beach. I may need to speak to you again.'

'Very good, sir. May I lock up here now?'

'You may. Tell me, is Mrs Blunden in the kitchen?'

'Of course, sir.' Beach's reply implied that there was nowhere else she could be.

'And Sir Adrian's two sons are still here?'

'Yes, sir. In the morning room. Did you wish to see them?'

'Not particularly, but I should perhaps let them know I'm here,' said Hardcastle.

'Ah, Inspector, I heard you were here,' said the elder of the two Rivers brothers. 'What can we do for you?'

'I've been questioning Beach about Sir Adrian's firearms, General. Somewhat remiss of me; I should have sought your permission first.'

Ewart Rivers waved a hand of approbation. 'Talk to whomever you like, Inspector.'

'I was just about to have a word with Mrs Blunden, as a matter of fact.'

'Carry on,' said Ewart.

'Thank you, General.' Not that Hardcastle would have brooked any opposition to his request. And he and Marriott descended to the kitchen.

'Good morning, Mr Hardcastle,' said Mrs Blunden, 'you're just in time for a cup of tea.'

'Thank you, Mrs Blunden,' said Hardcastle, 'that would be most welcome.' He got the impression that, whatever time of day he entered the kitchen, he would always be in time for a cup of tea.

'Take a seat, gents.' Mrs Blunden busied herself pouring tea from a large, brown teapot. Placing three cups of tea on the table, she put a sugar bowl, a milk jug and a plate of ginger snaps next to them.

'Ah, my favourites,' said Hardcastle, taking one and dipping it in his tea.

'Have you found out who killed the master yet, Mr Hardcastle?' Mrs Blunden sat down opposite the two detectives and added a spoonful of sugar to her tea.

'Not yet, Mrs Blunden,' said Hardcastle, stirring his tea. 'I have to say that Lady Rivers don't seem too distraught at his death.'

Mrs Blunden scoffed. 'Got her eye to the main chance, that one,' she said.

'What d'you mean by that?'

Mrs Blunden leaned forward and adopted a conspiratorial tone. 'She's only interested in the colonel's money, and now she's got it, I shouldn't wonder.'

'D'you think he left all his worldly goods to her ladyship, then?' asked Marriott.

'Wouldn't be surprised, Mr Marriott,' said Mrs Blunden, with a sniff. 'She could wind that poor man round her little finger.'

'She seems to be on very good terms with the butler,' suggested Hardcastle.

Mrs Blunden rose from her seat, and crossed the kitchen to close the door. Resuming her place, she said, 'That little madam is a sight too familiar with some of the servants,' she said.

'I noticed that she uses Beach's Christian name,' said Hardcastle. 'Does she use yours, Mrs Blunden?' he asked, more out of devilment than the need to know.

'That'll be the day,' said Mrs Blunden, with a toss of her

head. 'If she tries calling me Martha, I'll put her in her
place, her ladyship or not. Cooks is always called "Missus",
whether they're married or not. But you probably knew that
already. You're right though, Mr Hardcastle; she seems to
have taken a shine to *Mister* Beach.' She leaned even closer.
'And I'll tell you something else you won't know. When
we're down at Markham Hall in Wiltshire, we all have
rooms on the top floor, much the same as we have here.
Well, one night, I was coming out of my room – about
midnight, it was – on my way to the lavatory, when I see
Mr Beach's door opening, and he come out in his dressing
gown and bare feet. Well, I thought at first he was making
for the bathroom an' all, so I waited. But he went down
the stairs. I had a look over the banisters, and what d'you
think?'

'I've no idea, Mrs Blunden,' said Hardcastle, an amused
expression on his face.

'He went into her ladyship's room and closed the door
behind him. Never a knock nor nothing. Just barged
straight in.'

'What d'you think that was all about?'

Martha Blunden leaned back, folded her arms across her
ample bosom, and laughed. 'You're a man of the world,
Mr Hardcastle. What d'you think it was about?'

'I wouldn't have any idea,' commented Hardcastle drily,
and joined in Mrs Blunden's laughter.

'She also calls Mr Good by his first name,' said Marriott.
'D'you think that he and she . . .?'

'Bless you no, Mr Marriott.' Mrs Blunden dismissed the
suggestion with a nonchalant wave of her reddened hand.
'He's a good man, is Daniel.' She chuckled at her un-
intentional jest about the chauffeur's name. 'I suppose that's
why he's called Daniel Good. No, Mr Marriott, Daniel's as
straight as a die. Mind you, he has a lot to put up with,
and I'm surprised he sticks it. Her ladyship's always going
up the West End, spending Sir Adrian's money. Runs through
her hands like water. Daniel told me one time that she often
keeps him waiting outside Harrods or Dickens and Jones
for hours on end. So now I make up a pack of sandwiches

for him whenever he's going up London, otherwise he'd be
starved half to death by the time he got back, what with
all that hanging about. And I told him to buy one of them
thermos bottles so he could take some tea with him. Cost
fourteen shillings that did, but I gave him the money and
hid the cost in the meat expenses as half a lamb. Her ladyship never queried it, even though she's far more particular
over the household expenses than what she is over her own
spending, and that's a fact.'

But that interesting conversation was cut short by the
arrival of the footman. He took off his liveried coat and
hung it on a hook behind the door.

'Ah, Digby,' said Hardcastle, 'just the man I wanted to
see. What does her ladyship call you?'

Digby accepted a cup of tea from Mrs Blunden, and sat
down beside her. 'Why, Digby, of course, sir,' he said, with
a puzzled frown.

'But she calls the butler Thomas.'

'Well, that's different, sir. Mr Beach is the butler.' Digby
frowned at the question, as though the answer was obvious.

'Have you been in service in other households, Mr
Digby?' asked Marriott.

'Oh yes, sir. I've had a fair few positions over the years.'

'Well, I'd start looking for another one, if I was you,
John,' put in Martha Blunden, 'because I doubt that her
ladyship'll be staying here much longer. Come to think of
it, I'll probably start looking around myself. A friend of
mine got a good placing as cook down at the Sopwith
aircraft factory in Canbury Park Road.'

'Was the butler in your other houses ever addressed by
his first name?' asked Hardcastle, ignoring the cook's intervention.

'Now you mention it, sir, not as I recall.'

'What's so special about Beach, then?'

'He does a lot for her ladyship, sir, an' I s'pose that's why
she's so friendly. But being the footman, I don't have much
to do with her. And, of course, Mr Beach *was* Sir Adrian's
personal orderly when they was both in the army. I s'pose
that makes a difference. He's regarded as special, like.'

'You told my inspector that you always took Sir Adrian's cocoa to his room at ten o'clock every night, Mr Digby,' said Marriott.

'That's correct, sir.'

'Well, if the colonel thought so highly of Mr Beach, why wasn't it him who took it up?'

'I can't really say, sir. He used to do it, but then her ladyship said that Sir Adrian would rather have me taking it up.'

'When was that?'

'About six months ago, sir,' said Digby, after a moment's thought.

'Didn't Sir Adrian object to that arrangement?' asked Marriott.

'I don't know, sir, but not wishing to speak ill of the dead, I don't think Sir Adrian knew. Half the time I went up, he'd call me Beach. If he was awake, that is.'

But Hardcastle thought that maybe Beach was otherwise engaged. In Lady Rivers's bedroom. 'Were you in the army, Digby?' he asked.

'No, sir, never. Years ago I had a bit of a hankering to join the navy, when I was a boy, like, but nothing ever came of it. I got settled in service, and I've been a footman ever since. I wanted to join up when the war started, and saw them posters with Lord Kitchener on 'em, God bless him, but when I went down the drill hall in Orchard Road they wouldn't have me. Said I was too old, apart from which they said I'd got flat feet and me eyes was bad.'

'Is Daniel Good here this morning, Mrs Blunden?' asked Hardcastle.

'No, he's not. Her ladyship ordered up the car at about nine o'clock, and off she went for coffee with her high-falutin' friends. I think she was quite disappointed not being able to go shopping, it being Whit Monday.' Martha Blunden paused before making her final condemnation. 'She don't seem mortally affected by Sir Adrian's death, and that don't come as no surprise.'

'Thank you for the tea, Mrs Blunden.' Hardcastle stood up. 'I'd better take my leave of the general for now, but I'll probably be seeing you again.'

'Pop down for a cup of tea any time you're here, Mr Hardcastle,' said Martha Blunden. 'It's always interesting having a chat with you.'

Yes, thought Hardcastle, *but not half as interesting for you as it is for me.*

Six

It was a week after the death of Sir Adrian Rivers before Hardcastle visited the police station in London Road, Kingston. Built in 1864, it was beginning to show its age, and Hardcastle would have been appalled to know that another fifty years would pass before it was finally vacated.

'I'm DDI Hardcastle of A, Sergeant.'

'All correct, sir,' said the sergeant, making the automatic response required by the regulations. Even when things were *not* all correct.

'I should hope so,' said Hardcastle. 'Tell me how I get to the coroner's court from here.'

The sergeant rounded the counter and went to the front door of the station. 'Go straight down there, sir,' he said, pointing. 'Then follow the tramlines round into Eden Street, and turn left at the Druid's Head pub. Clattern House is a couple of yards down on the left-hand side. That's the assize court, but they hold inquests there. You can't miss it, sir, it's just by the stone.'

'Stone? What stone?'

'The Coronation Stone, sir,' said the sergeant smugly, and hurried back into the police station.

Hardcastle was mildly surprised to find that neither Lady Rivers nor Sir Adrian's two sons were present at the inquest. As a consequence, the first witness was Thomas Beach.

Somewhat nervously, the butler testified that the dead body, to which the footman had called him, was that of Sir Adrian Rivers, and that he had then called the police.

'Is the family represented?' asked the coroner, his voice straining as he peered officiously around the courtroom. 'Very well,' he said, having elicited no response, 'you may stand down, but do not leave the precincts of the court.' Clearly relieved that his ordeal was over, Beach scurried from the witness box, taking a packet of cigarettes from his pocket as he made for the doors at the back of the courtroom.

Dr Bernard Spilsbury was called next, and gave evidence of his findings in clipped and dry medical language, much of which, Hardcastle suspected, only the coroner – a medical practitioner as well as a lawyer – understood.

Finally, it was Hardcastle's turn. He took the oath, returned the New Testament to the usher, and announced himself to be Divisional Detective Inspector Ernest Hardcastle of the A or Whitehall Division.

'You are the officer appointed to investigate the death of Colonel Sir Adrian Rivers, baronet, of The Grange, Penny Lane, Kingston Hill, in the Royal Borough of Kingston upon Thames, are you not?' asked the coroner pedantically.

'I am, sir.'

'Tell the court what you know of this matter, Inspector.'

Hardcastle summarized his investigations to date, and waited for the inevitable routine questions.

The coroner shuffled through his papers, and then asked, 'Do you have a suspect in custody, Inspector?'

'No, sir.'

'Do you consider that there is the likelihood of an early arrest?'

'I can't say at this stage, sir.'

'Thank you, Inspector,' said the coroner, and waiting until Hardcastle had returned to his seat, asked, 'Are there any applications?'

'I make formal application for the release of Sir Adrian Rivers's body, sir,' said Hardcastle, rising to his feet.

'Is there no further police requirement for its retention, Inspector?'

'None, sir.'

'Very well. Sir Adrian Rivers's body may be released for burial or cremation in accordance with the wishes of his family. This inquest is adjourned until such time as the police inform my officer that there would be some benefit in reconvening these proceedings.'

'Well, that was over quicker than I thought it would be, Marriott,' said Hardcastle, as the two of them strode towards Market Place. 'According to that porter at Norbiton station, we ought to be lucky enough to find a taxi outside the Sun Hotel.'

'What's next, sir?' asked Marriott.

'Back up Kingston Hill to tell General Rivers that he can plant his father,' said Hardcastle bluntly.

The door of The Grange was opened by Digby, the footman. 'Mr Beach is at the inquest, sir,' he said, by way of explanation for the butler's absence.

'I know, Digby, I've just seen him there.' Hardcastle had later caught sight of Beach waiting at a tram stop, but had declined to offer him a lift in the taxi that took him and Marriott to the Rivers's house. 'Is General Rivers at home?'

'Yes, sir.' Digby hurried ahead of Hardcastle, and opened the door to the morning room. 'Inspector Hardcastle, sir,' he announced.

'Ah, come in, Inspector. You too, Sergeant.'

'I've just come from the inquest, General,' said Hardcastle, 'and the coroner has released your father's body. You can now go ahead with the arrangements for his funeral.'

'Thank you, Inspector. What happens next?'

'I shall continue with my investigations, General,' Hardcastle said stiffly.

'And d'you think you'll get the fellow?' asked Gerard Rivers.

'You may rest assured of that, Colonel,' said Hardcastle, expressing the opinion with a confidence that he was far from feeling. On the basis of what he had learned so far, he had concluded that he was seeking an opportunist burglar who had entered the house, stolen a few items of comparatively little value, and murdered Sir Adrian in the process. But the finding of such criminals was always fraught with difficulty.

'You'll take a glass of whisky, Inspector?' asked Gerard, his hand hovering over the decanter.

'Most kind, Colonel, thank you,' murmured Hardcastle.

'I'd be grateful if you'd let me know when the funeral will be, General,' he said, addressing the request to the elder son.

'Tomorrow, Inspector,' said Ewart Rivers, without hesitation. 'At two o'clock.'

'Tomorrow, General?' Hardcastle was amazed by the response. 'But I've only just told you that the body of your late father is to be released.'

Ewart Rivers laughed. 'Soldiers are accustomed to making decisions based upon probabilities, Inspector,' he said, raising his glass in a silent toast. 'I anticipated that the coroner would give his consent, but I'd arranged with the undertakers that the interment could be postponed if any, er, procedural problems arose. You'll understand, I'm sure, that my brother and I are both playing an important part in prosecuting the war. We have to return to the Front as soon as possible. Rumour has it there's a big push coming.'

'So I gather, General,' said Hardcastle. The newspapers had recently been full of hints that the British Expeditionary Force was about to break out of the inhibiting impasse of trench warfare. 'And where is this funeral to take place?'

'Putney Vale,' said Gerard Rivers. 'It's not far from here. Near Wimbledon Common, in fact.'

'Yes, I know it,' said Hardcastle.

'Are you intending to be there, Inspector?' Ewart Rivers raised an eyebrow.

'Indeed, General. It's part of my duty.'

'Incidentally, where is my father's body? I have to let the undertaker know, you see.'

'In the mortuary at St Mary's Hospital, Paddington General,' said Hardcastle. 'It's where Dr Spilsbury conducts his post-mortem examinations,' he added unnecessarily.

'I'd better get on to the undertaker straight away. He'll need to arrange for the collection, placing it in the casket, and all that sort of thing.' Ewart Rivers did not seem too distressed at the prospect of burying his father, but Hardcastle attributed that to his experience of dealing daily with death in Flanders.

*　　*　　*

Despite the short time available in which to make the arrangements, the Rivers sons had done their best to ensure their father's funeral would be a memorable one.

The family Rolls Royce, with a wreath of lilies attached to its radiator, drove slowly through the gates of the cemetery, and Lady Rivers, Ewart and Gerard emerged into the sunshine. The two men were in uniform with swords and black crêpe armbands, and Lady Rivers – a small figure between her two stepsons – wore a black serge costume, and a small black hat with a veil that completely covered her face. Moments later, a taxi disgorged Beach, Digby, and Daisy Forbes, the parlour maid. All were in black.

'Mrs Blunden not here, Beach?' whispered Hardcastle to the butler.

'Mrs Blunden doesn't do funerals, sir,' replied Beach. 'Anyway, she's back at the house preparing the food for the wake.'

At two o'clock precisely, an ornate hearse bearing Sir Adrian's coffin entered the cemetery, the sable plumes of its four black horses occasionally catching the light breeze. A guard of honour furnished by the Surrey Rifles from its tented camp at Epsom brought up the rear of the cortège, the pre-war splendour of their fur-trimmed caps, green tunics and patent leather belts replaced by drab khaki uniforms and webbing. With rifles reversed, they slow-marched in time to the muffled beat of a solo side drum.

The graveside service was short. The clergyman – an army padre – spoke the customary words from the Book of Common Prayer, and Sir Adrian's two sons saluted as the coffin was lowered into the grave. A lone bugler sounded the 'Last Post', and the Surrey Rifles detachment discharged a *feu-de-mort* over the grave. The committal was complete.

'You and your sergeant are very welcome to come back to the house for some refreshments, Inspector,' said Gerard Rivers, as the family was leaving.

'Most kind, Colonel,' said Hardcastle, 'but Marriott and me has other things to attend to.'

*   *   *

That Sir Adrian Rivers's funeral had been held on the
Wednesday prevented Hardcastle from going to Hurst Park
on that day as he had originally planned. It was, therefore,
the following afternoon that he and Marriott entrained at
Waterloo for the journey to Hampton Court. As Marriott
had said, the Derby had been held at Newmarket the
previous month – and styled the 'New' Derby – because
Epsom racecourse was now a huge army encampment.
However, meetings were still being held at Hurst Park.

But nowadays fewer people risked going to the races than
had been the case before the war. The fear of Zeppelin raids
had created a measure of unwarranted hysteria among some
sections of the population, and they tended to shun places
where there were likely to be large crowds. A panicky
government imposed lighting restrictions and, in some cases,
it was reported that entire factories stopped work when one
of these giant airships was spotted crossing the coast of
England. But the Zeppelins' vulnerability to searchlights
and British fighters soon became apparent, and the people's
fear lessened in proportion to the diverting spectacle of one
of these marauders plummeting to the ground in flames.

Despite all that, a festive air pervaded the substantial
crowd that thronged the racecourse, and Hardcastle recalled
what General Ewart Rivers had said about a nation divided.

The weather was idyllic: an earlier shower had freshened
the air without making the grass too wet. Now the sun shone
down on little groups of people enjoying picnics and
watching the impromptu entertainment that race meetings
always provided. A hurdy-gurdy man vigorously operated
his barrel organ while his pet monkey – attired in a fez and
a red waistcoat – sat atop the machine indifferent to the
hubbub around it. Nearby, a fairground roundabout attracted
children and adults alike.

An open-topped omnibus had become a grandstand for
some of the well-to-do who, indifferent – both physically
and socially – to the crowd beneath them, were surveying
the field through binoculars.

As the detectives pushed their way through the crowds
to the bookmakers' ring, Hardcastle heard a man in morning

dress and a top hat complaining bitterly that his wallet had been stolen. But today was not a day upon which Hardcastle could be bothered with cases of petty larceny. There were, after all, plenty of uniformed police about to deal with such comparatively minor infringements of the law. From time to time, either Hardcastle or Marriott was obliged to shove a lurching drunk out of his way.

At last they found what they had come for: a large board declaring that 'HONEST ALBERT NORTH' was 'the book-maker you can trust'. Beneath this claim of probity was a list of the day's runners and riders, together with the current odds.

Standing on a low platform in front of this board was a man with a ruddy complexion and a flowing moustache. Probably about sixty years of age, he was stocky, and some 5 foot 6 inches tall. His brown derby was pushed back on his head, and his suit – a loud, brown check – had seen better days. Behind him, on a small platform, stood a tic-tac man, energetically signalling the current odds to other bookmakers.

'Albert North?' enquired Hardcastle, having eventually fought his way to the front of the crowd surrounding the bookmaker's stand.

'At your service,' said North with a broad grin, as he pushed the forefingers and thumbs of each hand into his waistcoat pockets. 'What's your pleasure, sir?'

'A few words with you, Mr North.' Not wishing to announce either his office or his business, Hardcastle displayed his warrant card in such a way as to shield it from the punters around him.

'Can you give us a minute or two, guv'nor?' said North in a low voice. He pulled a turnip watch from his pocket and glanced at it. 'The three thirty's about due for the off.'

Not wishing to antagonize a man who might prove to be a useful source of information, Hardcastle agreed to the slight delay and stepped to one side.

A few moments later, North joined the two police officers. 'Right, guv'nor,' he said, tucking a pencil behind his ear, 'and what can I do for the law? I ain't a welsher, if that's what you're on about. Ask anyone round here. Albert North always pays out on the dot.'

'It's nothing like that, Mr North,' said Hardcastle, drawing the bookmaker away from the crush around his stand.

'Take over, Charlie,' shouted North to his assistant. 'Well, what's it all about?' he asked, turning back to Hardcastle.

'It's about your son-in-law.'

'What, young Fred? What's he been up to? He ain't run, has he?' North paused. 'Here, you ain't come to tell me he's been killed, have you?' he asked, a look of concern on his face.

'Fred? Who's Fred?' asked Hardcastle, momentarily taken aback by North's reply.

'Fred Simpson. Married to my Vera, he is. Used to run a stall down Brixton Market in Electric Avenue, till he joined the army. Sergeant, he is, in the Royal Engineers. Somewhere in France, so they say.'

'No, it's nothing to do with him. I'm talking about Sir Adrian Rivers.'

'Old Sir Adrian? Yeah, I seen he got topped, up Kingston way, weren't it? A bleedin' shame. A right toff was the colonel. Put a few quid on the gee-gees over the years. In fact he was an owner. Had one or two good little runners, did the colonel. You on that job, then, guv'nor?'

'Yes, I am. And Sir Adrian was your son-in-law.'

'You don't mean he was married to my Muriel, surely to God?' North took off his hat and scratched his scalp through thinning hair. 'I think someone's been selling you a pup, guv'nor,' he said, shaking his head.

'She was married to Sir Adrian Rivers in 1914, Mr North. There's a record of the marriage at Somerset House.'

'Well, I'll go to the foot of our stairs. I never knew that. The carney little bitch. You wait till I get hold of her.'

'When did you last see her, Mr North?' asked Marriott.

'Must've been a fortnight since, I s'pose, guv'nor. She come up my place down Wandsworth for afternoon tea with me and the missus.'

'And how was she dressed?' asked Hardcastle.

'Dressed?' North raised his eyebrows. 'Gordon Bennett,

how would I know?' He paused in thought for a moment. 'Well, ordinary like, I s'pose. Except she had a fur coat on. Bit funny that, I thought, being as how it was May. Still, as my Marge says: "Ne'er cast a clout till May be out."'

'Did she look as though she'd come into money?'

'Nah! Kitted out like she always was, except, like I said, for that fur coat.'

'You say she came to visit you. Does that mean she doesn't live with you any more?' Hardcastle knew perfectly well that that was the case, but was interested in what North had to say.

'No, she don't, guv'nor. Pushed off at the start of the war. Said she ought to do something for the war effort, so she got herself a job in an aircraft factory down Kingston way. Sopwiths, I think she said. Living in one of them hostels, so she reckons. And the pay's good by all accounts, that's how she got herself a fur coat, see.'

'She been spinning you a yarn, then, hasn't she, Mr North?' said Hardcastle. 'Because she's called Muriel, Lady Rivers now.'

'Well, I'm buggered,' said North. 'Pardon my French, but d'you mean she ain't working in no aircraft factory, guv'nor?'

'No, she's not, Mr North, and I doubt she's ever set foot in one. Seems she spends most of her time going up to the West End in the family Rolls Royce, and spending money in shops like Harrods, and Fortnum and Masons, and taking tea with her friends in posh hotels.'

'Well, you could knock me down with a feather, guv'nor, and that's no error,' said North. 'How did she meet a toff like Sir Adrian, then?'

'I was hoping you'd be able to tell me.' Hardcastle had no intention of revealing what he had been told: that Muriel had met Sir Adrian Rivers at Epsom racecourse, and he found it hard to believe that 'Honest Albert North' was telling the truth. But he was prepared to leave it for the time being. 'How well d'you know Thomas Beach?' he asked suddenly, making the question sound like a statement that brooked no denial.

'Tommy Beach? Yeah, I know him. He used to come down here quite a bit. Liked the horses, did Tommy. But I ain't seen him lately, guv'nor. Why d'you ask?'

'No particular reason,' said Hardcastle. 'It's just a name that's come up in my enquiries into the murder of Sir Adrian.'

'But why all the questions, guv'nor? I mean, my Muriel ain't done nothing wrong, has she?'

'No,' said Hardcastle, 'but I have to speak to everyone who knew Sir Adrian.'

'Well, I'm sorry I can't help you, but I ain't seen Sir Adrian since before this ding-dong with Kaiser Bill broke out.'

'What d'you make of that, sir?' asked Marriott, on the train back to London.

'Honest Albert North, my arse,' said Hardcastle. 'I don't believe a word of what he said, but the thing that puzzles me is why he's telling lies.'

'Unless Muriel put him up to what was in the Rivers's house, sir. Supposing she told her old man that there were a lot of valuables there. He set up a burglary, but it went wrong. Maybe whoever it was got challenged by Sir Adrian, and was shot dead for his pains.'

'There could be something in that, Marriott,' said Hardcastle thoughtfully. 'But everyone says that Sir Adrian was doolally-tap.'

'Yes, sir, but the burglar might not have known that. If Sir Adrian woke up and mumbled something, the burglar, whoever he was, might've thought he'd be recognized, so he topped him and did a shift.'

'It doesn't mean Lady Rivers was involved though, Marriott. Look at it this way: she tells North that she's married to Sir Adrian, and is swanking about how well off she is, and what sort of drum she's living in. If she did visit him in Wandsworth a couple of weeks ago, she might've turned up in the Rolls Royce, despite what North said. So North thinks he'll have a bit of what's on offer, and sets up a burglary without telling his daughter. But after Sir

Adrian gets topped, North decides that he's better off saying nothing. Even as far as denying he knew his Muriel was married to Sir Adrian, and was now Lady Rivers.'

'On the other hand, sir,' said Marriott, 'Beach might've given North the information.'

'That's more likely, Marriott, but I think we're going out on a limb here. When it comes down to it, it'll more likely have been a burglar who just picked a big house on Kingston Hill. But why he didn't just run when he was rumbled beats me. He didn't have to kill the poor old bugger.'

Seven

On Friday morning, Hardcastle was sitting at his desk, mulling over what he had learned from Albert North – or, more correctly, *not* learned – and pondering the future of his investigation into the murder of Sir Adrian Rivers.

'Excuse me, sir,' said Detective Sergeant Wood, tapping lightly on Hardcastle's open office door.

'Yes, what is it, Wood?'

'The station officer's just received a telephone call from General Ewart Rivers, sir.'

'Oh?' Hardcastle picked up his pipe from the ashtray, and teased the half-smoked tobacco with a letter opener. 'What did he want?'

'He never said exactly, sir, except that he would like to see you.'

'Oh, he did, did he? Well, just because he's a general, he needn't think I'll go running every time he whistles. I'm not in his bloody army. Have you got a telephone number for him?'

'Yes, sir.' Wood placed a slip of paper on the DDI's desk.

'Well, don't give it to me, Wood, get me connected. You know I don't know how to use those things.' That was not true. Hardcastle was perfectly capable of using a telephone, but often said that he did not bark himself when he kept a dog to do it for him.

'The instrument's downstairs, sir.'

'I know where the damned thing is, Wood. I wasn't born yesterday,' said Hardcastle testily, and followed the sergeant downstairs to a small cubicle near the front office of the police station. But Hardcastle's irritation was not with Wood, nor, for that matter, with General Rivers. The whole business of traipsing up and down to Kingston annoyed him; and for that he blamed Chief Inspector Wensley.

The telephone was answered by Beach, but eventually Hardcastle found himself speaking to Ewart Rivers.

'I'm most awfully sorry to bother you, Inspector, but a matter has arisen that I think you should know about.'

'Can't you tell me over the line, General?'

'I'd rather not, Inspector. It is rather confidential, and one never knows who's listening in to these things. We know for sure that the Hun often manages to tap into our telephones, and I've no reason to think that that sort of thing doesn't happen here.'

'Very well, General, I'll be down as soon as I can.' Hardcastle was not pleased at having to go down to The Grange again, and was unconvinced that the Germans might be listening in to calls from Kingston Hill. He wondered, briefly, whether Ewart Rivers was beginning to display the same paranoia from which his late father had suffered. But, of course, the general was talking about field telephones in France, not those operated by the General Post Office in Kingston upon Thames. However, Hardcastle would be the first to admit that he did not much care for this new-fangled equipment and, in common with many others in the force, did not think it would last. In fact, he frequently described it as 'a flash in the pan'.

Returning to his office, Hardcastle bellowed for Marriott, donned his bowler hat, and seized his umbrella.

'Yes, sir?' Marriott appeared in the doorway.

'We're going to Kingston again, Marriott. General Rivers has got himself in a two an' eight about something he won't discuss on that telephone thing.'

It was nigh on midday by the time Hardcastle and Marriott arrived, once again, at The Grange. As usual, Beach admitted them, and conducted them to the morning room.

General Rivers crossed the room with an outstretched hand. 'I do apologize for dragging you all the way down here, Inspector,' he said, 'but this is a matter I'd much prefer to discuss face to face.' He pointed to a 'candlestick' telephone on a side table. 'I know for a fact that the servants can listen in below stairs to calls made from that instrument.' His earlier allusion to Germans listening in had been a veiled hint that staff at The Grange might be doing so, but it had been a little too subtle for Hardcastle to grasp.

'I take it this is a serious matter, then, General,' said Hardcastle, accepting a glass of whisky from Gerard Rivers.

'My brother and I visited the family solicitor yesterday, Inspector,' said Ewart Rivers, indicating with a wave of his hand that the detectives should sit down. 'He's a dull old stick called Lawson Soames with chambers in Lincoln's Inn, and his firm has served our family for generations. We wished to discuss the question of our father's will, d'you see?'

'I imagine so, General,' murmured Hardcastle.

'To our utter astonishment, we learned that my father had changed his will last year, and has left his entire estate to his wife. Well, widow now,' he added. Ewart Rivers was a stickler for accuracy.

'Really?' Hardcastle was not as surprised as the Rivers brothers at this revelation, but he often described himself as a cynical old copper.

'When the war started, father assured us that we – Gerard and I – were to be the sole beneficiaries, with the greater part of the estate coming to me, of course, as the heir to the baronetcy. And in the event of my being killed, it would all go to Gerard.'

'When did you last see your father, General?' asked Hardcastle.

Gerard Rivers laughed outright. 'You sound like William Yeames, Inspector.'

'Who?' Hardcastle shot a confused glance at each of the two brothers in turn.

But it was Marriott who provided the answer. 'William Yeames painted a famous picture called *When Did You Last See Your Father?*, sir. We had a print of it in our classroom when I was at school.'

'Thank you, Marriott,' snapped Hardcastle brusquely, and turned to Gerard Rivers. 'My sergeant's a bit of a bookish fellow, Colonel,' he said, but determined that he would give Marriott a private ticking off for exposing him as an uneducated fool.

'However, to answer your question, Inspector,' said Ewart Rivers. 'It was August 1915 in my case, but I think . . .' He broke off and turned to his brother. 'I think you saw him after that, Gerry, didn't you?'

'Yes, just before last Christmas.'

'And did Sir Adrian say anything to either of you about changing his will, gentlemen?'

'Not a word, Inspector,' said Ewart Rivers. 'Not a word.'

'Nor to me,' said Gerard Rivers.

'D'you think your father's state of mind had anything to do with it?' asked Hardcastle.

Ewart Rivers pondered the question for a moment. 'Maybe so,' he said thoughtfully. 'I know that he'd been suffering from dementia since just before the war, but it seemed to manifest itself only in an occasional loss of memory. I suppose it could have got worse. But being on active service, neither my brother nor I was able to determine his state of mental health, d'you see? I suppose we might be able to prove a case of his being unfit to make a will.'

Hardcastle paused for some time before making what could be construed as a serious allegation, and one that could only involve Muriel Rivers. 'D'you think it's possible that the will was forged, General?' he asked tentatively.

Ewart Rivers thought that over. 'It's a possibility, I suppose, Inspector, but that's more your line of business than ours,' he said, including his brother in the comment. 'Although I would have thought Soames would have mentioned it if he'd had doubts about its authenticity.' He lowered his voice, even though the door of the morning room was closed. 'I've also considered the possibility that Lady Rivers somehow managed to persuade father to change his will in her favour. Given his mental state, he might have done so without actually knowing what he was doing.'

'If I could have sight of the will, General, I could show it to our forgery experts. Of course, I'd need to have a copy of Sir Adrian's signature so that they could compare the two. On the other hand – not that I know much about the civil law – it might be possible for you to contest the will. But that would be a matter for your solicitor.'

'Don't worry about that, Inspector,' said Ewart Rivers firmly. 'We've already discussed it with Soames, but we thought it necessary to tell you about it in case it impinged on your enquiries. However, I'll instruct him to allow you to have sight of the will.'

'That would be a help, General,' said Hardcastle. But he was uncertain that it would assist in finding Sir Adrian's killer. Indeed, he felt that he was being led into a side issue. 'Incidentally, I saw Albert North yesterday,' he continued, moving away from the subject of Sir Adrian's will.

'Who?' Ewart Rivers placed his whisky glass on a side table and stared at Hardcastle.

'Lady Rivers's father, General.'

'Good Lord! I'd forgotten about him. Some low sort of bookmaker, I believe.'

'You've not met him, then.'

'Not lately, Inspector.'

'Sergeant Marriott and I made a point of going to Hurst Park races, and speaking to him.'

'May I ask why you found it necessary to do so, Inspector?' There was no note of censure in Ewart Rivers's voice, rather one of curiosity.

'I don't really know, General,' admitted Hardcastle, with uncharacteristic candour. 'But in a murder investigation, one makes enquiries of anyone who might be able to shed some light, so to speak.'

'And did you learn anything that shed some light, as you put it?' asked Gerard Rivers.

'It was an interesting conversation, Colonel. For a start, he denied knowing that his daughter was married to your father.'

'I suppose that's just possible,' said Ewart Rivers doubtfully. 'Muriel's father wasn't at the wedding, but I'd've thought it was the sort of thing she'd've mentioned to him, eh what? Seems damned peculiar that she wouldn't have boasted about marrying a baronet.'

'North claimed that his daughter was working at the Sopwith aircraft factory, here in Kingston.'

Gerard Rivers threw back his head and laughed. 'Whatever gave him that idea?'

'He said that that's what his daughter had told him, Colonel,' said Hardcastle. 'He said that she turned up at his place in Wandsworth in a fur coat, even though it was May – this was a couple of weeks ago – and that she said she could afford such luxuries because she was well paid helping to build aeroplanes.'

'I've never heard such tosh,' exclaimed Ewart.

'May I speak in absolute confidence, General?' Hardcastle leaned forward, cradling his whisky glass in his hands.

'Of course you may, Inspector.' Ewart Rivers stood up and took Hardcastle's glass. 'Here, let me freshen that up for you.'

'The butler Beach told me that Sir Adrian first made the acquaintance of Lady Rivers – the current Lady Rivers, that is – at a race meeting at Epsom, just before the war.'

'Yes, that's so,' said Ewart, handing Hardcastle his recharged glass. 'It was a family day out, and we were all there. Can you remember how it was that the guv'nor met her, Gerry?'

Gerard leaned back in his chair and crossed his legs. 'We were having a picnic on the Downs, and this girl – Muriel, that is – was nearby. Only a yard or two away, as a matter of fact, sitting on a rug and looking very sorry for herself. She appeared to be on her own, and father took pity on her, I suppose. Always a soft touch for a pretty girl was the old man. Anyway, the upshot was that he asked me to invite her to join us for luncheon. A bit later on this fellow turned up wearing some awful tweed suit and a brown bowler hat. I ask you, a brown bowler!' The younger Rivers had clearly been unimpressed by Albert North's sartorial taste. 'And Muriel introduced him as her father.' Gerard smote his knee with his hand. 'I've just remembered something; father seemed to know the fellow.'

'That's probably explained by North admitting that your father had placed bets with him from time to time, Colonel,' said Hardcastle.

'Did Beach have any part to play in this apparently casual meeting, sir?' asked Marriott.

'Not that I'm aware of, Sergeant. He was busy serving the meal. I seem to recall that it was a light luncheon: salad, and cold chicken and ham, that sort of thing. And a bottle or two of Chablis that Beach had somehow managed to keep chilled. I seem to remember that the man North acknowledged Beach by raising his hat. But that's probably because he thought he was a member of the family. The damned fellow wouldn't've recognized a butler if one came up and bit him.'

'When I spoke to North, he said that he knew Beach of old, and that he was quite a gambler.'

'Is that so?' Ewart raised an eyebrow.

'While he was in the army, he was reduced in rank for borrowing money from subordinates,' said Hardcastle, throwing caution aside. But on reflection, he realized that the Rivers brothers would have had access to Beach's service record had they the desire to look at it.

'Really? I didn't know that. The old man seemed to think he was a good sort. Been with him for years apparently.'

'There is another more delicate question I have to ask, General,' interposed Hardcastle, lowering his voice, 'and it concerns Lady Rivers herself. I would ask that you don't mention it to her ladyship.'

'Of course.' Ewart frowned. 'What is it?'

'When I came to see you last Saturday . . .'

'I remember,' said Gerard, with a laugh. 'It was pouring with rain, and you and your sergeant turned up looking like drowned rats.'

'Exactly so, Colonel,' said Hardcastle tartly, before returning his gaze to Ewart. 'Well, on account of the inclement weather, Lady Rivers very kindly offered me and Marriott a lift to the railway station in the Rolls Royce.'

'Very generous of her,' murmured Gerard sarcastically.

'And during the course of that short journey, she mentioned that Sir Adrian had asked her to marry him shortly after that meeting at Epsom.'

'That's my understanding of the situation, Inspector,' said

Ewart, 'despite our attempts to dissuade him. But we didn't realize that his mind had started to go.'

'Quite so, General, but she also suggested that it was you, sir, who was, er, rather keen on her. She was of the view that you were the one what wanted to marry her.'

'Really? Well, I'm afraid she gravely misled herself in that regard, Inspector. I certainly gave her no encouragement to think that.' Ewart Rivers's response was remarkably restrained and his face expressionless, but Hardcastle was convinced that his outburst would have been far more voluble had it not been for his presence and that of Marriott.

'Am I to take it that there's no truth in her opinion, General?'

'Yes,' said Ewart Rivers curtly, 'you most certainly may, Inspector.' He opened a gunmetal cigarette case and offered it to the two detectives.

'I'm a pipe man myself, General, thank you all the same. But my sergeant indulges.'

'Do carry on.' Ewart Rivers's attitude relaxed as he offered Marriott a cigarette. 'If you're very fortunate, Inspector, my brother will offer you some of his tobacco.'

Gerard stood up and took a tobacco jar from an occasional table, and handed it to Hardcastle.

Once the four men were smoking, Gerard leaned forward. 'I have to tell you, Inspector, that my brother and I were very unhappy about our father's marriage to Muriel, and . . .'

'Gerry, I don't think we should discuss family matters in front of the inspector.' Ewart Rivers spoke sternly, and a frown settled on his face.

'For God's sake, Ewart, the inspector is trying to find out who killed the old man. He needs to know everything we can possibly tell him, however unpalatable.'

'But you surely don't suspect Muriel of killing father, do you, Inspector?' demanded Ewart, with a look of incredulity.

'I don't exclude anyone from my enquiries until I'm satisfied that they had nothing to do with it, General.'

'But God, man, she's only a slip of a girl.' Ewart gave his moustache a brief tug. 'Women like her don't go around murdering people. You said yourself that you thought it was a burglar who'd got into the house through the open window of father's bedroom.'

'That's only one of the theories I'm working on, General,' said Hardcastle. 'But crime is like that. You go down every road until you find it's a dead end. Then you go back to the crossroads and start off down another road, so to speak.'

'I see.' The tone of Ewart Rivers's response implied that he was not much impressed with this style of criminal investigation.

'Well, General, if that's all, Marriott and me'll be getting back to London.'

'Yes, of course, and once again I'm sorry to have dragged you all the way down here. You may wish to know that my brother and I are returning to the Front tomorrow evening. Should there be anything that you need to get in touch with us about, I'm sure the APM at London District will know the quickest and most secure way.'

'I'm much obliged, General.'

'Before you go, Inspector . . .' Ewart Rivers crossed to a small bureau and took out a wad of cheques. 'This is one of father's returned cheques – quite an old one – but it bears his signature. Your fellows may wish to use it for comparison with the signature on the will.'

'Thank you, General.' Hardcastle pocketed the cheque as he and Marriott stood up. 'I hope you'll keep your heads down over there, gents,' he added.

'You may rest assured that we shall, Inspector,' said Ewart Rivers, an amused smile on his face. He did not think that much harm would befall him in the chateau that housed Fourth Army's headquarters, some four miles from the foremost trenches.

'Get hold of Catto, Marriott,' said Hardcastle, once he and his sergeant had returned to Cannon Row police station. 'I've got a job for him.'

A few minutes later, Henry Catto appeared in the doorway. 'You wanted me, sir?' he asked apprehensively, obviously wondering what dereliction of duty Hardcastle had discovered.

'Albert North is a bookmaker, Catto.'

'Yes, I know, sir.'

'I should hope you do, Catto, seeing as how you did the Somerset House searches on him and Lady Rivers. But don't interrupt. He's got a pitch at Hurst Park races, and he lives in Wandsworth.'

'Whereabouts in Wandsworth, sir?' asked Catto unwisely.

'I don't know, lad. That's for you to find out. You're supposed to be a detective. For the next few days you'll be following him about. I want to know all about him. Who he meets, where he goes, and generally what he's up to. Start tomorrow.'

'Yes, sir.' Catto was not a little disturbed by this instruction.

'And dress rough, so's he won't spot you for a copper,' said Hardcastle. 'Not that he'll have much of a problem in that regard, not with the state of your suit.' The DDI glanced at the calendar on his desk. 'Report back on Tuesday, or sooner if you've got something interesting. Got that? And don't go nicking no crown-and-anchor merchants, nor none of them find-the-lady men. I know you have a liking for feeling a collar.'

'Yes, sir. Er, no, sir.' Catto was unsure what would constitute 'something interesting', but was not prepared to seek a definition from the irascible Hardcastle for fear of yet another reproof.

'Well, don't stand there, Catto. Get on with it.'

'Yes, sir,' said Catto, and fled from the DDI's office.

'What d'you hope to learn by setting Catto on to North, sir?' asked Marriott.

'I haven't the faintest idea,' said Hardcastle airily. 'But one of the things you learn in this game is to cast your bread on the waters. You never know when something'll turn up.'

Eight

B eing uncertain what he was supposed to be looking for, Detective Constable Henry Catto had mixed feelings about his assignment. Although it would get him away from the demanding Hardcastle, Catto knew there would come a time when he had to report back to the DDI. And that would be when the results of his surveillance of Albert North would, in all probability, be found wanting by the exacting inspector.

On Saturday morning – having deliberately not shaved – he left the police section house in Ambrosden Avenue, Westminster, attired in a pair of tattered trousers, an old seaman's sweater that had seen better days, and a cloth cap with a hole in it. Catching an Underground train to Waterloo railway station, he purchased a third class ticket for the service to Hampton Court.

As it was a Saturday, Hurst Park racecourse was even more thronged with people than when Hardcastle and Marriott had visited it on Thursday. And, as Hardcastle had forecast, there was a proliferation of illegal gamesters, each with a lookout keeping an eye open for the police. But Catto, recalling the DDI's admonition, regretfully ignored them.

He soon found Albert North's pitch, and for a few moments he stood at a distance from it, wondering what, if anything, to do next. It was all very well for Hardcastle to say that he should identify North's acquaintances, but what should he do? Follow them, and in the process miss someone more important? Or perhaps return only to find that North himself had disappeared. It was the sort of dilemma that Catto frequently found himself facing.

He felt a firm tap on his shoulder, and turned to find a young policeman standing behind him. 'I've been keeping an eye on you, cully, and I know what you're up to, my lad. Just waiting for someone with a bulging dummy so's you can dip him.'

'I'm in the Job, you bloody idiot,' snarled Catto in a stage whisper. 'I've got more to do than watch for punters with fat pockets so's I can filch a wallet.' Palming his warrant card from his trouser pocket, he displayed it in such a way that only the policeman could see it.

'Sorry, mate,' said the PC.

'Well, don't stand there blowing my cover, piss off, you stupid bastard,' muttered Catto out of the corner of his mouth.

The chastened policeman moved away, disappointed that he was not, after all, about to make an arrest of a suspected person loitering with intent to commit a felony.

For the remainder of the afternoon, Catto kept a close watch on Albert North's stand, changing his position from time to time in an attempt to appear uninterested. But the only people who approached the bookmaker were obvious punters intent upon placing a bet. Around mid-afternoon, Catto took advantage of a brief thinning of the crowd around North's stand, and slid away to purchase a couple of hot dogs, and have a pint of beer. At one point, he visited another bookmaker and risked half a crown on Copper's Might in the three thirty to win. It came in last.

At six o'clock, the day's racing having finished, North began to pack up. He dismantled his stand and placed its constituent parts in a large canvas bag that was fitted with a shoulder strap, then placed his day's takings in a leather bag and locked it. Eventually, he made his way to a beer tent and sank three pints of best bitter in quick succession before making his way to Hampton Court railway station.

To Catto's frustration, the train was crowded with race-goers returning to London, most of whom – including Albert North – found it necessary to change at Clapham Junction. And it was there that Catto almost lost his quarry. Fighting his way upwards through the crowd of home-going workers descending the steps from one platform, and climbing those to another, he was constantly buffeted by people going in the opposite direction. But luck was on his side, helped by the fact that North was easily distinguishable, and encumbered, by the canvas-covered bookmaker's board he was carrying.

As Catto reached the distant platform, he was fortunate enough to see Albert North struggling to board the train, and the detective just managed to throw himself into a compartment as it began to move off.

'Stand away,' shouted the guard. 'You'll get yourself bloody killed.'

Because Catto had been forced by circumstances to enter the compartment next to North's, he was obliged to poke his head out of the window every time the train stopped to see if North was alighting. Finally, at Wandsworth Town station, he was rewarded by the sight of North making for the exit, and promptly set off in pursuit. Again, he almost lost track of him, this time thanks to the intervention of an officious ticket collector.

'This ain't the right ticket for here, mate. That'll be another fourpence.'

'Urgent police business,' said Catto, and ignoring the official's protests that he would still have to pay, pushed past him and rushed out to the street just in time to see North entering the Railway Arms public house.

Half an hour later, North emerged and, now a little unsteady on his feet, made his way into Podmore Road. A hundred yards further on, the bookmaker turned into Flavell Road, and it was here that Catto had a stroke of good fortune.

It would have been obvious to any onlooker that not only had North had his fill of beer, but doubtless had been drinking for much of the day. Staggering drunkenly across the road, he tripped on the kerb and went flying. His cumbersome board hit the ground with a clatter and skidded across the pavement.

With no thought for what should have been a discreet surveillance, Catto rushed towards the bookmaker who, by now, was lying full length on the flagstones and swearing volubly.

'Are you all right, guv'nor? Here, let me give you a hand up.' Catto seized hold of North's arm and helped him to his feet.

'Very good of you, mate. Yes, very decent,' said North, his speech quite slurred.

'Are you sure you ain't hurt, guv'nor?' asked Catto, at his solicitous best, as he picked up North's battered bowler hat.

'Not at all, guv'nor,' said North with a rueful grin. 'Nothing that a large whisky won't put right.'

Catto picked up North's board and handed it to him. 'Got far to go?' he asked.

'No, this is where I live,' said North, nodding at the house outside which he had fallen. 'Thank Gawd the missus weren't looking out of the window. She'd've thought I'd been drinking.' He accompanied this comment with a throaty laugh. Lurching unsteadily up the garden path of number 22, he stood his board against the front wall, and opened the door with a latchkey. 'Come in and have a tipple, guv'nor.' He beckoned in Catto's direction. 'Least I can do for you for giving me a hand.'

Once inside, North led Catto into the parlour. 'Marge,' he yelled, 'I've got a visitor.'

A woman wearing a flowered overall entered the room. She cast a searching glance at her husband and shook her head. 'Have you been drinking again, Bert North?' she demanded. It sounded as though it were a daily accusation.

'Only my usual pint at the Railway, love,' lied North, and quickly diverted the conversation from any further enquiry into his drinking habits. 'This young gent very kindly gave me a hand carrying my board,' he continued, enlarging on the fiction. 'I'm going to give him a glass of whisky as a sort of thank you. This here's my missus, Marjorie,' he added, as an afterthought.

'Oh, that was very good of you.' Marjorie North held out one hand while primping her hair with the other. 'Delighted, I'm sure,' she said. 'And to whom do I have the honour?'

Catto shook hands. 'I'm, er, Jim Cook,' he said, conjuring up the first name that came into his head. He thought it would be unwise to tell the Norths who he really was, and even less to explain *what* he was.

'Well, I'll leave you to your whisky while I finish off supper, Bert,' said Marjorie. She paused at the door. 'Perhaps you'd like to join us, Mr Cook. There's plenty.'

'Thank you, Mrs North,' said Catto. 'That's very generous of you.' He was driven to accept not only by overwhelming hunger, but also the thought that he might get into Hardcastle's good books by acquiring a little more information about the North family.

Albert North crossed to a side table and poured two substantial measures of whisky from a decanter. 'There you are, Jim. Don't mind if I call you Jim, do you?'

'Not at all, Mr North.'

'Bert's the name, Jim. Honest Albert North, the bookmaker you can trust.' He laughed, and took a swig of Scotch.

Catto glanced at a framed photograph on the mantelpiece. It was of a coarsely good-looking young woman in a bridal gown on the arm of a much older, distinguished man in morning dress.

'Who's that, Bert?' asked Catto, half guessing.

'That's our eldest, Muriel,' said North, puffing himself up with pride. 'Done well for herself, she has. She's Lady Rivers now. Married a baronet. A colonel, he was.'

'Is that a fact?' said Catto, pretending surprise at this revelation. 'How'd she manage that, then?'

'Bit of a long story, really.' North waved at an armchair. 'Take the weight off of your plates, Jim,' he said, and sat down opposite Catto. 'A mate of mine, Tommy Beach, introduced them, in a manner of speaking. Tom's butler to Sir Adrian Rivers, or was before the old boy got hisself topped up Kingston way. I knew him an' all. Great racing man was Sir Adrian. A true gent of the turf, and always good for few quid on the favourite.' He shook his head. 'Bleedin' tragedy, and that's a fact. Gawd knows who'd've wanted to do him in. Anyway, Muriel was with me at Epsom one day – a few months before the war broke out – and Sir Adrian and his brood turned up, along with Tom. Well, Tom knew as how Sir Adrian was a widower, and hinted to Muriel that she might do herself a bit of good by settling on the grass near where the Rivers clan was having a picnic. Tom reckoned the old man had an eye for a pretty girl, and our Muriel's a bit of a stunner. But you could've knocked me down with a feather at what happened next, Jim, and that's no error.' He chuckled at the recollection. 'Believe it or not, Sir Adrian sent one of his lads across to invite our Muriel to join 'em for lunch. The next thing Marge and me knew was that she was getting wed to him. There, what d'you think of that, eh?'

'Was it a big society wedding, Bert?'

'I s'pose so.'

'Weren't you there, then?' Catto again expressed surprise.

'Nah! It was held some place down Wiltshire, but more to the point it was Derby Day, third of June, 1914. A big day in my game, and not one I'm likely to forget.'

'What game's that?' asked Catto innocently, making a pretence of forgetting that North had already told him he was a bookmaker.

'Like I told you, Jim, turf accountant. What the hoi polloi calls a bookie,' said North with a grin. 'Anyway, where was I? Oh yes, if I'd known then what I know now, I'd've been better off giving it a miss. The Derby, I mean, not the wedding.' He glanced at Catto, a rueful expression on his face. 'Durbar the Second was first past the post at twenty-to-one, Mick MacGee up. Cost me a bloody fortune. And a few others in the profession, an' all.'

'I don't suppose you see much of your daughter now, then, Bert,' said Catto. 'Now she's mixing in high society.'

'On the contrary, Jim. She gets down here to see us whenever she can. What's more, she comes in a Rolls Royce with a chauffeur all kitted out in the proper gear. Done better than our other girl, Vera. Married a market trader from Brixton, she did. Well, he's a sergeant in the Royal Engineers now. Somewhere over in France, the last we heard. That's her.' North pointed to another photograph of two young people in a stiff wedding-day pose.

But further conversation was interrupted by the re-appearance of Mrs North. 'Supper's ready,' she said, poking her head around the door of the parlour.

The 1914 Derby might have cost Albert North a fortune, but if the spread on the kitchen table was anything to go by, he had clearly recovered his losses. Marjorie North, a capable cook, had produced a banquet, at least in Catto's eyes.

'You tuck in, Mr Cook,' said Marjorie, as Albert North joined them bearing two tankards of beer, and a cup of tea for his wife. 'Bert knows a few people who manage to get round the shortages,' she added confidentially, 'but don't tell anyone.'

There was a huge boiled ham, its knuckle adorned with a paper frill, Cumberland sauce, and a cold savoury pie. On a plate in the centre of the table were chunks of homemade bread, and a dish of freshly churned butter, alongside an assortment of pickles and chutney. A large bowl of salad stood on the sideboard.

Albert North set to with gusto, occasionally holding his knife and fork vertically on the table while pausing to make some comment.

'Bert, put your cutlery down, and don't talk with your mouth full,' reproached Marjorie. 'Shouldn't behave like that when we've got a guest.'

'Sorry, dear,' said North, contriving to look sheepish. 'Been married nigh on forty years now, Jim,' he continued, 'but she still nags me.'

'Are you married, Mr Cook?' asked Marjorie.

'No, Mrs North,' said Catto. 'Never seem to have found the right girl.'

'I'm sure you will one day,' commented Marjorie. 'A well set-up young man like you ought to have a girl looking after him.'

'Where d'you live, Jim?' asked North.

It was an innocent question, but it flummoxed Catto momentarily. 'Er, Victoria,' he said eventually.

'Oh yes. Whereabouts?'

'Strutton Ground,' said Catto, recovering his composure,

and naming one of the few streets in the area where it was feasible he might have accommodation.

'What were you doing down here in Wandsworth, then?' Again, Catto had to think quickly. 'I was supposed to be meeting a mate of mine, but he never turned up.'

'I've got mates like that,' muttered North, but to Catto's relief did not press the matter further.

'I'm sure you'd fancy some of my pudding,' said Marjorie North, placing a fruit tart and an apple cheese-cake on the table, and setting down a large jug of cream. 'Young single fellow like you needs building up, I can see that.'

It was gone nine o'clock before Catto was able to make his excuses and depart, having thanked Mrs North profusely for the supper.

'Any time you're in the area, drop in and have a chinwag,' said Albert North, as he conducted Catto to the front door. 'And if you're ever at Hurst Park races, look me up. Mind you, I'm not always there. You might find me at Gatwick, Lingfield, Kempton or Sandown. To tell you the truth, I'd rather have Epsom, but it's full of soldiers now. I got to know the punters there, see, and you can't beat having regulars you know. But fortunately most of 'em have shifted to Hurst Park.' He grasped Catto's hand in a firm grip. 'Thanks for helping me up, Jim,' he whispered. 'And thanks for not letting on to the missus about me falling arse over tit because I was half pissed.'

In something of a quandary, Henry Catto walked slowly down Flavell Road towards the railway station. Although he had obtained what the DDI might consider to be valu-able information, he had also compromised himself by becoming known to the Norths. That, of course, would rule out any further surveillance on his part. In any event, he did not think any useful purpose would be served by keeping a watch on Albert North's house the following day, a Sunday, but he was now unsure what he should do on the Monday. Somewhat reluctantly, he decided there was only one course of action he could take: see Hardcastle and seek directions. It was that decision, and contemplation of the DDI's possible reaction, that completely ruined the rest of Catto's weekend.

At nine o'clock on Monday morning, Catto tapped on Hardcastle's office door. In view of the DDI's earlier comments about his turnout, Catto presented himself in as immaculate a condition as was possible. He had donned the better of his two suits, having risen early to spend half an hour carefully pressing it. Highly polished shoes and a clean shirt with a perfectly knotted tie completed his sartorial elegance.

Hardcastle looked up in surprise, but made no comment about his DC's appearance. 'What are you doing here, Catto?' he demanded accusingly. 'I thought I'd given you an observation to do.'

'I've got a problem, sir,' said Catto nervously.

'So have I, and it's called Catto,' said Hardcastle cuttingly. 'So you'd better tell me why you're here and not following Albert North about. And you'd better tell me a bit *jildi*, an' all, because I ain't got time to waste.'

As succinctly as possible, Catto explained about tailing Albert North from Hurst Park races to his home in Flavell Road, Wandsworth, on Saturday afternoon and evening. With grave apprehension, he then recounted how he had come to share a meal with the Norths, and what he had learned about Muriel Rivers, her first meeting with Sir Adrian, her marriage to him, and her frequent visits to her parents' home in Wandsworth.

This exposition was followed by a long silence on the DDI's part, during which he filled his pipe. Catto waited, fiddling with the bottom button of his waistcoat, and wondering if Hardcastle's oft-threatened promise to return him to uniform duty was about to come to pass.

'You've done bloody well, lad,' said Hardcastle eventually, as he expelled pipe smoke towards the nicotine-stained ceiling of his office.

'Thank you, sir.' Catto could not believe it, but was careful not to look too pleased at this singular compliment from the DDI.

'I think there might be some advantage in continuing to keep an eye on this cove,' mused Hardcastle.

'But he knows me now, sir.'

'Well, of course he does, Catto. No, I'll have to use someone else.' Hardcastle looked thoughtful for a while. 'Wilmot,' he said suddenly. 'Fetch Wilmot in here.'

Catto dashed out to the detectives' office and told Fred Wilmot that the DDI wanted him urgently. Hardcastle had not actually used the word 'urgently', but it was common knowledge at Cannon Row police station that when the DDI said he wanted something or somebody, it was automatically assumed the instruction should be complied with expeditiously.

'Wilmot, I've got an observation for you to do,' said Hardcastle, when the DC appeared. 'Catto here'll tell you what's what, and he'll tell you the tale so far. Don't make a Mons of it, and report back here . . .' He paused and glanced at his calendar. 'Friday. That's all.' And with that he waved a hand of dismissal, but as the two detectives turned to leave the office, he said, 'Not you, Catto.'

'Sir?'

'When you've told Wilmot what he's got to do, tell Sergeant Marriott what you found out on Saturday.'

'Yes, sir.'

Ten minutes later, Marriott joined his DDI. 'Catto seems to have turned up some useful information, sir,' he said.

Hardcastle nodded. 'Certainly gives the lie to this nonsense North was talking about Lady Rivers working in an aircraft factory, Marriott. So much for him pretending he didn't know she was married to Sir Adrian. I wonder what his game is.'

'D'you think he had something to do with the burglary, sir?'

'Right now, your guess is as good as mine, Marriott. But why should he make up a cock-and-bull yarn like that otherwise?'

'Are you going to front him with it, sir?'

'Not yet, Marriott, not yet. The bugger's up to something, and I want to find out what before I start in on him. I'm wondering if he put Muriel up to having Sir Adrian's will changed. But if what Catto said is right, then our Mr North don't seem short of a bob or two. Of course, Muriel might be feathering her own nest, on account of Honest Albert not being disposed to parting with any of his money in her direction. In my experience, bookmakers are notorious penny-pinchers. Nearly as bad as pawnbrokers.'

And divisional detective inspectors, thought Marriott, but kept his counsel.

Nine

Lawson Soames was a tall man of severe countenance. Dressed in black jacket and striped trousers, he rose majestically from his chair and crossed the room ponderously to shake hands with his visitors.

'Divisional Detective Inspector Hardcastle of the Whitehall Division, sir, and this is Detective Sergeant Marriott.'

'Do take a seat, gentlemen, and tell me what I can do for you.'

'I understand that General Rivers has spoken to you regarding Sir Adrian Rivers's will, Mr Soames.'

The Rivers family solicitor returned to his place behind his desk. 'That is so. But what is your interest?'

'General Rivers, and his brother, Colonel Rivers, were surprised that the will had been changed solely in favour of Lady Rivers,' began Hardcastle.

With the professional taciturnity of lawyers, Soames expressed no opinion about that, but clipped on a pair of pince-nez and drew a document across the broad expanse of his desk. Removing the pink tape, he carefully unfolded the sheets of parchment comprising Sir Adrian Rivers's last will and testament.

'I personally drew up this will, Inspector, and was present when it was signed by Sir Adrian. It was witnessed by . . .' Soames paused to peer more closely at the signature. 'One Thomas Beach.' He looked up. 'I understand that Beach was Sir Adrian's butler.' He appeared faintly bemused that a man of Sir Adrian's calibre should have had his butler witness his signature. 'However, Sir Adrian assured me that he had known Beach for a long time, and trusted him.

Apparently the man had been Sir Adrian's batman in the army before entering the Rivers's household as butler.' He pushed the will away, and took off his spectacles. 'I understand from General Rivers that you believe the will may have been forged, Inspector.' It sounded like an accusation, emphasized by the almost sarcastic half smile on his face.

'No, sir, not as such. When General Rivers told me that Sir Adrian's will had been unexpectedly changed, I expressed the view that it *might* have been forged. But now you assure me that you were present when it was signed, that removes that possibility.'

'Well, that seems to conclude our business.'

'One other thing, Mr Soames,' said Hardcastle. 'I have been told by various members of the household that Sir Adrian was suffering from some sort of dementia.'

'So I understand.'

'Are you satisfied that Sir Adrian was quite lucid when he made his new will?'

'Perfectly, Inspector.' Soames steepled his fingers and leaned back in his chair. 'One of the duties of a legal advisor is to ensure that a testator is sound of mind. And I'm quite satisfied in that regard.' There was an air of hostility in the reply, almost as if the solicitor's professional competence had been impugned.

'Did Sir Adrian happen to say why he had changed his will in favour of his wife?' persisted Hardcastle, even though it was clear that Soames was intent upon bringing the interview to a close.

'No, he did not, and I would not be able to tell you even if he had. Conversations between client and lawyer are privileged, as I'm sure you know.' The solicitor stood up, and returned the will to his safe.

'That Soames is a pompous arse,' muttered Hardcastle, as he and Marriott walked out into the sunshine of Chancery Lane in search of a cab. 'But it seems that forgery don't come into it, Marriott.'

'It certainly looks like a dead end on that score, sir.'

'Seeing what Soames said about his conversation with Sir Adrian being privileged, I doubt that he'd even tell

General Rivers what his old man said about changing his will. If he said anything. Like getting blood out of a stone, getting anything out of that Soames. But I'm still sure there's been some jiggery-pokery going on somewhere, Marriott.'

'But d'you reckon this had anything to do with the break-in at The Grange, sir?' Marriott was somewhat concerned that Hardcastle seemed to be developing a conspiracy of some sort out of what, at first sight, appeared to have been a straightforward burglary, albeit one that resulted in murder.

'I think that Honest Albert North's hand is involved in this somewhere,' said Hardcastle, ignoring Marriott's observation. 'I'd trust him about as far as I could sling a grand piano, and that's a fact. But I'm not sure he'd have the wit to get involved in bending a will. Not when you've got a baronet, a general and a colonel involved. And if there was anything a bit suspicious about it, Soames would've come down on whoever was responsible like a ton of bricks.'

'What now, then, sir?' asked Marriott.

'Seeing as how it was Beach who witnessed the will, Marriott, I think we'll have a word with him. Give him a bit of a rattling,' said Hardcastle, as he waved his umbrella vigorously at a passing cab.

The Rolls Royce, with Daniel Good behind the wheel, was drawn up outside the front door of The Grange when Hardcastle and Marriott arrived at nine o'clock on the Tuesday morning.

'Good morning, sir.' Beach, as immaculate as ever, opened the door wide, and stepped back to admit the two detectives. 'I presume it's Lady Rivers you're wishing to speak to, sir.'

'No, it's you, Beach,' said Hardcastle, handing his bowler hat and umbrella to the butler.

'Very good, sir.' Beach did not seem at all disturbed that Hardcastle had further questions for him.

'Lady Rivers off out, is she?'

'Yes, sir. I understand her ladyship is going into Kingston to meet friends for coffee.'

As if to confirm what the butler had said, Muriel Rivers

appeared at that moment. This morning, she was wearing a knitted cashmere jacket with a fluted skirt, both in white. A Spanish straw hat and a Japanese paper parasol completed the outfit.

'Good morning, Inspector.'

'Good morning, Lady Rivers.'

'I'm afraid that Ewart and Gerard have both returned to the Front. Or was it me you wished to see?' Muriel Rivers shot Hardcastle an engaging smile.

'No, ma'am. I wanted a word with Beach here.'

Muriel Rivers flashed a quick appraising glance in Marriott's direction before returning her gaze to Beach. 'Take the gentlemen into the morning room, Thomas,' she said. 'You can speak to them there. And order some coffee for them.'

'Very good, m'lady.' Beach half bowed, and swiftly crossed the hall to open the front door. Once Lady Rivers had departed, he ushered the two detectives into the morning room. 'I'll just arrange the coffee, sir,' he said, making for the door.

'Her ladyship don't seem too distressed at the death of Sir Adrian, Marriott,' said Hardcastle, not for the first time, as he gazed around at the paintings adorning the walls. 'Not by the jaunty way she was off, doubtless to spend some more of his money.'

'It strikes me that she's almost relieved to see him gone, sir,' said Marriott.

'If Sir Adrian's will is proved, she'll be bloody delighted, I shouldn't wonder, Marriott, but she ain't counted on the brothers. Nor, for that matter, on snooty Mr Soames. I've got a feeling it'll be a while before she can lay her hands on the family spondoolicks.'

Moments later, Beach returned. 'The coffee will be here shortly, gentlemen.' He sat down on a sofa opposite them, something, Hardcastle surmised, he would not have done when Sir Adrian was alive. And certainly not if either of the Rivers brothers had still been in the house.

'I suppose you know that Sir Adrian changed his will so that all his estate goes to Lady Rivers, Beach.' Hardcastle did not believe in polite preamble, particularly when dealing with the butler.

'Really, sir?' Beach contrived to look surprised.

'It's no good you drawing the long bow in my direction, Beach. You know bloody well that's the case, because you witnessed Sir Adrian's signature in the presence of Mr Soames, the family solicitor.'

Beach's expression did not change. He displayed neither surprise nor irritation at Hardcastle's allegation that he might have known. 'I'm afraid I was unaware of the contents of the colonel's will, sir,' he said. 'Mr Soames summoned me to the master's bedroom to watch Sir Adrian sign the document, and then I appended my own signature as witness.'

'Appended, eh?' said Hardcastle sarcastically. 'That's a nice word. So you were unaware that Sir Adrian's two sons had been cut out of the will?'

'I had no idea, sir.' Beach raised his eyebrows. 'I imagine that they're not best pleased.'

'You can say that again,' muttered Hardcastle.

Further discussion was stemmed by the arrival of Daisy Forbes, the parlour maid, bearing a tray of coffee.

'Shall I pour it, Mr Beach?' she enquired.

'No, you can leave that to me, Daisy.' Beach stood up and addressed himself to dispensing coffee into bone china cups.

Once the detectives had been served, Beach took a cup for himself, and sat down again. 'Is there anything else I can assist you with, gentlemen?' he asked. Although the butler presented an unruffled demeanour, Hardcastle sensed that he was anxious to end the interview as soon as possible. And that interested him.

'I've been told by several people – you included, Beach – that Sir Adrian was not in the best of health.'

'He did have trouble with his memory, sir, as I mentioned before. He'd forget things that had been told him only minutes previously. But he had a good memory for things that had happened way back. I think I told you that he was writing his memoirs at one time. And he never had any trouble remembering something that had happened years ago. At least, not at first, as I think I told you before. Sometimes he even came up with things I'd forgotten. Things that had happened when I was there, like.'

'D'you think he knew what he was doing when he signed that will?'

'I'm sure he did, sir,' said Beach, smoothing a hand over his pepper-and-salt trousers.

'Is it possible that Lady Rivers might have influenced your late master into making the change, Mr Beach?' asked Marriott, looking up from the notes he was making in his pocketbook.

'I wouldn't know, sir. I'm not exactly privy to her ladyship's thinking,' replied Beach smoothly.

'I'm told you like a flutter on the gee-gees,' suggested Hardcastle, in an offhand sort of way.

'I have been known to risk the occasional shilling, sir.'

'Win, do you?'

Beach smiled. 'As often as I lose, sir.' But he was obviously wondering how Hardcastle knew about his gambling. And wondering how much more he knew. He did not have long to wait to find out.

'Would you describe yourself as an honest man, Beach?'

'I have to say that I wouldn't have remained in Sir Adrian's employment for long were I not, sir.'

'Did he know about your court martial?'

'That was a mistake,' Beach blurted out, looking decidedly uncomfortable. 'But how did you hear about that?'

'When I'm investigating a murder, Beach, I talk to all manner of people, and you'd be surprised what they tell me. And what they did tell me was that you was busted down from sergeant for borrowing money from private soldiers to feed your gambling habit.'

There was a distinct pause before Beach answered. 'I don't know how much you know about the army, sir, but when the powers-that-be get their knife into you, there's not much you can do about it. The incident you're talking about arose because the regimental sergeant major had it in for me. And when a senior warrant officer goes to the colonel and puts what he calls the facts in front of him, there's nothing you can do about it. It was all lies, of course.

The main witness had been promised a corporal's tapes if he gave evidence against me, and that was that. The RSM was out to get me, come what may.'

'I take it the colonel you're talking about wasn't Sir Adrian,' said Hardcastle.

'No, sir, it wasn't. You can rest assured that if it had been, none of that business would've happened.'

'So, it was after your court martial that you became Sir Adrian's orderly. Is that right?'

'That's correct, sir. A very fair man was Sir Adrian. He said that just because a man had fallen by the wayside once, there was no cause to keep him there.'

'And I suppose, from what you say, that he knew all about you getting broken.'

'Must've done, sir. You can't keep secrets in the army. I suppose it's much the same in the police.'

'Don't you worry about that, Beach,' said Hardcastle. 'All you need to know about the police is that they'll keep nagging away at a crime until they find the truth. And I shall delight in seeing whoever was responsible for Sir Adrian's topping taking the eight o'clock walk.'

'I suppose so, sir,' said Beach, forcing a smile.

'Which brings me to my next point.'

'Er, more coffee, sir?'

'No thank you. You told me that Sir Adrian kept a strict inventory of all the valuable property in the house.'

'Yes, sir. That's how I was able to tell you the items that had been stolen.'

'I'll need to see it.'

Beach hesitated. 'I'm afraid Lady Rivers keeps it locked in her bureau, sir. And as her ladyship's gone out, I'm not able to lay hands on it immediately.'

'In that case we'll wait. I imagine that Lady Rivers is returning for luncheon.'

'Those are my instructions, sir,' said Beach miserably. He was obviously not happy that Hardcastle wanted to see the inventory.

'Very well, Beach, I won't need to detain you further. Perhaps you'd let me know when Lady Rivers returns.'

'That Beach is a lying bastard, Marriott,' said Hardcastle, after the butler had closed the door.

It was not until noon that Hardcastle heard the crunch of Rolls Royce tyres on the gravel outside the morning room window. During the time that the two detectives had been waiting, Hardcastle had reviewed the case at some length. But Marriott got the impression his DDI was merely going over the facts for his own satisfaction, rather than wanting to elicit any thoughts Marriott might have had.

Hardcastle and Marriott rose to their feet as Lady Rivers swept into the morning room.

'Oh, do sit down, gentlemen,' she beamed, and took a seat on the sofa opposite them. 'Thomas tells me you wish to speak to me.'

'Yes, Lady Rivers, I was . . .'

But Muriel Rivers cut Hardcastle short with an imperious wave of her hand. 'Just let me order something to drink before we start, Inspector. Perhaps you'd be so good as to give that bell cord a pull for me.'

Beach responded to the summons within seconds. 'M'lady?' he murmured, appearing in the doorway.

'I think I'm in need of a glass of champagne, Thomas.' Lady Rivers glanced at the policemen. 'Perhaps you'd care for a glass of bubbly, or even a whisky, gentlemen?'

'No thank you, ma'am. But another cup of coffee would be welcome.'

When Beach had departed to do Muriel Rivers's bidding, she faced Hardcastle. 'Such a wearying morning, Inspector,' she said, unpinning her hat and laying it on the sofa beside her. 'I went to Nuthall's to meet a friend of mine, but we were joined by the most awful wife of some town councillor. There is a tendency among such people to suck up to anyone with a title, you know. Always wanting you to contribute to some charity, or say a few words at some wretched bazaar. Last year, they wanted me to open the extension to the Malden sewage works, would you believe. The audacity of it. Well, I turned that down. It's very tedious having to look pleasant and cut a ribbon with a pair of scissors while those dreadful newspaper people are taking photographs.'

'I imagine so, Lady Rivers,' murmured Hardcastle, taken aback at the presumptuousness of the woman. That the daughter of a bookmaker should assume such airs and graces quite amazed him. He knew from experience that a real lady would never have adopted such an attitude.

Beach reappeared bearing a salver on which was an ice bucket containing a bottle of Moët champagne. He was followed by Daisy with a tray of coffee. Beach busied himself opening the champagne and pouring a glass, which he then handed to his mistress.

'Will that be all, m'lady?'

'Thank you, Thomas.' Muriel Rivers flashed the butler a winsome smile, and turned to Hardcastle. 'Now, Inspector, what was it you wished to discuss?'

Waiting until Beach was out of the room, Hardcastle said, 'The inventory, Lady Rivers.'

'The inventory? What inventory?'

'Beach tells me you keep the inventory of the valuables locked in your bureau.'

'Did he? I don't know where he got that idea.' This time Muriel Rivers crossed to the bell cord herself to send for the butler.

'M'lady?' As deferential as ever, Beach appeared. But in view of what Mrs Blunden, the cook, had said about the secret assignation she had witnessed between Muriel Rivers and Beach, Hardcastle was not fooled by the formality.

'What's this about me keeping some sort of inventory in my bureau, Thomas?'

'I was assured by Sir Adrian that you kept it, m'lady. Your ladyship might recall that when the, er, unfortunate incident occurred, I was obliged to obtain it from you in order to apprise the inspector of the losses.'

'Of course. I'd quite forgotten, Thomas.' Lady Rivers opened a small crocheted reticule and extracted a key. 'There you are. You know where my bureau is. Perhaps you'd fetch the inventory for me.'

'Very good, m'lady.' Unbidden, Beach refilled Lady Rivers's champagne glass, and left the room.

'Beach is so dependable, Inspector,' said Lady Rivers with a sigh. 'I really don't know what I'd do without him. Particularly at this distressing time.' She reached across for her champagne glass, and took a sip.

'I understand that Sir Adrian held him in high regard,' said Hardcastle.

'Oh, indeed he did. He'd been with him through the South African wars, you know. As honest as the day is long, but then Sir Adrian wouldn't have taken him on had he been at all unreliable.'

'I imagine so,' murmured Hardcastle, deciding against mentioning Beach's court martial.

Beach returned with the inventory, although Hardcastle was by no means certain that it had been in Lady Rivers's bureau. More perhaps the excuse had been used as a device to prevent him from seeing it.

Lady Rivers glanced at it briefly, and handed it to Hardcastle. 'I don't know why you want it, Inspector, but perhaps you'd let me have it back. Thomas said something about it being needed for the insurance people.' She turned to the butler. 'Isn't that right, Thomas?'

'Indeed, m'lady,' murmured Beach.

Hardcastle glanced at the document. It was a full list of all the valuable items in the house, together with their exact location. 'This won't take long, m'lady, but I need to make sure that nothing else was taken at the time of the burglary.'

'I thought Thomas had checked that for you.' She raised an eyebrow, and glanced in Beach's direction, but Beach remained silent.

'He certainly gave me a list of the items that were missing, Lady Rivers, but I have to make sure for myself.' Hardcastle smiled apologetically. 'My chief is a stickler for detail, and if I haven't checked the list myself, he'll ask why, and then send me back to do it. I'm sure you understand.' He glanced at the butler. 'And I'm sure Beach understands too, having been in the army.'

'Quite so, sir,' said Beach. 'Would you like me to accompany you round the house, sir?'

'There's no need for that, Beach. I wouldn't want to take up your valuable time, and I'm sure you have other duties to attend to.'

'Very good, sir.' Glancing briefly at Lady Rivers, Beach departed. With some reluctance, Hardcastle thought.

'There's no need for me to delay you any longer, Lady Rivers.' Hardcastle and Marriott stood up. 'I'm sure my sergeant and me can manage.'

'If you have any difficulty do please call Thomas, Inspector. Or, for that matter, ask me. I shall just be sitting here enjoying my glass of champagne.'

It had not escaped Hardcastle's notice that Muriel Rivers was now on her third glass of Moët.

Beach was hovering outside the door to the morning room. 'Cook has prepared luncheon for you and Mr Marriott, sir. In the kitchen.'

'Thank you, Beach. Perhaps you'd tell her we'll be down directly.'

'I've done a nice roast for her ladyship, Mr Hardcastle,' said Mrs Blunden, 'and I thought I might as well put in enough for you and Sergeant Marriott.'

'That's very kind of you, Mrs Blunden,' said Hardcastle. 'I must admit to being a bit peckish.'

The two detectives sat down at the large kitchen table where Mrs Blunden had already laid places for them. Then she carved slices from a joint of roast beef, and produced Yorkshire puddings, roast potatoes and cabbage.

'There's horseradish there, Mr Hardcastle. It's home-made, of course,' said Mrs Blunden. 'Or some redcurrant jelly if that's what you prefer. And you can't have roast beef and Yorkshire pudding without a decent drop of gravy,' she added, putting a sauceboat on the table.

'That's splendid, Mrs Blunden,' said Hardcastle, rubbing his hands together. 'Aren't you joining us?'

'In just a minute. I've got to get her ladyship's luncheon ready first, then I can have a bite to eat myself.'

Once Lady Rivers's meal had been winched upstairs in the hoist, Mrs Blunden took a seat opposite the two detectives.

'I was surprised to see you down here again, Mr Hardcastle. Are you any nearer finding out who did for Sir Adrian?'

'A little bit closer,' said Hardcastle mysteriously, a comment that came as a surprise to Marriott. 'But these things often take a long time. Rest assured, though, that we'll find whoever was responsible. I've never failed to catch a murderer yet.'

'I did hear tell that Master Ewart and Master Gerard have been left out of the will in favour of her ladyship,' commented Mrs Blunden.

'How did you know that?' asked Hardcastle, pausing with a potato-laden fork in mid-air.

'There's not much as misses the servants in a house like this, Mr Hardcastle, and that's a fact.'

Deciding that Mrs Blunden was probably his most valuable informant in the Rivers ménage, Hardcastle decided to pursue the point.

'It seemed to come as a surprise to General Rivers,' he said.

'I'll wager a month's wages it did. And between you, me and the gatepost, I reckon her ladyship had a hand in it,' said Mrs Blunden, leaning closer to the DDI. 'Sir Adrian doted on them two boys, and I'm sure he'd never have cut 'em out if he'd been in his right mind. You should have seen him when he heard that Master Ewart had been made a general. Well, brigadier-general to be precise. Over the moon, he was, and sent a couple of bottles of champagne down below stairs so's all of us could have a drink to celebrate. The most generous man I ever worked for, and no mistake. No, Mr Hardcastle, there's something fishy about that will getting changed.'

'Speaking in confidence, Mrs Blunden, Mr Soames, the family solicitor, assured me that Sir Adrian was compos mentis, so to speak, when he signed that will.'

'So he might've been, Mr Hardcastle,' said Mrs Blunden

dismissively, 'but did he know what was in it when he signed it? Anyway, I wouldn't trust that Soames. A snooty snake in the grass, so he is.'

'Mr Beach witnessed the signature,' said Marriott quietly.

'Pah!' snorted Mrs Blunden. 'I wouldn't trust him to run a whelk stall in the Mile End Road. Like I said before, Mr Marriott, him and her ladyship's got something going. And it'll all end in tears, you mark my words.'

'That was splendid, Mrs Blunden,' said Hardcastle, pushing his plate away.

'I hope you'll stay for a slice of plum duff and custard, Mr Hardcastle. It's my speciality.'

Ten

'There's a lot of stuff on here, Marriott,' said Hardcastle, flourishing the inventory. 'But it's detailed, so we shouldn't have too much trouble seeing if anything else has gone adrift.'

Slowly and methodically, the two detectives worked their way through the large house, meticulously checking the property against the inventory. An hour later, they had come to a startling conclusion.

'There's more to this business than meets the eye, Marriott,' said Hardcastle, when he and his sergeant had returned to the morning room. 'According to this list, and from what we've seen, there's a few things missing that Beach never told us about.' He sat down in an armchair, and rested the inventory on his knee. 'Make a note of the following what can't be accounted for: a bronze Japanese sleeve vase – whatever that is when it's at home; a pair of nineteenth-century brass candlesticks; an ivory carving of a man, thirteen inches high; a French bronze figurine of a nude bather, fourteen inches high; and a pewter muffin dish and cover measuring nine and a half inches in diameter.' He took off his glasses. 'And God knows what else that wasn't on this list.'

'That means that the burglar must've come downstairs, sir,' said Marriott, glancing up from his pocketbook, 'because the candlesticks were in the drawing room, and the muffin dish was in the dining room. The nude bather was in the gunroom, and the rest were in here.'

'Exactly, Marriott. Now then, how come this tea-leaf of ours gets to roam about the house, but no one hears him?' Hardcastle stood up. 'I think we'll have a poke around in the garden. Never know, but our man might've panicked and chucked the stuff out there if he'd worked out he couldn't carry it all. In my experience villains of this sort get greedy, and they pick up too much stuff. Then, at the last minute, they realize that some enterprising copper might catch them wandering about in the dead of night with a sack marked "Swag".'

'The garden, then, sir?' Marriott forbore from pointing out that the missing property was too large to have been secreted about the burglar's person. Neither did he mention that the burglar had had adequate time to return and collect his spoils at a later date.

'Having had a look out of the window, Marriott, I reckon the grounds are too big for you and me. Anyway, I'm too old to go messing about in gardens looking for stolen property. I'll speak to the nick and ask 'em to send three or four coppers up here a bit *jildi*. No sense in keeping a dog and barking yourself.' It was one of Hardcastle's favourite expressions, which Marriott and the other detectives knew to their cost.

As if by some sixth sense, Beach appeared in the hall at the same time as the two police officers. 'Everything all right, gentlemen?'

'Yes, thank you, Beach,' said Hardcastle, not wishing to talk to the butler about the missing items. At least, not yet. 'Perhaps you'd show me where your telephone is. I need to call the police station.'

'Certainly, sir. But there's an instrument in the morning room.'

'Haven't you got one in the kitchen?'

'Well, yes, sir, but I thought . . .'

'I'll use the kitchen one.' Hardcastle knew from what General Rivers had told him that the staff would sometimes listen in to telephone conversations. By using the kitchen instrument, he hoped to prevent that from happening.

'Certainly, sir.' Beach led the detectives downstairs to the basement.

Although he often professed to his staff that he did not know how to use the telephone, Hardcastle was quite able to do so. Seeing Beach hovering, he said, 'This is a private conversation, Beach. Be so good as to close the door after you.'

Once the butler was out of earshot, Hardcastle asked the operator to connect him to Kingston police station. When, eventually, he was put through to the sub-divisional inspector, he asked for the services of three constables to assist him in a search of the garden at The Grange. Cutting off the SDI's lame excuse about shortage of manpower, Hardcastle forcefully pointed out that he was an A Division officer doing V Division's work for them.

Even though he had emphasized the urgency, Hardcastle was pleased to witness the arrival of the three officers within half an hour of his call to Kingston police station. He sent them around the side of the house, and told them to wait there.

Next, Hardcastle went looking for Lady Rivers. 'I should like your permission to search the garden, ma'am,' he said, once he had found her in the drawing room.

Muriel Rivers looked up from the magazine she was reading. 'Search the garden, Inspector?' she asked in surprise. 'Whatever are you hoping to find?'

'I've received information that there might be some of the missing property out there, Lady Rivers.' Hardcastle decided that he would not at this stage reveal the discrepancy between what he had been told by Beach, and what the inventory indicated had been stolen. Nor did he say where his 'information' had come from.

'How splendid,' exclaimed Muriel Rivers. 'I do hope you find it. Beach will show you the way.' And before Hardcastle could protest that the butler's assistance was unnecessary, she had summoned him.

'M'lady?'

'The inspector wishes to search the garden, Thomas. Perhaps you'd show him the way.'

'Very good, m'lady. If you'll follow me, sir.'

Beach led the two policemen to the back of the house and into a conservatory furnished with cane chairs. A number of exotic plants and flowers gave the area a tropical ambience.

'Very keen on his rare plants was the master, sir,' Beach commented. 'Mind you, he'd lost interest towards the end. The gardener looks after them now, although her ladyship seems quite keen on getting rid of them.'

'Oh, there's a gardener, is there?' asked Hardcastle. 'You never mentioned him before.'

'I didn't think it was important, sir. You see, he's only part time. He doesn't live in. Shows up about three times a week, just to keep everything in order, and to mow the lawn. As you can see, sir, it's a very simple sort of garden. Large, but simple. D'you wish me to show you around, sir?'

'No, I think we can manage on our own without getting lost, Beach.'

The butler opened the double doors, and stood back. 'I'll leave you to it, then, gentlemen.'

Hardcastle and Marriott stepped out on to the terrace and surveyed the garden. As Beach had said, it was uncomplicated, most of it being well-tended lawn, but with a few flowerbeds around the edges, and two or three oak trees shielding the far end of the garden.

Hardcastle walked round to the side of the house to where the Kingston policemen were waiting. 'Put those bloody fags out,' he barked. 'This isn't a picnic.'

'Sorry, sir,' muttered one of the constables, as the three of them hurriedly stubbed out their cigarettes.

'I want the garden searched. And I want it searched thoroughly. Sergeant Marriott here will tell you what you're looking for.'

Marriott itemized the property that had been listed on the inventory, but of which there was no trace in the house.

'Right, get to it, lads.' As the three policemen fanned out and began to walk slowly through the garden, their eyes on the ground, Hardcastle took out his pipe and filled it. 'I'll be surprised if they find anything, Marriott,' he commented. 'But like I said, there's more to this caper than springs out at you, and we've got to try.'

'Sir!' One of the constables waved an arm from a far corner of the extensive grounds. 'There's a man here, sir, skulking about in the undergrowth.'

'Well, don't stand there shouting at me, man, bring the bugger up here.'

The policeman approached, firmly clasping an ageing man by the arm. 'Like I said, sir, he was skulking in the undergrowth.'

'All right, lad, you can leave go of him now. He looks too old to run,' said Hardcastle. 'And who are you?' he demanded. The man was dressed in moleskin trousers with leather straps buckled just below the knees, and a rough tweed jacket.

'Jethro Parker, sir,' said the man, snatching the cloth cap from his head. 'And I weren't skulking, sir, begging your pardon. I'm the gardener, and I was weeding the herbaceous border.'

'Is that so? And how often d'you come here, Parker?'

'About three times a week, sir. Just to do what I can to keep the garden in order, and to do a bit of mowing. Not that I get here much in the winter on account of me arthritis. Gets into me bones something chronic in the cold, sir. Apart from me back playing up. I used to send me boy up if anything needed doing in the winter, but he's gone for a soldier on account of the war. I think he's up near that Wipers place. It's in Belgium, so I've heard.'

'I see,' said Hardcastle, not much interested in the gardener's arthritis, or the current whereabouts of his 'boy'. 'And who took you on for this job?'

'Mr Beach, sir. He's the butler.'

'And when was this?'

Parker scratched his stubble with a dirty fingernail. 'Must be about a year since, sir.'

'How did he come across you, then?'

'Him and me meet up in the George and Dragon pub from time to time, sir. That's just down the hill. I only lives round the corner. I've got lodgings in Crescent Road.'

'I know the George and Dragon,' said Hardcastle, who recalled seeing the public house on his way up to The Grange. 'So you and he are drinking mates, are you?'

Parker smiled crookedly. 'I reckon you could say that, sir. We has the occasional pint together.'

'Sir Adrian was murdered a fortnight ago,' continued Hardcastle. 'And some things were stolen from the house.'

'Aye, sir, I know. Tom Beach told me.'

'So you'll have been here about six times since then,' mused Hardcastle. 'Did you come across anything here in the garden? Stuff that might've been nicked and then dumped.'

'No, sir, nothing.'

'All right, Parker, I'd better let you get on with your weeding. But don't get in the way of my policemen.'

'Right you are, sir.' And with that, the bow-legged Parker ambled off towards the far end of the garden.

'Looks as though we've drawn a blank here, Marriott,' said Hardcastle, knocking out the dottle of his pipe against his heel.

'I've found this, sir,' said the policeman who had brought Parker to the DDI. Suspended on a pencil through the trigger guard, he held a Webley & Scott service revolver.

Taking his handkerchief from his pocket, Hardcastle wrapped it round the weapon and broke it. 'Unloaded,' he said. 'Unless I'm much mistaken, Marriott, I think this officer's found our murder weapon.'

'It was in the undergrowth right down the end, sir,' volunteered the constable.

'Show me exactly where, lad,' said Hardcastle, and he and Marriott followed the policeman to the far end of the garden.

'It was there, sir. I accidentally kicked it with my foot. It looked as though it'd been covered up with them leaves.'

'Now I wonder why the murderer did that,' said Hardcastle. 'Why didn't he dig a hole and bury it?'

'Either he didn't have time, or he was planning on using it again, sir,' suggested Marriott.

'Yes, I think you might be right, Marriott,' said Hardcastle thoughtfully. 'Although I'd've thought he'd've wrapped it in oilskin if he hadn't finished with it. On the other hand, he might not have known how to look after a weapon.'

The other two policemen joined their colleague, and one of them said, 'We've been through the garden thoroughly, sir, and we couldn't find any of the stuff the sergeant said might be there.'

'I never really expected you to,' said Hardcastle, 'but I reckon you've done a good job.' He held up the pistol before putting it in his pocket. 'Well done, lads. You can get back to the nick now, and be sure to give the SDI my thanks for his help.'

Beach was waiting in the hall when the two detectives returned to the house.

'Everything all right, sir?' he asked.

'Yes, thank you, Beach. Where's Lady Rivers?'

'In the drawing room, sir.'

'Good. We'll have a word with her.'

Muriel Rivers was reclining on a sofa with her feet up when Hardcastle and Marriott entered.

'Inspector, you're still here,' she said, swinging her legs on to the floor. 'Did you find what you were looking for?'

'No, Lady Rivers, I'm afraid not.'

'But I don't suppose you really expected to find anything as small as cufflinks and a pocket watch and . . . What else was it? Oh, do sit down, both of you.'

'Sir Adrian's medals, ma'am.' Hardcastle had no intention of revealing that the police had discovered what was probably the murder weapon in the garden of The Grange.

'Yes, of course. Very sad that his medals were taken. He was very proud of those, particularly that thing he used to wear round his neck. Not that I ever saw him wearing it, of course.'

'It appears that other property was stolen as well, Lady Rivers,' said Hardcastle.

'Oh?' Muriel Rivers flicked open her fan and waved it in front of her face. 'It's so hot today. Other property, you say?'

'Tell Lady Rivers about the other items, Marriott.'

Marriott read out the details of the missing items that he and Hardcastle had been unable to find.

'Sir Adrian was very particular about that inventory, Inspector,' said Lady Rivers, 'but when his memory started to go, he rather let it slide. It's probably not up to date. On the other hand, I do know that certain pieces were taken down to Markham Hall. That's our country house in Wiltshire. They'll most likely be there. I shouldn't worry about it.'

'Is Markham Hall kept locked when the family's not in residence, Lady Rivers?' asked Marriott.

Muriel Rivers gave Marriott an engaging smile. 'Yes, of course. But we do have an estate manager called Harry Ryan down there. A good man. He has a look round the house from time to time, just to make sure everything's in order.'

'That's probably where it is, then,' said Hardcastle. 'I'm sorry to have bothered you again, Lady Rivers, but I have to check up on things that don't seem to tally, so to speak.'

'Of course, Inspector. Please feel free to consult me at any time. I'm as anxious as you are to find my poor dear husband's killer.' Muriel Rivers glanced at an ormolu clock on the mantelpiece. 'Good gracious! Six o'clock already. Can I tempt you gentlemen with a drink?'

'That's very kind of you, Lady Rivers,' said Hardcastle, 'but we have to get back to London.'

Hardcastle had no intention of returning to London immediately, however. Once outside the drawing room he told Marriott that they would be going via the George and Dragon public house on Kingston Hill.

'Pubs are good places to pick up local gossip, Marriott,' he said.

'Yes, I know, sir,' said Marriott, who had been a detective for twelve years.

The landlord of the George and Dragon eyed the two strangers who entered the saloon bar with some apprehension, half guessing who they were. In common with his clientèle, he knew of Sir Adrian Rivers's murder, and surmised that there would be some important policemen in the area. In fact, he was rather surprised that he had not had a visit earlier.

'Evening, gents. What can I get you?'

'Two pints of your best bitter, landlord,' said Hardcastle.

The licensee busied himself pouring the ale, and placed the two glass tankards on the bar.

'I'm Divisional Detective Inspector Hardcastle of the Whitehall Division.'

'I s'pose you're doing that murder up at The Grange, then, guv'nor,' said the landlord, as he pushed the beer towards the two detectives. 'On the house, sir.'

'Very kind, I'm sure,' said Hardcastle, who would have been somewhat affronted had he been obliged to pay. 'Yes, I'm dealing with Sir Adrian Rivers's murder. What d'you know about it?'

'Only what I've heard, guv'nor. And seen in the newspapers, of course.'

Hardcastle beckoned the landlord to the far end of the bar, out of earshot of the other customers. 'I'm told that Beach – Sir Adrian's butler – gets in here.'

'That he does. Tom Beach is a regular.'

'And Jethro Parker?'

'Aye, him an' all. Why, have they got something to do with it?'

'Only that they work at The Grange,' said Hardcastle, draining his glass.

'Dreadful thing to have happened,' said the landlord, refilling Hardcastle's tankard. 'Yeah, Tom Beach has been coming in here for nigh on three year now, I s'pose.'

'I'm told he likes a flutter,' put in Marriott.

The landlord scoffed. 'Likes a flutter? That's putting it mildly. Blimey, guv'nor, I reckon he's kept a few bookies in clover over the years. Mind you, he was on his beam-ends a couple of years back. I even had to refuse him credit. He'd run up a pretty heavy slate, and I had to tell him to pay up or else.'

'Or else what?'

'Or I'd bar him. I have to make a living, you know.'

'When was this?'

The landlord drew back his lips and sucked through yellowing teeth in an expression of thoughtfulness. 'Not long after the war started, I s'pose. Maybe a bit before.

It were certainly 1914, that I do remember, 'cos I lost my potman about the same time when he went off and joined the East Surrey Regiment down the barracks in King's Road, daft hap'orth.'

'But then Beach paid what he owed, did he?'

'Yeah, come breezing in here round about the end of August, and settled up. Said he'd had a good win on the horses. He must've done because he bought drinks all round.'

'Ever hear tell of a bookie called Albert North?' asked Hardcastle, taking a pull of his beer.

The landlord ran a hand round his chin. 'No, guv'nor, don't ring any bells.'

'I wondered if Beach had ever mentioned him.'

'Not as I recall, no.'

'Well, thanks for your help, and for the drink,' said Hardcastle. 'And when Beach or Parker next come in for a wet, I'm sure you won't mention our little conversation, will you?' It was more of a threat than a request, and the landlord clearly understood that it would be bad policy to upset the police rather than two customers.

Back at Cannon Row police station, Hardcastle examined the revolver that had been found in the garden at The Grange, and then put it in his safe.

'That needs to be got across to Mr Franklin's magic grotto first thing in the morning, Marriott. I'm sure he'll be able to tell us if the round that did for Sir Adrian came from that weapon.'

'I was wondering if the serial number might be a help in finding out who was issued with it, sir.'

'I'd thought of that, Marriott. We'll have a word with Colonel Frobisher,' said Hardcastle, who had not thought of it at all. 'Where exactly is this Markham Hall where Lady Rivers thought the missing property might be?'

Years of working with Hardcastle had conditioned Marriott always to have answers to any questions his DDI might ask. 'Tolney Reach, sir. It's a village about seven miles from Warminster.'

'I think we might have a run down there and see what

this estate manager has to say. What was his name, Marriott?'

'Harry Ryan, sir.'

'On the other hand, I might ask the Wiltshire Constabulary to pay him a visit, although I'm not too sure they can be relied on. Don't suppose they have much in the way of murders in that neck of the woods.' Hardcastle took out his hunter and glanced at it. 'Nine o'clock. I think we'll have an early night, Marriott. And my respects to Mrs Marriott.'

'Thank you, sir, and mine to Mrs H.'

Eleven

Hardcastle put the revolver on Detective Inspector Percy Franklin's bench, and explained that it had been found in the garden at The Grange.

'See what you can make of it, Mr Franklin.'

'I take it that it's been checked for fingerprints, sir,' said Franklin, rubbing his hands together in anticipation.

'I got DI Collins to take a look at it, Mr Franklin, but there aren't any prints on it. Been wiped clean. I'd say whoever used it had read about the Deptford oil shop murders.'

'With any luck, I should be able to tell you if this is the weapon that killed your victim, sir. I'll do a test firing, and let you know.'

'How long will that take?'

'About an hour, sir.'

'Good. In the meantime, I'll have a word with the military, and see if they can shed any light on who it was issued to.'

Lieutenant Colonel Ralph Frobisher took the piece of paper bearing the serial number of the weapon that had been found in Sir Adrian Rivers's garden, and placed it squarely in the centre of his desk.

'A Webley & Scott, you say, Inspector.'

'Indeed, Colonel.'

Frobisher sighed. 'There are over a million men under arms on the Western Front, Inspector. To trace the officer or other rank to whom this weapon was issued would be an impossible task. Apart from anything else, firearms are being lost on the battlefield every day, and they're replaced without question. In the circumstances, the weapon you found could have come into anyone's possession, and there'd be no record of who that person was if they'd just found it lying about. It's even possible that your burglar – whoever he is – picked it up somewhere in France or Belgium, and then deserted, came home and committed your murder.'

Hardcastle was not comforted by this theory, logical though it was. 'How about I give you a couple of names, Colonel, and then you could start from the other end, so to speak.'

Frobisher spent a few moments considering that proposition. 'It might help,' he said eventually. 'Who did you have in mind?'

'Well, there's Colonel Sir Adrian Rivers himself, and then there's Daniel Good, Sir Adrian's chauffeur, who's an ex-lance bombardier in the Royal Field Artillery.'

'That might make it easier, I suppose. Leave it with me, Inspector, and I'll see what can be done. But I wouldn't hold out too much hope.'

And with that, Hardcastle had to be satisfied.

Impatient, as always, that enquiries left to others did not proceed as quickly as he would have liked, Hardcastle cast around for something else to do.

'I think we'll go down to this Markham Hall and have a chat with the estate manager, Marriott. What was his name?' asked Hardcastle again.

'Harry Ryan, sir.'

'So it is. And Markham Hall's where?'

'Tolney Reach, sir. About seven miles from Warminster.' Marriott paused. 'And the trains go from Waterloo, sir,' he added, as usual forestalling Hardcastle's next question.

'I wonder if they've got cabs in Warminster,' said Hardcastle, 'because sure as hell I'm not walking seven miles. And it'll probably be raining.'

Marriott did not know the answer to that. 'I could try to find out, sir.'

'D'you think the Wiltshire Constabulary have got telephones, Marriott?'

'I could try to find that out too, sir.'

'Yes, do that, Marriott. After all, we're saving them time going to Markham Hall to make enquiries for us, so the least they can do is to provide us with some transport. And while you're about it, you'd better tell 'em why we're tramping about on their bailiwick.'

Marriott hurried away, to return some fifteen minutes later. 'It seems that only their headquarters and one or two police stations have got the telephone connected, sir, so I took the liberty of making a call to HQ. I told them what we were about, and they'd be happy to send a car to take us to Markham Hall. And they said that if we'd like to meet the local PC at Tolney Reach at his police house, he'll do anything he can to assist. He's a PC John Dodds.'

'Very civil of them, Marriott,' said Hardcastle, 'but I don't suppose they have much to do down there. Bit of sheep stealing, and that sort of thing, I'd imagine.'

'Very likely, sir,' said Marriott, chuckling inwardly that his DDI never seemed able to be complimentary about other police forces.

The motor car that met Hardcastle and Marriott at Warminster was, in fact, the chief constable's, and proved to be the only one in the Wiltshire force. The driver, an elderly constable, was waiting in the station forecourt. Sighting the two unmistakable policemen, he alighted and saluted.

'I've had instructions from the chief constable to take you two gentlemen to Tolney Reach, sir, and anywhere else you need to go. And when you've finished your business, I'm to bring you back here to the railway station.'

'Very kind of the chief,' murmured Hardcastle, as he and Marriott climbed in to the Vauxhall car.

The drive to Tolney Reach took twenty minutes through winding country lanes.

'Bit different from the Smoke, Marriott,' commented Hardcastle. 'But somehow I don't fancy this country coppering.'

PC John Dodds, the Tolney Reach village policeman, had

been keeping watch for the arrival of his visitors and, sighting the vehicle, donned his helmet, and walked quickly down the pathway of his house, a cottage that was distinguished from its neighbours only by a blue lamp over the front door bearing the inscription POLICE.

'Good afternoon, sir.' Dodds saluted as Hardcastle and Marriott alighted from the chief constable's car. 'Perhaps you'd care to come in and have a cup of tea before we go up to the hall. Must be a long journey from London.'

'Thank you,' said Hardcastle, as he followed Dodds into the living room of his house.

'This is my wife Mary, sir.'

'Pleased to meet you, sir, I'm sure,' said Mrs Dodds, only just restraining herself from curtseying.

'How d'you do,' said Hardcastle, as he looked around the comfortably furnished sitting room. 'You seem to do all right for yourself down here in the sticks, Dodds.'

Dodds smiled. 'We get by, sir.'

Tea was already prepared. Not only were there cups and saucers set out on a lace cloth on the table, but a selection of small cakes and biscuits too.

'Everybody seems very helpful in this part of the world,' said Hardcastle, as he sat down and accepted a cup of tea and a couple of ginger snaps from the PC's wife. He was genuinely taken aback by the co-operation of the local force.

'The chief constable was a great friend of Sir Adrian Rivers, sir,' said Dodds, by way of explanation for the courtesy that was being shown to the London officers. 'They used to do a bit of rough shooting together in the old days, and a spot of fishing. There's some handsome trout to be had hereabouts. The chief was fair cut up when he learned that Sir Adrian had been murdered.'

'I suppose you know Markham Hall quite well, Dodds.'

'That I do, sir. It's part of my beat, of course, and I make it my business to have a look round the grounds from time to time.'

'So you'll know Harry Ryan quite well.'

'Not all that well, sir. He's only been estate manager for a year or so.'

'Presumably you've met Beach, Sir Adrian's butler.'

Dodds hesitated. 'I don't go much on him, sir, to tell you the truth. He's the sort of fellow I'd have a word with if I come across him in the night. Bit shady, if you ask me.'

Hardcastle sat forward in his chair. 'In what way?'

'Difficult to say, sir, but I suppose it's best called copper's instinct, if you know what I mean.'

'Oh yes, Dodds, indeed I do,' said Hardcastle warmly.

'Well, he's – how shall I put it? – a bit too eager to please, but probably only because I'm a copper. I've had a chat with him from time to time, when he's been down with the family, but one thing I noticed is that he don't much care for answering questions about his past.'

'Probably because he was court-martialled when he was in the army, and busted down from sergeant,' said Hardcastle, seeing no harm in giving the local policeman a bit of background information about one of his occasional residents. 'Ever hear of a bookmaker called Albert North, Dodds?'

Dodds pondered the question for a minute. 'No, sir. The name don't mean anything. A local is he?' It was obvious that the PC, who must have had a very good knowledge of the characters who lived on his manor, had never heard of the man.

'No, he comes from Wandsworth in London, but he's a friend of Beach.'

'How long have you been stationed in Tolney Reach, Dodds?' asked Marriott.

'About seven years, Sergeant. I'm due for promotion in six weeks, so I'll likely get a transfer to Devizes.' In common with most policemen, Dodds knew precisely when he was to be promoted, and where he would be posted.

'So you'd've known Sir Adrian's previous butler.'

'Indeed, Sergeant. Len Parry had been with Sir Adrian for donkey's years.'

'What happened to him?'

'Dropped dead one night while he was serving at dinner, up at the hall. Terrible shock, that was, but he was getting on for seventy, so I s'pose no one was really surprised.'

'When was this?' asked Hardcastle.

'Four years back,' replied Dodds promptly.

'So that would've been 1912,' mused Hardcastle. 'Just when Beach conveniently retired from the army, and turned up on Sir Adrian's doorstep at Kingston Hill.' He put his empty cup on the table. 'Thanks for the tea, Mrs Dodds. Much appreciated.'

'My pleasure, sir,' said Mary Dodds.

'I suppose you'll be looking forward to moving to Devizes when your husband's made sergeant.'

'Not really, sir. We've been very happy here in Tolney Reach. The children have made friends at the local school, and they've not known anywhere else. It'll be an upheaval, but when the force says you've got to go there's not a lot you can do about it.'

'Yes, I know,' said Hardcastle, who had himself been the victim of several unwelcome forced moves during his service.

'Well, if you're ready, sir, we'll make our way up to the hall,' said Dodds.

'Be a treat for you, having a ride in the chief's car, won't it, Dodds?' said Marriott.

Dodds grinned. 'It will that, Sergeant,' he said, 'but it'll probably be the first and last time.'

The chief constable's Vauxhall staff car wound its way up the long, beech-lined drive at Markham Hall, and stopped at the front door.

Harry Ryan, the estate manager, was standing on the steps, having been alerted by Dodds earlier that day to Hardcastle's impending visit.

'When I heard from headquarters that you were coming down, sir, I let Harry know. Be no point in your coming if he weren't going to be there.'

'Very good of you, Dodds,' murmured Hardcastle.

Dodds effected introductions, and Ryan held out a hand, while raising his bowler hat with the other. 'Welcome to Markham Hall, sir,' he said, in a mellifluous Irish accent.

'We'll not keep you long, Mr Ryan, but we've one or two things to check. You've heard about Sir Adrian, obviously.'

'Indeed, sir. A terrible tragedy. I hope you'll find the spalpeen responsible.'

'Don't fret about that,' said Hardcastle, following Ryan into the great hall. 'He'll be dangling on the end of a rope once I've laid hands on him.'

'Very pleased to hear it, sir. Now what exactly was it you wanted?'

'Tell Mr Ryan here what we're looking for, Marriott,' said Hardcastle.

Marriott listed the items that were missing from The Grange. 'Lady Rivers suggested that they might've been brought down here at some time, Mr Ryan.'

Ryan shook his head. 'I'm pretty well aware of what goes on here, Mr Marriott, and I don't recall anything having been brought down from Kingston in my time. But just to make sure, we'll have a look round.'

The estate manager led the detectives from one room to another in the large rambling house, but no trace of the ornaments was found anywhere. They returned to a room on the first floor that Ryan described as the long gallery.

'Have a seat, gentlemen, and I'll get the missus to arrange some tea.' Ryan paused. 'Unless you gentlemen would fancy a glass of the Irish.'

'That would be most acceptable, Mr Ryan,' said Hardcastle. He glanced at the village constable. 'If you care for a tot too, Dodds, I won't let on to the chief constable.'

Dodds laughed. 'Very good of you, sir.'

Ryan disappeared, returning moments later with a tray on which were four glasses, and an unopened bottle of Bushmill's Irish whiskey.

'There you are, sir.' Ryan handed a tumbler of neat whiskey to Hardcastle. 'You'll not be taking water with it, sir, will you now?'

'Certainly not,' said Hardcastle, wondering how an estate manager could afford whiskey that cost at least four shillings a bottle. But he assumed that Ryan did what most domestic servants did, and filched it from his employer.

'It looks as though you came down here on a wild goose chase, sir,' said Ryan, taking a hefty swig of his whiskey.

'To tell you the truth, Mr Ryan, I think someone's playing fast and loose with us,' muttered Hardcastle.

'When was Mr Beach last down here, Mr Ryan?' asked Marriott.

'That'd be Christmas, Mr Marriott. The family always comes down for Christmas, so I'm told. I've only been here since May of last year.'

'I take it you've escaped Lord Derby's conscription scheme, then.' Hardcastle, who estimated that Ryan had yet to reach thirty-five, was aware of the new legislation that enlisted men of certain ages into the armed forces, whether they liked it or not.

'The Irish are exempt, sir, and I don't really see why I should fight England's war for her,' said Ryan, but his partisan statement was softened by a broad grin.

'Tell me, d'you see much of the family when they're down here?'

'They've only been down a couple of times since I was taken on, sir,' said Ryan, 'apart from the Christmas I mentioned. But no, I see more of the staff. I usually pop down to the kitchen and have a cup of tea with Mrs Blunden. She's the cook, sir, and a very handsome woman, so she is too.'

'Did you ever get up to Kingston, Mr Ryan?' asked Marriott casually. Like Hardcastle, he did not dismiss anyone from the list of suspects until their innocence had been proved to his satisfaction.

'Bless you no, Mr Marriott,' said Ryan. 'I can't abide the big towns. I'm country born and bred. I've never even been to Dublin. All that noise, and the people rushing about everywhere, and them newfangled motor cars threatening to run you down if you don't keep your wits about you. No, sir, this is the place for me. Quiet and peaceful, and the occasional wet is all I ask. Will you be taking another, gentlemen?' he asked, lifting the whiskey bottle.

The chief constable's driver had dropped PC Dodds at the police house before delivering Hardcastle and Marriott to the railway station. And it was late that evening by the time they returned to Cannon Row police station.

'Well, Marriott, despite what I said earlier, it looks very much as though our burglar did take the missing property. But the thing that puzzles me is why Beach never said anything about it.'

'I reckon he's a bit slapdash, sir,' said Marriott. 'If you ask me, he didn't do a thorough check. He saw that the cufflinks, the watch and the medals were adrift, and didn't bother to look anywhere else.'

'Perhaps you're right, Marriott. I don't reckon that an army batman would have the skills needed of a proper butler.' Hardcastle glanced at his watch. 'I think we'll call it a day.'

'Success, sir,' said Detective Inspector Franklin jubilantly. 'I carried out a couple of test firings, and the weapon you found is definitely the one that was used to murder Sir Adrian. Incidentally, sir, it's a Webley & Scott Mark Four. Without doubt, a military issue.'

'Ah, now we're getting somewhere,' said Hardcastle, even though the problem of where the weapon came from still remained. There was no point in pestering Colonel Frobisher until he advised Hardcastle that he had exhausted his enquiries. And the DDI feared that those enquiries might prove to be negative. It was all very well finding the weapon that killed Sir Adrian Rivers, but until such time as Hardcastle could identify who had pulled the trigger – and that meant finding who had possessed the gun – he was not much further forward. The revolver could have been dumped in the garden by almost anyone, but the most likely suspect was the as-yet-unidentified burglar. However, there were other lines of enquiry to be pursued.

'Marriott, what was the name of that first-class from Kingston nick who put in an appearance the morning the body was found?'

'DS Atkins, sir.'

'That's the fellow. Get him up here.'

'What, to Cannon Row, sir?'

'When a DDI wants a sergeant, Marriott, the sergeant

comes to him, not the other way round. You should know
that.'

'Very good, sir.'

'You took your time, Atkins,' said Hardcastle brusquely, as
the Kingston sergeant was shown into his office.

'I'm sorry, sir, but I was dealing with a burglary.'

'Oh? And where was that?'

'One of the big houses on Kingston Hill, sir.'

'Tell me about it,' said Hardcastle, showing a spark of
interest.

'It was on the main road, sir, between the Black Horse
and the George and Dragon pubs. Entry was effected during
the night, and a quantity of silver taken. According to the
householder, the haul was worth about two hundred pounds.'

'Any violence used?'

'No, sir. The master of the house never knew that anything
had happened until he found a broken pane in the front door.'

'Method?' barked Hardcastle, impatient that the sergeant
appeared to be dithering in his explanation.

'The thief used brown paper covered in treacle, sir. He
applied it to the glass pane in the front door and cut round
it with some sort of device, probably a diamond ring. The
idea of the brown paper and the treacle was to prevent the
noise of breaking glass if the pane fell to the ground, you
see, sir.'

'I'm familiar with methods of entry, Atkins,' snapped
Hardcastle. 'I've investigated more burglaries than you've
had hot dinners. Any fingerprints at the scene?'

'Not that we could find, sir.'

Satisfied that there appeared to be no similarity to the
burglary at The Grange, Hardcastle moved on to the reason
he had summoned Atkins to London.

'How many jewellers and hockshops have you got on
your toby, Atkins?'

There was only a brief hesitation before Atkins replied.
'About thirty in all, sir. Fifty-fifty, I should think.'

'What the blue blazes are you talking about, Atkins?
Either it's thirty or it's fifty.'

'I meant that half of them are hockshops and half of them are jewellers, sir.'

'Well, I wish you'd said so. Doubtless you'll be asking them if they've seen any of your silver.'

'Yes, sir.'

'Well, while you're at it, you can make a few enquiries about our murder. Sergeant Marriott will give you a list of the booty that's missing from Sir Adrian's crib. If you come across it, seize it, and get a description of whoever fenced it. Understood?'

'Yes, sir,' said Atkins, after Marriott had given him the list, and explained in more detail what was missing.

'Right, well don't delay, Atkins. I can see you're a busy man.' Waiting until Atkins had left the office, Hardcastle said, 'I don't know what they get up to down at Kingston, Marriott, but if I ever commit a crime I want to get away with, I'll do it on Kingston's bailiwick.'

Twelve

A s it turned out, Lieutenant Colonel Frobisher had obtained a result remarkably quickly. Even so, it was not until Monday that Hardcastle received a message to say the APM had got some information for him. And, happily, things started to progress quite rapidly from then on. Or at least, Hardcastle thought they had.

'It proved to be very useful that you were able to give us those two names, Inspector,' said Frobisher, referring to a sheet of paper. 'The revolver in your possession was originally issued to 12947 Lance Bombardier Daniel Good of the RFA at Woolwich in 1908.' The APM looked up, a grave expression on his face. 'There is no record of the weapon ever having been handed in.'

'That sounds like pretty slack bookkeeping,' suggested Hardcastle. Not that the Metropolitan Police had anything to boast about. When, at the turn of the century, the force recalled all its revolvers for repair, it was found that Scotland Yard itself held sixty-six more weapons than it was credited with holding.

'These things happen, even in the best regulated of circles, Inspector,' said Frobisher with a disarming smile. 'Of course, it may be that Lance Bombardier Good lost the weapon in some campaign, and it was replaced by another that he did hand in. I have to say that some quartermasters are not always as honest as they should be. But there's no way of knowing, not now, what with the war.'

'That's a possibility, I suppose,' said Hardcastle reluctantly, 'but it's enough for me to feel his collar.'

'As a matter of interest, on what grounds?' Not for the

first time, Frobisher appeared at once amused and mildly alarmed by Hardcastle's instant decisions.

For his part, Hardcastle was surprised at the APM's question. Frobisher was, after all, an army policeman and, to the best of the DDI's knowledge, possessed the same powers of arrest as the civil police. Indeed, some of the powers of the military police were even more draconian that those that Hardcastle could deploy.

'Quite simple, Colonel. That weapon was used to top Sir Adrian Rivers. Daniel Good was his chauffeur, and was present in the house at the time of the murder. He'll have to come up with some pretty smart answers to satisfy me.'

Hardcastle rose to his feet. 'Thank you for your assistance, Colonel.' He paused. 'And once this case is over and done with, I'll ensure that the weapon is returned to the military.'

At noon on that Monday, three weeks after the murder of Sir Adrian Rivers, Hardcastle and Marriott arrived, once more, at The Grange.

'Good morning, sir.' Beach opened the door, but expressed no surprise at the return, yet again, of the two detectives. 'Is it her ladyship whom you wish to see, sir?'

'That'll do for a start, Beach,' said Hardcastle.

'Her ladyship is in her boudoir, sir. I'll enquire if she's happy to see you there.' And without waiting for a response, Beach slowly mounted the stairs.

'Boudoir be buggered,' said Hardcastle, as he and Marriott followed at a distance. 'He's assumed a few airs and graces, has that Beach. I'll wager he never behaved like that in the army, the pompous arse.'

'Her ladyship will see you up here, sir,' said Beach from the top of the staircase.

'Very gracious,' muttered Hardcastle.

Lady Rivers was reclining on the chaise longue she had been occupying when Hardcastle and Marriott interviewed her on the day of her husband's murder. Her peignoir was of a frothy, pink material with a feather ruffle, and her feet were shod in white satin slippers.

'Have you come with news, Inspector?' she asked, without changing her position.

'In a manner of speaking, Lady Rivers. I've come to arrest your chauffeur, Daniel Good.'

'Christ!' exclaimed Muriel Rivers, returning rapidly to her cockney roots. In a most unladylike way she swivelled her body round, and placed her feet on the floor. 'What the bloody hell for?'

'On suspicion of murdering your late husband, ma'am.' Hardcastle, somewhat taken aback by Lady Rivers's profane language, saw little point in keeping from her that which would become common knowledge throughout the household within minutes of Good's apprehension.

'Well, Inspector, I'm afraid you're too late. Daniel gave notice last Wednesday morning, and asked if he could be allowed to go immediately. I saw no reason for him to work out his notice. The only problem is finding another chauffeur, although I have learned to drive myself. But it really is a frightful chore.'

Last Tuesday was the day upon which police had found the murder weapon in the garden, and the following day Good had handed in his notice. He had no way of knowing of the discovery; it had been a secret between Hardcastle, Marriott, the officer who had found it, and his two colleagues. But it was too much of a coincidence for Hardcastle's liking.

'Have you any idea where he might've gone, Lady Rivers?'

'Oh, for God's sake do sit down, Inspector,' said Muriel Rivers, waving an imperious hand towards the other chairs. 'No, I've really no idea where he went. But what makes you think he had anything to do with the death of my husband? I suppose that's what you're suggesting.'

'I'm afraid I'm not at liberty to disclose information that may have to be given in evidence, ma'am,' said Hardcastle, somewhat stiffly.

Lady Rivers shook her head. 'I find all this very hard to believe, Inspector,' she said. 'Daniel always struck me as being as honest as the day is long. I do hope you're proved wrong.'

'Thank you, ma'am,' said Hardcastle, declining to be drawn on what he now knew of Daniel Good. 'Before I go, I'll have a word with the staff, if you've no objection.' The request was purely a formal one; the DDI was going to speak to the staff whatever Lady Rivers said.

'Of course.'

Hardcastle made straight for the kitchen.

'Hello, Mr Hardcastle,' said Martha Blunden. 'You're just in time for tea.'

The two officers sat down at the kitchen table. 'D'you mind if I smoke, Mrs Blunden?' asked Hardcastle.

'Bless you, no. You carry on.'

Hardcastle began to fill his pipe while the cook poured tea for him and Marriott.

'I've just heard that Daniel Good has left, Mrs Blunden.'

'Don't blame him. I think he'd had enough of her ladyship. I told you the other day that she sometimes keeps him waiting for hours outside some fancy shop up the West End. That's no way to treat a chauffeur, particularly one as obliging as Daniel. Between you and me, I'm surprised he never went ages ago.'

'Have you any idea where he's gone, Mrs B?' asked Marriott.

'No idea, Mr Marriott. It was all a bit sudden. He came across from the stable at about eight o'clock, said he'd told her ladyship that he was off. And by midday he was gone. Bit of a surprise, mind you.'

But Hardcastle had thought about Good's departure, coming, as it did, so quickly after the discovery of the revolver. And he had arrived at what he thought was a solution. 'Does PC Draper ever drop in for a cup of tea?' he asked, at last getting his pipe going.

Mrs Blunden glanced guiltily at the DDI. 'I don't want to get Charlie into trouble, Mr Hardcastle,' she said.

'You needn't worry about that, Mrs Blunden. All coppers call in for tea at various places on their beat. I did it myself when I was a young constable. It's how policemen keep in touch with what's going on. You'd be surprised what they

learn over a cup of tea.' It was also true of an illicit pint
of beer at the back of a pub, but Hardcastle was not going
to mention that. In fact, the spectre of disciplinary sanc-
tions hung over every policeman found guilty of 'loitering
in the vicinity of licensed premises with a view to solic-
iting alcoholic refreshment there from'.

'Yes, well, he does drop in when he's on this beat. Usually
about half past six in the morning, or at sevenish in the
evening when he's on the late turn. And sometimes he'll
call in at the start of night duty to get his flask filled. He
was telling me that they has this habit of leaving a flask of
tea next to the burner in gas lamps, so's it heats up by the
next time they get round their beat.'

Hardcastle was familiar with that age-old practice, but
what Draper did with himself on night duty was of no great
interest. 'And did he happen to drop in the morning that
Daniel Good gave his notice?'

Mrs Blunden wiped her hands on her apron and sat
down opposite the two detectives. 'Yes, as a matter of
fact, he did.'

'I thought he might've done,' said Hardcastle, only just
containing his annoyance at what he was now certain had
happened thereafter.

Hardcastle's fury had not abated by the time he and Marriott
reached Kingston police station.

'Can I help you, sir?' enquired the officer on duty at the
counter, his four stripes proclaiming him to be a station
sergeant.

'Yes, you bloody well can. I'm DDI Hardcastle of A, and
I want to see PC Draper right now.'

The station officer moved across to a large book that
rested at one end of the counter. 'He's on eight beat, sir.'

'I don't give a fig where he is, Sergeant. I want to see
him *now*.'

The sergeant glanced at the clock over the door leading
to the charge room. 'He's due to make a point with the
section sergeant at four o'clock, sir, at the Black Horse,
foot of Kingston Hill.'

'And where's the section sergeant now?'

'I think he's having a cup of tea in the canteen, sir,' said the station sergeant hesitantly.

'Is he indeed? Well, fetch him down here this instant.' It was obvious that the station officer had emphasized the urgency, doubtless inferred from Hardcastle's irascibility, because the section sergeant appeared within seconds.

'Sir?'

'I'm told you've got a point with Draper at four o'clock, Sergeant.'

'Yes, sir.'

'I want you to bring him back here to the nick, as soon as possible.'

'Very good, sir. Can I tell him what it's about?' the sergeant asked unwisely.

'Don't stand there arguing with me, Sergeant, just do as you're told.'

'Yes, sir.' The chastened sergeant rapidly disappeared to get his bicycle from the backyard of the police station. It was evident that something unpleasant was afoot and he did not want to be involved in it.

At twenty past four, PC Charles Draper appeared in the front office of the police station.

'You wanted me, sir?'

Hardcastle opened the door to the interview room, just to the right of the station's main entrance.

'In there, Draper.'

PC Draper obviously did not like the sound of that. 'Is something wrong, sir?'

Hardcastle slammed the door, and turned to Marriott. 'Take notes, Sergeant,' he said. 'Now then,' he continued, addressing his remarks to Draper. 'You told Daniel Good that a firearm had been found in the garden of The Grange?'

'Well, sir, I, er . . .'

'Don't shilly-shally with me, man,' snapped Hardcastle.

'I think I might have mentioned it to him, sir.'

'And this was when you were having a cup of tea in the kitchen up at Sir Adrian's house, was it?'

'Not quite, sir. I met Daniel outside the garage where

the Rolls Royce is kept. Daniel lives over the garage, you see, sir.'

'And it was then that you told him, was it?'

'Yes, sir. You see, sir, he was very interested to know whether we were any nearer catching the burglar who did for Sir Adrian, sir.'

'And how did you know that a firearm had been found, Draper?'

'One of the PCs who was sent up to The Grange to do the search told me, sir,' admitted Draper miserably. He knew that he was in serious trouble, and feared that this hostile DDI might well bring about his dismissal from the force.

'It might interest you to know,' continued Hardcastle relentlessly, 'that your actions have resulted in Daniel Good – a strong suspect for the murder – disappearing. And no one seems to know where he's gone.'

'I'm very sorry, sir.'

'Not half as sorry as you will be, Draper. Did Good tell you where he was going?'

'No, sir. I didn't know he was going anywhere.'

Hardcastle turned to Marriott. 'Get the patrolling officer in here, a bit sharp, Sergeant,' he said.

'Yes, sir.'

A few minutes later, Marriott returned with the duty inspector of the relief.

'This officer,' began Hardcastle, having introduced himself, 'is to be placed on the report for divulging information about a murder case to a member of the public. And when you find him, Inspector, the officer who gave Draper this information is also to be placed on the report. Detective Sergeant Marriott here will give you a full statement. Is that clear?'

'Yes, sir,' said the inspector.

'Right, Marriott, and now, thanks to this idiot Draper, we've got to set about finding Daniel Good.'

Hardcastle's first step was to have details of the errant coachman-cum-chauffeur inserted in the *Police Gazette*, but he knew that it would probably be weeks rather than days before the suspect was apprehended. And for that reason, he intended to do what he could to find Good himself.

That done, Hardcastle went from Kingston police station back to The Grange to speak to Martha Blunden, the one member of staff who seemed to know everything about everything.

'Goodness gracious, Mr Hardcastle, you'll be taking root here soon.'

'Did Daniel Good ever mention any family, Mrs Blunden? Or say where he came from?'

Mrs Blunden paused in the act of pouring tea. 'I did hear him mention a younger sister who was in service up Chelsea way. Housekeeper, she is. Now, let me see, where was it he said . . .? Yes, Parson's Green. The house of a barrister, a King's Counsel, he said.'

'D'you remember the name of this KC, Mrs Blunden?' asked Marriott.

'Sir John Green,' replied the cook promptly. 'Yes, I'm sure that's what it was. Is Daniel in some sort of trouble, Mr Hardcastle?'

'No,' said Hardcastle airily. 'We just want to talk to him.' Mrs Blunden was a useful informant, but the DDI knew that she was free with her information. And that meant that anything he told her would probably be similarly disseminated; passed on perhaps to people he would prefer to be kept in ignorance. 'Now then, Marriott, I want you to—'

But at that moment, Beach appeared in the kitchen. 'Good afternoon, sir. I didn't expect to see you again so soon.'

'You're the very man I want, Beach,' said Hardcastle. 'Is there a copy of *Who's Who* in the house?'

'Of course, sir.' Beach gave the impression that no properly run household could possibly manage without such a publication. 'It's in the library. Shall I get it for you, sir?'

'No, I'll go up there.' And leaving Beach and Mrs Blunden wondering what was going on, Hardcastle led Marriott upstairs to the library where, ironically, he had first interviewed Daniel Good.

The address for Sir John Green, KC, that Hardcastle had

found in *Who's Who* proved to be in Parsons Green Lane, Fulham. And it was close to eight o'clock in the evening by the time Hardcastle and Marriott arrived there.

'Yes?' demanded the rather superior butler, casting a discerning glance at the two men on the doorstep.

Having told the manservant who they were, Hardcastle and Marriott were led across the hall. 'I reckon Beach could learn a few lessons from him, Marriott,' whispered Hardcastle.

'Two men from the constabulary to see you, Sir John,' intoned the butler in nasal tones, as he threw open the door of the drawing room. He was clearly unimpressed by the arrival of the police.

'I'm Divisional Detective Inspector Hardcastle of the Whitehall Division, Sir John, and I must apologize for calling so late.'

'Not at all, not at all.' Sir John Green was a bluff fellow with full sideburns and fleshy rubicund cheeks. 'What can I do for the police?' He placed his cigar in an ashtray, and picked up a glass of brandy.

Briefly, Hardcastle explained about the murder of Sir Adrian Rivers, and went on to describe the finding of the murder weapon. Finally, he told the barrister of the connection between Daniel Good and the revolver.

'The moment Good found out that we had recovered the weapon, Sir John, he disappeared. Obviously we need to speak to him urgently.'

Green nodded. 'Yes, I imagine you would, Inspector,' he said. 'But what can I do to assist? I have to admit that I've never heard of the fellow.'

'My information is that Good's sister is – or was – employed by you as housekeeper, sir.'

'Ah! You'll be speaking of Mrs Wright, I presume.'

'I don't know her name, sir, but if she is Daniel Good's sister then she might be able to tell us where he is.'

'It's very likely to be her, then. She's been with the family for at least ten years, possibly longer.' Green strode across to the fireplace and pressed a small button next to the light switch. 'An electric bell system, Inspector,' he said proudly. 'Had it installed last year.'

'You rang, sir?' queried the butler, appearing in the doorway of the drawing room.

'Roberts, be so good as to ask Mrs Wright to see me, will you?'

'Very good, sir.'

The woman who entered the room a few minutes later was about forty years of age. Dressed in a black, high-necked bombazine dress, she wore a leather belt from which a bunch of keys was suspended.

'Mr Roberts said you wanted to see me, sir.'

'Yes, Mrs Wright. These gentlemen are from the police. They want to talk to you about your brother.'

Hardcastle was impressed that the barrister had not asked if the housekeeper had a brother, or even if that brother was called Daniel Good; he had put the statement to her as though there was no doubt. The DDI made a mental note to be very careful if ever he found himself being cross-examined by Sir John Green.

The housekeeper reddened and put a hand to her cheek. 'Oh glory be,' she said.

'I see you know something about him, Mrs Wright,' said Hardcastle.

'He hasn't done no harm, sir, and that's gospel.'

'That remains to be seen, Mrs Wright, but more to the point, I need to know where he is.'

'He's upstairs, sir,' admitted the housekeeper guiltily.

'*Upstairs!*' roared Sir John. 'What in the name of Hades is he doing upstairs? I think you'd better explain yourself, woman.'

'I never meant no harm, sir, but he came here last Wednesday in a terrible state. He said as how the police were after him, but that he'd not done nothing wrong.'

'Don't you think the police are better placed to judge that, Mrs Wright?' said Sir John severely. 'He should have surrendered to them immediately. You had no business bringing a man wanted by the police into my house. In fact, you have no business bringing anyone into my house without permission, never mind a wanted man.'

'I knew you'd hand him over, sir.'

'I most certainly would, Mrs Wright. Now take these officers upstairs to where your brother is hiding. I'll speak to you later.'

A tearful Mrs Wright led the way to the servants' quarters on the top floor of the old house, and opened the door to a room at the back.

'I'm sorry, Daniel, but the police is here.'

Daniel Good was sitting on a chair reading a newspaper, and leaped up at the sight of Hardcastle.

'I'm sorry, Edna,' he said. 'I hope I haven't got you into any trouble.'

'Trouble, Daniel Good. You've likely cost me my position. And ten years or more I've been here.'

'I'm sorry, love,' said Good again.

'Daniel Good, I'm arresting you for the wilful murder of Sir Adrian Rivers on Tuesday the sixth of June 1916. I shall now take you to Kingston police station.'

'I never did it, sir, as God is my witness,' protested Good.

Sir John Green was waiting in the hall when Hardcastle and Marriott brought their prisoner downstairs.

'I'm sorry to have disturbed you, Sir John,' said Hardcastle, 'but we have our man.'

'Perfectly all right, Inspector,' said Green with a smile. 'I am in the trade, after all.' But then his expression changed to one of annoyance. 'Mrs Wright, come into the drawing room. I want a word with you.'

'Well, Good, it looks like you've got your sister the sack,' said Hardcastle, as he bundled Good into a taxi.

'And all for nothing,' muttered Good. 'I never had nothing to do with Sir Adrian getting murdered, sir, and that's the truth.'

'They all say that,' said Hardcastle, as he directed the cab driver to Kingston police station.

Thirteen

'I really can't let you go, Ewart,' said General Sir Henry Rawlinson, smoothing a hand over his bald pate. 'Yesterday I signed the operation order for the attack. As you'll be aware, two days ago we started to lay down the biggest barrage that warfare has ever known, and it is my hope that by the time of the assault, the constant artillery fire will have completely destroyed the German defences.'

Brigadier General Ewart Rivers needed no reminding. Even at four miles behind the lines, he and the army commander had to shout to make themselves heard above the noise of the guns.

'On the morning of Friday the thirtieth of June,' Rawlinson continued, 'British, Empire and French troops – all half a million of them – will walk across no man's land and seize the enemy's frontline positions with little or no opposition. As you know, we cease the barrage from time to time in the hope that the Hun will open up and show us where his guns are.' He spoke with an enthusiasm that was not shared by the frontline troops. 'It's the big push that could end the war.' He paused to correct himself. 'At least it'll put an end to trench warfare.' In fact, bad weather delayed the start of the assault, and the attack was destined to take place on the first of July, a day that would forever be etched in the minds of thousands of bereaved families.

'You make it sound easy, sir,' said Ewart Rivers.

Rawlinson played with the watch chain stretched between his two tunic pockets. 'I've never said it'll be easy, Ewart, but at least the war will become mobile. And I shall need every staff officer that I have. I'm afraid that the problem of your father's will is going to have to wait until after Saturday.'

'I quite understand, sir.' Ewart Rivers had not asked for leave, but had been responding to the army commander's questions about the death of Sir Adrian Rivers, and Ewart Rivers's expressed determination that he would challenge the surprising change of legatee that his father's last will and testament had contained. 'My solicitor is in the act of contesting it.'

'That's all right, then, Ewart. Now come over here.' Rawlinson walked across to a large relief map that had been constructed by the Royal Engineers and mounted on two tables. Extending a forefinger, he prodded various places along the depiction of the British, French and German lines, and explained, once again, the order in which various units would leave their trenches when the first whistles blew at seven thirty.

But neither Rawlinson nor Rivers could have known that Saturday the first of July, 1916, was a date that would forever mark the greatest disaster in the history of the British Army. A disaster that would be spoken of in dread terms as 'The Somme'.

On his return to Kingston police station, Hardcastle sensed an air of hostility, doubtless due to his insistence that PC Draper should be disciplined for telling Good about the finding of the murder weapon in the garden of The Grange. But it would take more than a few malevolent looks to dissuade the DDI from his duty.

As it was now gone ten o'clock in the evening, there was a different station sergeant on duty. He carried the huge tome known as the occurrence book through to the charge room, and set it down on the desk before taking a seat.

'Name?' he asked, dipping his pen in the inkwell.

'Daniel Good, sir.'

'Date of birth?'

And so it went on until the station sergeant had recorded all the information required of him by the regulations.

'Detained for questioning, sir?' he asked, looking up at Hardcastle.

'That's correct, Sergeant. In connection with the murder of Sir Adrian Rivers.'

'Very good, sir.' The station officer – jocularly known as 'the stationmaster' – having concluded his business, closed the book. 'Are you putting him down for the night, sir?' he asked, glancing at the clock.

'No, I'll question him now,' said Hardcastle.

'As you wish, sir.' The station sergeant could never understand the urgency that CID officers attached to the interrogation of suspects.

Escorting Good into the same interview room where he had earlier questioned PC Draper, Hardcastle motioned to his prisoner to take a seat. He glanced at Marriott to make sure that his sergeant had his pocketbook out. It was an unnecessary habit of Hardcastle's; Marriott was always ready to take notes.

'Tell me why you murdered Sir Adrian Rivers, Good,' began Hardcastle.

'I didn't, sir, I swear,' protested Good, his face working with emotion as his hands clasped and unclasped on the table in front of him.

Hardcastle sighed. 'Stop wasting my time, Good. Your revolver – the one the army issued to you back in 1908 – was found covered with leaves in the garden at The Grange. We've had it examined by an expert, and he's in no doubt that it was the weapon used to kill Sir Adrian.'

'I don't know how it got there, sir.'

'Really?' Hardcastle posed the question cynically. 'Why wasn't it handed in when you left the army?'

'I don't know, sir. I s'pose I must've forgotten,' said Good lamely.

'And the army forgot as well, did they?' Hardcastle's question was redolent with sarcasm.

'The army's not very good at keeping track of weapons, sir, and I thought it might come in handy at some time.'

'For killing your master with, I suppose,' commented Hardcastle.

'What did you do, square the bloke in the quarter-master's stores with ten bob to fiddle the records?' asked

Marriott, who was more familiar with the army than was his DDI.

'Something like that,' said Good miserably.

'Where did you keep this revolver?' asked Hardcastle.

'In a cupboard in my quarters over the garage, sir. It was well hidden. I'd wrapped it in an old sock, and stuck it inside a riding boot. Once I became a chauffeur, I never had cause to use them boots again.'

'Did you ever tell anyone that it was there?'

'No, sir, never.'

'When did you find that it was missing, then?'

'Not until I heard that it had been found in the garden, sir.'

'And who told you that?'

Good hesitated. 'I can't remember,' he mumbled.

'It's as well that my memory's better than yours, Good. It was PC Draper who told you, and he told you on Wednesday morning, the day after my officers turned it up. And it was one of the policemen who found it who told Draper.'

'How did you know that?' Good blurted out, seemingly surprised that Hardcastle knew so much about that conversation.

'Because I'm a detective, Good, and I'm paid to detect things. So, why did you run, eh?'

'I thought you'd think that Sir Adrian's murder was down to me, sir.'

'You're right about that, Good, and that's a fact. See, it all makes sense to me. Sir Adrian is murdered in his bed, and the man who possessed the weapon that did for him runs the day after it was found. So I don't see why I shouldn't put you on the sheet for the wilful murder of Sir Adrian Rivers.'

'It's not true, sir,' cried Good, anguish apparent on his white face. 'I tell you I'd never have hurt a hair of Sir Adrian's head. He was very good to me, taking me on when I was on me uppers. All right, so I shouldn't have hung on to the iron when I left the kate, but I wasn't the only one.'

'What sort of excuse is that?' muttered Hardcastle.

'I s'pose if I hadn't kept a hold of it, none of this would've happened,' said Good, looking down at the table that separated him from the DDI.

'It's a bit late to be full of remorse now,' commented Hardcastle brutally. But he was unhappy about the story that Good had related. With years of interrogation experience behind him, he sensed that Daniel Good was telling the truth. And that indicated that someone else – possibly someone in the household – knew of the existence of the revolver, and had removed it from Good's hiding place. Whether that same person had committed the murder was open to conjecture, and ultimately to proof.

'What's going to happen now, sir?' asked Good, fearful of the answer.

'You'll spend the night in one of Kingston's nice comfortable cells until I decide,' said Hardcastle. Then he posed a sudden question. 'How well d'you know Albert North, the bookmaker?'

Good stared at the DDI, a puzzled frown on his face. 'I've never heard of him, sir. I'm not a betting man. I s'pose I know too much about horses. And them high-bred ones can be a bit fickle. Not worth putting your money on 'em if you takes my meaning.'

'Put him down, Marriott,' said Hardcastle impatiently, 'and then come back here.'

When Marriott returned from locking up the prisoner, Hardcastle was leaning back in his chair, puffing at his pipe, and staring out of the window of the smoke-filled interview room.

'What d'you think, sir?'

'I don't know what to think, Marriott. Right from when I first set eyes on him, I thought Daniel Good was as straight as a die. I think he was telling the truth. But that begs the question, who found out about the revolver, and who nicked it and used it to top Sir Adrian?' Hardcastle pulled out his hunter and stared at it. 'Good heavens, Marriott, d'you know it's nigh on midnight?'

'Yes, sir.' Marriott was only too well aware of the time.

'I think we'd better get off home, then. We'll meet back

here at nine o'clock tomorrow morning. Let the station
officer know what's what, will you?'

When Hardcastle arrived at Kingston police station on the
Tuesday morning, there was a surprise awaiting him in the
form of Detective Sergeant Dennis Atkins.

'Good morning, sir.'

'Morning, Atkins. What d'you want?'

'I think I may have some information regarding the property stolen from The Grange, sir.'

'Have you now? Well, are you going tell me, or is it a
secret?'

'I had occasion to visit an antiques dealer in Thames
Street, sir, and . . .'

'Just get on with it, Atkins,' snapped Hardcastle irritably.
'You're not giving evidence in court. Yet!'

'He took in the figure of the nude bather three days after
the murder, sir.'

'What's he talking about, Marriott?' asked Hardcastle,
turning to his own sergeant.

Marriott flicked open his pocketbook. 'A French bronze
figurine of a nude bather, fourteen inches high, sir,' he replied
promptly.

'That's the one,' confirmed Hardcastle. 'Well, what about
it, Atkins?'

'The dealer – his name's Joseph Levy, sir – got it from
his brother who runs a similar establishment in Wandsworth,
and . . .'

'In Wandsworth?' Hardcastle took a sudden interest in
what Atkins was saying.

'Yes, sir. The brother's name is Benjamin Levy. He took
the figure a day after the murder, but decided that his clientèle was not likely to be interested in it, so he passed it over
to his brother in Kingston. He said that people in Kingston
would likely have more money than them in Wandsworth.'

'He's probably right about that,' muttered Hardcastle.
'Where's this piece now?'

'In accordance with your directions, sir, I seized it. It's
in the property store here.'

'Have you spoken to the antiques dealer in Wandsworth?'

'No, sir. But if you want me to go over there, I'll—'

'No, don't do that, Atkins. Sergeant Marriott and me'll pay this Benjamin Levy a visit. Give Marriott the address.'

'D'you want the figure, sir?'

'Yes, we'll take it with us.'

'What about Daniel Good, sir?' asked Marriott.

'He can stew, Marriott,' said Hardcastle. 'Right now, we've got bigger fish to fry.'

Benjamin Levy conducted his business from a pokey little shop in Wandsworth High Street, ironically almost opposite the police station.

A bell rang as Hardcastle pushed open the door. A small, wizened man wearing a yarmulke and a woollen cardigan was seated behind a desk, strategically placed so that he could keep an eye on his entire stock. He peered at the detectives through pebble-lensed spectacles.

'Good morning, gentlemen.'

'Mr Benjamin Levy?' asked Hardcastle.

'At your service, sir. Who have I the honour of addressing?' Levy had immediately surmised that these two men were not there to buy antiques.

'We're police officers,' announced Hardcastle.

'Ah!' Levy, having guessed that already, rose to his feet. 'And how may I help you, gentlemen?'

Marriott took the figurine from his briefcase and placed it on Levy's desk without comment.

'A beautiful piece, and quite valuable,' said Levy, running a loving hand over the small statuette.

'So I believe,' said Hardcastle, 'which is probably why it was stolen.'

'Stolen!' Levy sounded shocked, although Hardcastle guessed it was a ploy.

'Yes, stolen, Mr Levy, and you accepted it in exchange for cash. And I somehow doubt that you paid anything like its true value for it.'

'I had no idea, sir.' Levy hunched his shoulders, and spread his hands in an expression of defeat. 'Are you sure it's the same one?' he asked hopefully, but in reality he was under no illusion that it was.

'Without a doubt,' continued Hardcastle relentlessly. 'Your brother Joseph told the police that you handed it over to him. The suggestion was that your customers here in Wandsworth weren't as well-heeled as his in Kingston.'

'That's true,' said Levy. 'I hardly make enough to keep the wolf from the door. It's this terrible war, sir. People just aren't spending.'

'Dreadful,' muttered Hardcastle, without any show of sympathy. 'However, you'll doubtless be interested to know that only this year a law was passed dealing with receiving stolen property. It's called the Larceny Act and, what's more, it provides for punishment according to the offence by which the same property was obtained.'

'But, sir . . .'

'Furthermore,' continued Hardcastle, 'this particular piece was obtained as the result of a murder. And that means you could be charged with a felony.' He turned to his sergeant. 'How much is that worth, Marriott?'

'Life imprisonment, sir,' said Marriott, 'if he's lucky enough not to be hanged.' He had played this game with Hardcastle many times before.

Benjamin Levy blanched visibly and leaned on his desk for support. 'If you give me an Old Testament, sir, I'll swear on it that I never knew that figure was stolen.'

'Really? Well, you'll have plenty of time for swearing on the Bible when you get to court.' Hardcastle gazed at the unfortunate dealer. The only flaw in the argument he had put forward was that police had to *prove* that Levy knew the figurine was stolen when he bought it. And that, he knew from previous experience, was virtually impossible. But he was banking on Levy not knowing.

'The client who brought it in seemed to be a trustworthy sort of gentleman,' said Levy, anxious to demonstrate his lack of culpability in the matter of the nude bather. 'He was well-dressed, and certainly didn't look like a thief.' He paused. 'Or a murderer,' he added in a whisper.

'Just have a look round and see if you can spot any of the other property that was taken, Marriott.'

'Yes, sir.' Marriott opened his pocketbook and started round the shop, carefully examining anything that seemed to fit the description of the stolen items. 'This could be one, sir,' he said, picking up a pewter dish. 'A pewter muffin dish and cover measuring nine and a half inches in diameter.' He read the details aloud from his pocketbook and then looked again at the dish.

'And where did you get that, Mr Levy?' demanded Hardcastle.

'From the same gentleman, sir,' said Levy miserably. 'But I never knew it was stolen.'

'And did you buy anything else from this man?'

'No, sir, I swear it.'

'Nothing that you might have handed over to your brother Joseph in Kingston? Like a gold watch, or cufflinks, or medals?'

'No, nothing, sir.'

'Seize that dish, Marriott,' said Hardcastle, and turned again to the wretched dealer. 'Now's your chance to assist me, Mr Levy. And if you're very helpful, you might just avoid any trouble.'

'Anything, sir, anything,' pleaded Levy, wringing his hands.

'The identity of this man who sold you the figurine and the pewter muffin dish would be a start.'

'I don't know, sir. I didn't ask his name.'

'How did you pay him?'

'In cash, of course,' said Levy, as though Hardcastle had asked a silly question.

'Describe him, then.' Hardcastle did not imagine for one moment that Benjamin Levy was a man who dealt much with cheques and banks.

Levy gave careful thought to the question. 'He had a red face, sir, and a moustache. Quite a big moustache, a bit like Lord Kitchener's, God rest his soul, but not waxed like his lordship's was.'

'Age?'

'About sixty, I'd think.'

'Height?'

'About the same as me, sir.'

'And you're about five foot six, I should think.'

'Indeed, I am, sir,' said Levy.

'Anything else? How was he dressed, for instance?'

'I can't remember, sir.'

'Well, Marriott, I suppose we'll have to make do with that,' said Hardcastle, realizing that the description was one that could fit hundreds of men. But before leaving, he gave the antiques dealer a final warning. 'If I find that you're lying, Mr Levy, I'll be back here with a search warrant and half a dozen policemen, and I'll take this shop apart. Just before I arrest you. That clear?'

'I've told you the God's honest truth, sir,' whined Levy.

But, as Hardcastle and Marriott left the shop, Benjamin Levy disappeared into the back room and made a telephone call.

'What d'you make of that, Marriott?' asked Hardcastle, as he and his sergeant clambered into a taxi.

'Well, the man who sold him the stuff could be Albert North, sir. And he doesn't live far from here.'

'Yes, it could be, I suppose,' said Hardcastle thoughtfully. 'And I'm wondering – if it is him – whether he's still got the other items that went adrift.'

'Search warrant, sir?'

'Yes, but not yet, Marriott. Before we get all hot under the collar, we'd better make sure that the two pieces we've got really are the ones that were nicked from Sir Adrian.' Hardcastle leaned forward and tapped on the glass screen with the handle of his umbrella. 'Make it The Grange in Penny Lane, Kingston Hill, rather than the nick, cabbie.'

'It was bad luck that they were fenced in Wandsworth, but finished up in Kingston, not three miles from where the murder occurred, sir,' said Marriott. 'Just because Benjamin Levy had a brother who kept a shop there.'

Hardcastle laughed. 'Yes, it is. And it might just prove to be our man's undoing, Marriott.'

* * *

'Lady Rivers, I'd like you to take a look at these two items of property, and tell me if they're the ones that are missing.'

Muriel Rivers peered at the muffin dish and the figure of the nude bather that Marriott had set down on the table in the morning room.

'Yes, Inspector, they are indeed. So you did find them at Markham Hall, as I suggested. I heard you'd been down there. But why did you bring them back?'

'I didn't bring them back from Wiltshire, Lady Rivers. They were recovered from antiques shops in Wandsworth and Kingston.'

'What on earth were they doing there?'

'That's what I'm attempting to find out.' Hardcastle forbore from mentioning that, in his view, Lady Rivers's father was a strong suspect in the matter.

'Did you find the other things? You know, Sir Adrian's watch, and his . . .'

'Not yet, Lady Rivers, but I'm sure we will, given time.'

'I must say you've been very thorough, Inspector.' Muriel Rivers raised her fan and held it pensively to her lips.

'Incidentally, I've found Daniel Good,' said Hardcastle casually.

'You have? Where?'

'He was staying with his sister in Parsons Green.'

'I really don't understand why he left like that. So quickly, I mean.'

'I've had a few words with him, and I don't think he can help us any further, Lady Rivers.' Hardcastle had earlier made up his mind to release the Rivers's ex-chauffeur.

'I knew you were wrong about him, Inspector. And if you can possibly persuade him to return to my employment, I'd be forever in your debt. I just can't manage without a chauffeur.'

'No, it must be very difficult for you, ma'am,' said Hardcastle, just managing to control his sarcasm. Having read of the privations of the soldiers in France and Flanders, he was sick of this pampered woman's protestations about so-called difficulties.

*　　*　　*

'What d'you know about the property missing from The Grange, Good?' asked Hardcastle, once the prisoner had been brought up to the interview room.

'Nothing, sir, apart from what Mr Beach told me.'

'And what did Beach tell you?'

'Only that Sir Adrian's watch was missing, and his medals and some cufflinks. That's all, sir.'

'Nothing else was mentioned?'

'No, sir.'

'All right, Good. I've decided not to charge you with Sir Adrian's murder.'

'Thank you, sir,' said Good, with a gratitude that Hardcastle found slightly nauseating.

'But only on condition that you return to Lady Rivers's employment. It seems she's suffering something cruel, having to manage without you. And I might want to talk to you again, so I want you somewhere I can find you.'

'Thank you, sir,' said Good again. 'I'm most grateful. But d'you think her ladyship will have me back?'

'I think I managed to talk her into it, Good. Now, be off with you before I change my mind.'

'Are you sure it was a good idea to release Good, sir?' asked Marriott, as the grateful chauffeur left the police station.

'Not altogether, Marriott,' said Hardcastle enigmatically, 'but if we give him enough rope he'll hang himself.'

Fourteen

'Come in the office, Catto,' bellowed Hardcastle, as he passed the open door to the detectives' room.

Hastily, Henry Catto donned his jacket and buttoned his waistcoat. 'Yes, sir?' he said breathlessly, as he skidded to a halt in front of Hardcastle's desk.

'For God's sake, slow down, Catto. I'm not going to eat you,' said Hardcastle, which came as a relief to Catto who always imagined – not without some justification – that the DDI had found some fault with his work, and was about to berate him for it. 'About ten days ago, you made the acquaintance of Albert North.'

'Yes, sir.'

'Is the door still open?'

'What, the front door, sir?' queried the bemused Catto.

'There are times when I think you're as dim as a Toc H lamp, Catto.' Hardcastle had been quick to latch on to an expression that derived from the light outside the mission founded the previous year by the Reverend 'Tubby' Clayton in the little town of Poperinge, near Ypres in Belgium. The saying had quickly become current to describe someone who was not very bright. 'What I want to know is whether you'd be welcome there again,' he explained patiently.

'Oh, I see, sir. Yes, sir. Albert said if ever I was passing to be sure to drop in and see him.'

'Oh, it's Albert now, is it? Well, you can do just that.' Hardcastle glanced at the calendar. 'I don't know if there's a race meeting on anywhere today, but if you're a bit *jildi*, lad, you might be in time to catch him before he leaves home.'

'What d'you want me to say to him, sir?'

'Please yourself, so long as you don't tell him you're a copper. But what I want you to do is to have a good look round, discreetly like. What are them other two pieces that are adrift, Marriott?'

'There are three, sir,' corrected Marriott, somewhat apprehensively. He opened his pocketbook, and reeled off the details of the outstanding missing property. 'A bronze Japanese sleeve vase, a pair of nineteenth-century brass candlesticks, and an ivory carving of a man, thirteen inches high. And, of course, the medals, cufflinks and watch.'

'What's a sleeve vase, Sergeant?

'I've no idea, Catto,' said Marriott, with an amused smile. 'Look it up.'

Further bemused, Catto took out his pocketbook and began to write down what Marriott had dictated.

'What are you doing now, Catto?' demanded Hardcastle.

'Er, making notes, sir.'

'And what are you going to do when you arrive at North's drum, Catto? Pull out your official pocketbook and ask if you can have a look round? Memorize them, lad, memorize them.'

'Yes, sir.' Catto put away his pocketbook. 'What shall I do if there are any of those things there, sir? D'you want me to seize them?'

'No, I don't, Catto. You'll just report back to me. Sergeant Marriott and me will take care of it. Well, don't just stand there – get going. Oh, and Catto . . .'

'Sir?'

'You'd better change into them clothes you was wearing the first time you met Honest Albert. Otherwise he might think you've come into money.' Hardcastle made a point of staring at Catto's suit. 'No, on second thoughts, I doubt he will. But change anyway.'

Despite rushing back to the police section house, changing, and hastening to Waterloo, Catto did not arrive at Flavell Road in Wandsworth until midday.

He banged loudly on the door of number 22, but it was at least a minute before Mrs North opened it.

'Why, Mr Cook, how nice to see you again. Come on in.'

Despite welcoming Catto so warmly, Marjorie North seemed flustered and her face wore a harassed expression.

'I was just passing, Mrs North, and I was wondering if Albert was at home. He said I was to drop in, if I was in the area.'

Mrs North led Catto into the kitchen before answering. 'I don't know where he's gone, Mr Cook. He had a telephone call yesterday morning, and said he had to go out. And I haven't seen him since. He never came home last night, and I'm terribly worried that something might have happened to him, what with the Zeppelin raids and all that. It's most unlike him.'

'I'm sorry to hear that, Mrs North.' Catto was at a loss as to what he should say next. Hardcastle had told him there might be some missing property somewhere in the North household, but had not told him the full story, and certainly had not suggested that such property might have been stolen. He certainly had not told Catto that it might be connected to the murder of Sir Adrian Rivers. Furthermore, if the DDI had revealed that stolen property had been found at the establishments of the brothers Levy in Kingston and Wandsworth, and that Albert North was a suspect for receiving it, Catto might have been better equipped to deal with the situation.

'I was wondering if I should call the police, Mr Cook.'

'Please call me Jim, Mrs North,' said Catto, remembering, just in time, the name he had used the last time he was at the Norths'. 'I suppose that might be a good idea,' he added, although he was uncertain what Hardcastle's reaction would be to his having made such a suggestion. 'Has he ever stayed away that long before?'

'Only the once, and that was last year, when he went to a race meeting at Towcester. That's in Northamptonshire. But he told me he'd be away overnight on that occasion. Yesterday though, he said he was only popping out for a few minutes.' Despite her anguish, Marjorie North suddenly remembered her duty as a hostess. 'Sit down, Jim, and I'll make you a cup of tea.'

'I don't know what to suggest, Mrs North,' said Catto.

He was concerned that if he encouraged Albert's wife to contact the local police and file a missing person report, it might upset Hardcastle's plans. Whatever they were.

'Perhaps I should wait a bit longer, Jim.' Although Marjorie North was visibly concerned about the disappearance of her husband, she was obviously in two minds about whether to involve the police. Nevertheless she finished brewing the tea, and set out the tea things on a tray.

'Here, let me take that for you, Mrs North,' said Catto, standing up as she moved to pick up the tray.

'Thank you, Jim. Perhaps you'd bring it into the parlour. It's more comfortable in there.'

For the next twenty minutes or so, Mrs North and Catto made small talk, mainly about the unexplained absence of Albert North, and how out of character it was. Meanwhile, the detective's eyes were darting everywhere. It took time, because the room was full of bric-à-brac, most of it in glass-fronted cabinets. But then his eyes lighted upon an ivory carving of a man. Admittedly it was about thirteen inches high, but Catto assumed that such an ornament was not uncommon in households like the Norths'. If he reported its existence to the DDI, and it turned out not to be the item that was missing, Catto would doubtless be in trouble. But if he failed to report it, that could spell trouble too. To the unfortunate Catto, it was a dilemma.

'That's a nice little chap there, Mrs North.' Catto pointed at the ivory statuette.

'D'you like it? I think it's a horrible thing. I don't know where Albert got it from, but he often comes in with bits and pieces like that. To tell you the truth, Jim, my Albert's a bit of a magpie. He's always picking up things like that, but he usually sells them again quite quickly. And at a profit. It's a sort of sideline.'

'How long's he had that, then?' Catto hoped he was not being too obvious.

Marjorie North gave the question some thought. 'Only a few days, I think. He never tells me when he's bought something new, and usually I only find out when I come in to dust. Are you interested in that sort of stuff?'

'Not really,' said Catto. 'But I've got an uncle who's in the business, up Islington way,' he added, extemporizing madly. 'He's a bit like Albert in a way. Always collecting things.'

Marjorie North glanced at the ormolu clock on the mantelpiece. Catto realized that it had not been there on the occasion of his last visit, and wondered whether he should mention it to the DDI when he got back to the police station.

'Good heavens, one o'clock,' exclaimed Marjorie North. 'Will you stay for a bite to eat, Jim?'

'That's very kind of you, Mrs North,' said Catto, 'but I'm meeting a pal of mine in London at half past two.' That was true in a way, although he did not think the DDI would much care for being described as Catto's 'pal'. 'I do hope Albert turns up safe and sound. Do give him my best, and tell him I'll call in again next time I'm in the vicinity.'

'You're more than welcome, Jim. I miss having a young-ster about the place, although Muriel does drop in from time to time.'

'Oh yes,' said Catto. 'Albert was telling me the last time I was here that she had got married to a "Sir".'

'She did that. She's called Lady Rivers now. Who'd've thought it? Done very well for herself, has our Muriel.' Marjorie North gazed dreamily at the wedding photograph of her daughter and Sir Adrian Rivers.

It was three o'clock when Catto returned to Cannon Row. He had decided to chance turning up in the rough clothing he had assumed for his visit to the Norths, despite what the DDI might have to say about it.

Hardcastle examined his detective's outfit closely when he appeared in the office.

'If anything, that's an improvement, Catto,' he said jocu-larly. 'Well, what did you find out?'

Catto began by explaining about the disappearance of Albert North, but was immediately interrupted by Hardcastle.

'Disappeared? Hold on a minute, and get Sergeant Marriott in here.'

Catto crossed the corridor to the detectives' office and summoned the first-class sergeant.

'Right, Catto, give me that again,' said Hardcastle, once Marriott had joined them.

Once more, Catto told Hardcastle about Albert North's sudden departure, and the fact that Marjorie North had no idea where he was. He also mentioned that North had vanished shortly after receiving a telephone call yesterday morning.

'Did Mrs North say who the call was from, Catto?' asked Hardcastle.

'No, sir, she said she didn't know.'

Hardcastle smote the top of his desk with the flat of his hand. 'Guilty knowledge, Marriott. I wouldn't mind betting that our friend Benjamin Levy got in touch with Honest Albert the minute we'd left his shady little emporium.'

'There was an ivory carving of a man in one of the cabinets in the parlour, sir,' Catto continued.

'Did it fit the description Sergeant Marriott gave you, lad?'

'It seemed to, sir, and Mrs North said Albert had only brought it into the house a few days ago. She said collecting things like that was a sort of hobby of Albert's. She also said he usually sells them on at a profit, too.'

'Did she now?' Hardcastle rubbed his hands together. 'The man's a bloody fence as well as a bookie, Marriott. I do believe we've got the bugger.'

'I also noticed an ormolu clock on the mantelpiece that hadn't been there the last time I called, sir.'

'Did you indeed?'

'Search warrant, sir?' asked Marriott.

'Yes, and as soon as you like. Get up to Bow Street, Marriott, and swear one out.' Hardcastle paused. 'On second thoughts, I'll come with you, then we can go straight on to Wandsworth from there.'

'D'you want me to come with you, sir?' asked Catto.

'Don't be bloody silly, Catto,' said Hardcastle. 'I want to keep you in reserve, just in case I need you to go in there again and talk nicely to Mrs North.' Once again he examined Catto's apparel. 'In your Sunday best.'

'There was one other thing, sir,' said Catto. 'Mrs North didn't seem to want to tell the police that her husband was missing. I was wondering whether she knew he was a fence, and didn't want the likes of us turning the place over.'

For a moment or two, Hardcastle gazed at the young DC. 'D'you know, Catto, you might have the makings of a detective after all.'

'Thank you, sir.'

'Given another ten years,' added Hardcastle.

After taking a taxi to Bow Street, and having advised the warrant officer why he was there, Hardcastle mounted the witness box and swore his hurriedly prepared 'information'. But despite the fact that they took another taxi from there to Wandsworth, it was still gone five o'clock that evening before Hardcastle and Marriott were hammering on the door of 22 Flavell Road.

'Mrs North?' Hardcastle raised his hat as the woman came to the door.

'Yes.' Marjorie North stared apprehensively at the two men on her doorstep.

'We're police officers, Mrs North,' said Hardcastle, and introduced himself and Marriott.

'Oh, glory be. I knew it. What's happened to him? Is he dead? Something terrible's happened, hasn't it?'

Hardcastle feigned surprise. 'Are you talking about your husband, Mrs North? Were you expecting something to have happened to him?'

'Albert's been missing since yesterday, and I don't know where he's gone. He's just disappeared. He got a telephone call and said he was popping out for a few minutes. It's so unlike him. I'm sure something dreadful's happened to him.'

'I'm afraid I know nothing about your husband, Mrs North, but it's him we wanted to see.' Hardcastle convincingly continued the fiction of knowing nothing about Albert North's absence.

'Well, you'd better come in, Inspector. I'm not sure if I can help, but if it's about Albert's business, I don't know much about it. He's a turf accountant, you see.'

'Really?' said Hardcastle. 'As a matter of fact, we've had information that your husband might be able to assist us,' he continued, as he and Marriott followed Marjorie North into the parlour. 'I believe he sometimes buys antiques.'

'Yes, that's true, but I don't know anything about that. Except that I have to dust them. As if I haven't got enough to do.'

Hardcastle glanced at the ivory figurine of a man in the glass case where Catto had said it would be. 'Have you any idea where he got that from, for instance?'

'No. All I can tell you is that he brought it home a few days ago.'

'How long ago exactly?'

Marjorie North gave the question some thought. 'Having said a few days, I suppose it must've been at least a fort-night back. To tell you the truth, Inspector, I can't keep up with all the junk he brings in. And it's usually here for only a day or two, and then he sells it again. It's a sort of hobby of his.'

'Have you an idea who he buys it from, or sells it to, Mrs North?' asked Marriott.

'No, I'm afraid not.' Marjorie North paused in thought for a moment. 'But funnily enough there was a young man here only today who was very interested in that little figure.' And she pointed at the ivory statuette that had attracted Hardcastle's attention.

'D'you happen to know his name?' asked Hardcastle, his interest aroused.

'Yes, Jim Cook. A nice young man, and he's been here before. He's quite friendly with Albert. In fact, Albert told him to call in anytime he happened to be passing.'

'Any idea where this man comes from, Mrs North?' Marriott asked. Catto had neglected to tell either Hardcastle or Marriott that he had used the name Jim Cook.

'Let me see . . . Yes, I think he mentioned Victoria. Strutton Ground, I think he told Albert, although I'm not certain.'

'Did he suggest that he might want to buy that partic-ular piece?'

'No, but he said he had an uncle in the antiques business. Up Islington way, is what he said. So I suppose he might have a word with that uncle of his, to see if he's interested like. I'd be grateful to see the back of it. It's quite horrible.'

'An uncle in the antiques business, eh?' Hardcastle glanced meaningfully at Marriott. 'Well, Mrs North, I have reason to believe that that particular item is stolen property, and I'm obliged to seize it. I also have a warrant issued by the Bow Street magistrate that empowers me to search these premises.'

Marjorie North stared at the two detectives in stark disbelief. 'Oh, but this is terrible. If only Albert was here.' She was a picture of despair as she stood in front of the empty fireplace, wringing her hands. First her husband had disappeared without a word, and now the police were here insisting on searching the house. 'I don't know where he's gone, Inspector, but I'm sure he'd be able to answer all your questions if he was here.'

'Are you connected to the telephone, Mrs North?' asked Hardcastle, even though Catto had told him there was one in the house.

'Yes, it's in the hall.'

'D'you mind if my sergeant uses it?'

'No. Please help yourself.'

'Telephone Wandsworth nick, Marriott, and ask them to send a couple of CID officers round here to carry out a search.' Hardcastle had no intention of involving himself in a time-consuming rummage of the premises. If there was any other stolen property here that had a connection with the murder of Sir Adrian Rivers, the Wandsworth officers could be relied upon to find it. But so far, it was only the ivory figurine that seemed to fall into that category.

A quarter of an hour later, a detective sergeant and a detective constable from the local station arrived at the house.

'DS Grimes, sir, from Wandsworth,' said the sergeant, 'and this is DC Walker.'

Hardcastle explained what they should look for,

mentioning the ormolu clock in particular, and handed the
Wandsworth sergeant the warrant.

'If you happen to come across a gold watch, gold cufflinks
or medals, seize them and let me know, Sergeant. Any other
stolen property you find you can deal with at Wandsworth.'
Hardcastle turned to his own sergeant. 'Tell them what
medals are adrift, Marriott.'

Once Marriott had given the Wandsworth officers details
of Sir Adrian Rivers's missing decorations, watch and
cufflinks, Hardcastle seized the ivory figurine, and he and
Marriott departed. But not before Hardcastle had asked Mrs
North to tell her husband to contact him when eventually
he returned home. Not that he had much hope of Honest
Albert North complying with that request.

Catto was summoned to Hardcastle's office the moment the
DDI returned to Cannon Row.

'What d'you know about a man called Jim Cook who
called on Albert North, Catto? Apparently he's got an uncle
who runs an antiques business in Islington.'

'Er, that's me, sir.' Catto looked apprehensively at
Hardcastle, then at Marriott, and back again.

'What d'you mean, it's you?' snapped Hardcastle angrily.
'Your name's Catto. Or have you changed it by deed poll
without telling me?'

'No, sir, but I thought it best not to use my own name
when I met Albert North, sir, so I made one up. And when
Mrs North asked me if I was interested in the ivory figure,
I pretended I'd got an uncle in Islington who was in the
trade. Just to show interest, like.'

For some seconds, Hardcastle stared at Catto, who, not
for the first time, firmly believed that his detective career
was about to come to an inglorious end.

'Well done, lad,' said Hardcastle eventually, and laughed.

At nine o'clock that evening, the two officers who had
carried out the search of the North family home appeared
in Hardcastle's office.

'We found nine pieces of stolen property at 22 Flavell

Road, sir,' said Detective Sergeant Grimes. 'All of which had appeared in the *Police Gazette*, including the ormolu clock. Been nicked from a country house in Ripley apparently.'

'Good work,' said Hardcastle.

'We also found these, sir.' The sergeant opened his brief-case and took out a Distinguished Service Order, medals for the Sudan and Africa campaigns, and the neck insignia of a Companion of the Most Honourable Order of the Bath. 'They were in a drawer in the Norths' bedroom. Wrapped up in a handkerchief, they was, sir.'

'You've done a good job there, Grimes.' Hardcastle examined the medals, slowly turning each one over in his hands. The name of Adrian Rivers was engraved on the rim of each decoration. 'I think that's good enough for an arrest warrant, Marriott,' he said. 'Now all we've got to do is find the bugger.'

'I've got a feeling that might take some time, sir,' said Marriott.

'What was it that Boy Scout Baden-Powell said, Marriott? Softly, softly, catchee monkey?'

'I do believe so, sir,' said Marriott, trying to work out what Lord Baden-Powell's famous quote had to do with the apprehension of Honest Albert North.

Fifteen

Although Hardcastle had ordered that details of Albert North be included in the next issue of the *Police Gazette*, he had no intention of sitting back and waiting for detectives from another division to arrest him.

On Thursday morning, he summoned all the available CID officers from across A Division, and by eight o'clock they were lined up in the parade room at Cannon Row police station.

'Albert North is a bookmaker who's wanted on warrant by the police at Wandsworth for receiving stolen property,' Hardcastle began, and in an aside, added, 'And he has the cheek to call himself *Honest* Albert North.' There were a few laughs at that, but the DDI silenced the outbreak with a frown. 'The stolen property found at his home address points to him being a professional fence, and I'm convinced that he had a hand in the topping of Sir Adrian Rivers at Kingston.' There was no need for the DDI to expand on that; A Division's detectives were well aware that their chief was spending a lot of time on V Division investigating the baronet's murder. 'Sergeant Marriott will tell you what he looks like, so get your pocketbooks out.'

There was a rustle of movement, and Marriott read the detailed description that he and Hardcastle had compiled of Albert North; a description added to by DC Catto.

'He's resident at 22 Flavell Road, Wandsworth, and is known to frequent racecourses around London,' Hardcastle continued. 'Hurst Park – that's the most likely place he'll be – Kempton Park, Lingfield, Gatwick Park and Sandown Park for certain. His missus told us he once went to Towcester, but it seems he don't make a habit of it.'

'Where's Towcester, sir?' asked a Rochester Row detective constable.

'In Northamptonshire, lad, but don't worry yourself about that; you won't be going there.'

There was another laugh from the assembled officers, but Hardcastle let it go. He knew there was nothing his officers liked more than a spell of detached duty out of town, mainly because it meant distancing themselves from his authority.

'I want this man found, and found quickly. Use any noses you've got, and ask around other bookies, tipsters, or anyone who might've seen him lately. I want him to know he's being threatened so that if he hears we're after him, he might do something stupid. And if you do feel his collar, just tell him you're nicking him for receiving stolen property. If any one of you mentions to North that I suspect him of the murder of Sir Adrian Rivers, who happens to be his son-in-law—'

'Blimey, that's a turn up,' said a voice.

'Just shut your rattle, lad,' snapped Hardcastle. 'As I was saying, if any one of you mentions the topping of Sir Adrian to North, that officer will be wearing a pointed hat and a blue suit with shiny buttons on it within the hour. Now then, Sergeant Marriott has drawn up a list of the racecourses that each of you is going to cover, but DS Wood and DC Catto will take Hurst Park, on account of that being the most likely venue, and that Catto knows what North looks like. Where are you, Catto?'

'Here, sir,' said Catto, raising a hand.

'I still want you to keep out of North's sight, lad, but only if you can. If he's there, point him out to DS Wood, and let him run him in. But if North cuts up rough, you'll have to weigh in. That's if there aren't any uniforms about. There never are when you want them,' added Hardcastle in an aside. 'Got that, have you, Catto?'

'Yes, sir.'

Hardcastle pulled out his hunter and glanced at it. 'That's it, lads. Make sure you get something to eat before you go, and then move off. I want you all in place at your assigned courses by midday, and you're to stay there until after the last race. Carry on.' Then he added a caution that years of experience told him would be ignored. 'And no drinking on duty.'

There was an excited buzz of conversation as the group of detectives broke up and filed away.

'Well, Marriott,' said Hardcastle, as they went back upstairs to Hardcastle's office. 'We'll see if that brings the bugger in.'

'I hope it does, sir,' said Marriott, although he was not too sanguine that Albert North would reappear at any of his usual stamping grounds. And neither was Hardcastle.

Herbert Wood and Henry Catto arrived at Hurst Park race-course at midday, as Hardcastle had instructed they should. Being a Thursday, there were fewer racegoers than if it had been a Saturday.

'Where does this bloke North set up his pitch, Henry?'

'Alongside the ring usually, Sergeant,' said Catto. 'It's probably best if I show you. It's down this way.' And he led DS Wood to where he had seen Albert North on the day he had followed him to his house in Wandsworth. 'He normally sets up over there, next to that bearded bookie in the brown trilby hat.' His eyes searched the array of book-makers. 'Ah, but he's not here.'

'That comes as no surprise,' commented Wood who, in common with the other detectives, was unconvinced that North would appear at any racecourse, let alone his usual one. 'Go down and have a word with that bookie, Henry. If he clocks me for the law, he won't say a dickie bird. But seeing as how you claim to be a mate of North's, he might open up.'

Catto wandered casually towards Albert North's profes-sional neighbour whose board proclaimed him to Horace Dabbs.

'What's your fancy, guv'nor?' asked Dabbs.

'I'm looking for Albert North,' said Catto. 'He told me to look him up next time I was down this way so's I could buy him a pint.' He gestured towards the vacant space next to Dabbs's stand. 'He's usually there.'

Dabbs laughed. 'Yeah, that'll be Bert North,' he said. 'Never known to refuse a pint. But he's not here today.'

'I suppose I'll find him at another course, then,' commented Catto, contriving to look disappointed. 'Any idea where he might be? Or maybe he's at home at Flavell Road.'

'Oh, you know where he lives, then.' The bookmaker leaned forward confidentially. 'You won't find him there, mate,' he said in a low voice. 'Between you and me, Bert's got a bit of grief with the law.'

'Bloody hell!' exclaimed Catto, giving a passable impression of shock. 'What's he been up to, then?'

Horace Dabbs shrugged. 'Dunno, mate, but he reckoned it was a bit serious. I saw him yesterday, and he said he was going to stay with a mate of his down Woolwich way.'

'Any idea where?' asked Catto. 'I owe him some money, see,' he added, making up his story as he went along.

'Half a mo,' said the bookmaker. 'He gave me a note of it in case anyone was asking after him.' And he paused to chuckle throatily before adding, 'Apart from the bleedin' rozzers, o'course.' Taking a small diary from his pocket, he thumbed through the pages. 'Got it. Number 12 Nelson Street guv'nor. It's hard by Woolwich Arsenal.'

'Thanks, mate,' said Catto.

'Give him my best if you sees him, guv'nor. And tell him he's losing money hand over fist. Whatever he's got himself tied up in must be serious.'

Catto waved a hand of acknowledgement over his shoulder as he turned away and set off to impart this valuable information to DS Wood.

'Well done, Henry. I reckon we'll make time for me to buy you a pint, and then we'll get back to the nick and give Mr Hardcastle the glad news.'

'Well?' said Hardcastle, when Wood and Catto appeared in his office. 'Nicked him, have you?'

'He wasn't there, sir,' said Wood, 'but Catto had a word with a mate of North's who saw him yesterday.'

'Oh? And who is this mate, Catto?'

'Name of Horace Dabbs, sir, he's a bookie an' all.'

'And what did he have to say?'

'He said that North had told him he was in trouble with the law and had decided to lie low for a few days.'

'He's dead right about that.' Hardcastle emitted a coarse laugh. 'Did he say where he was holed up?'

'Yes, sir.' Catto opened his pocketbook. 'Number 12 Nelson Street, Woolwich. It's close to Woolwich Arsenal by all accounts, sir.'

'D'you want me to alert R Division, sir?' asked Wood hesitantly.

'No, I bloody don't, Wood. He's mine and I'm going to nab him myself. Tell Sergeant Marriott to come in here, Catto. And well done, lad.'

'Thank you, sir,' said Catto, preening himself.

'Well don't stand there grinning like a Cheshire cat, Catto. Bugger off and get Sergeant Marriott.'

'I hear that Wood and Catto have located North, sir,' said Marriott, entering Hardcastle's office a few moments later.

'Nelson Street, Woolwich, Marriott.' Hardcastle pulled out his hunter and stared at it. 'Half past six. We'll have a bite to eat and then go and feel his collar.' The DDI rubbed his hands together. 'We'll leave it for a bit in case he's out.'

Nelson Street in Woolwich consisted of a row of mean, terraced houses owned by an insurance company. Its rent collector – who wore a bowler hat and a raincoat, winter and summer – took a sadistic delight in the relentless pursuit of those who had neither the inclination nor the wherewithal to pay their dues.

Most of the families who lived there relied for their income on the nearby Woolwich Arsenal where the breadwinners, aided nowadays by young girls, were engaged in the manufacture of huge shells and other armaments for the army and navy. Those wives who were not themselves working kept their houses immaculate, regularly whitening the doorsteps, cleaning the windows, washing the curtains and, in summer, removing carpets – from those dwellings that possessed them – and mercilessly beating them in the open air.

'Ah!' said Hardcastle, sighting the Goose and Duck public house on the corner of Nelson Street, 'I think we'll stop off here for a wet, Marriott. According to Catto, Albert North likes his pint, and we might just be lucky enough to find him in here propping up the bar.'

'Evening, guv'nor. What'll it be?' The ruddy-faced land-lord gave the top of the bar a cursory wipe with a dirty cloth.

'Two pints of your best bitter,' said Hardcastle, and glanced at Marriott before casting his gaze around the crowded saloon bar.

Marriott, aware that he and Hardcastle were off their manor, knew the beer would have to be paid for, and also knew he would be the one paying for it.

'There we are, guv'nor.' The landlord placed two tankards on the bar.

'Seen Albert North in here lately?' asked Hardcastle casually.

The landlord frowned. 'You the law?' he asked, displaying that sixth sense all licensees seem to possess.

'Yes. Divisional Detective Inspector Hardcastle of the Whitehall Division.'

'Didn't think I'd seen you in here before, guv'nor.' The landlord pushed Marriott's money away, and lowered his voice. 'No, as a matter of fact, I ain't seen him since last night. It was the first time I'd met him. He ain't a regular.'

'No, he wouldn't be,' said Hardcastle. 'But he was here?'

'Yes. He come in with a mate of his, Joe Fraser. Lives down the far end of the road. Number 12, I think.'

For the next twenty minutes, the two detectives listened to a raucous singsong accompanied by a less-than-competent pianist on a badly tuned piano. The songs were mainly those said to be popular with the troops in the frontline – *Take Me Back to Dear Old Blighty*; and *It's a Long Way to Tipperary* – but sung with more gusto, Hardcastle suspected, than the soldiers who were actually out there.

It was at about ten o'clock that the drinkers in the Goose

and Duck heard the dull, throbbing engines of an airship, searching for the prime objective of Woolwich Arsenal.

The pianist stopped playing and the singsong ceased abruptly.

'That's a bloody Zeppelin,' complained the landlord tersely. 'Those square-headed bastards are after the Arsenal again.'

Hardcastle and Marriott followed the pub's customers out into the street, but remained only long enough to watch the giant machine hovering overhead, searchlight beams criss-crossing beneath it in an attempt to provide the anti-aircraft gunners with a target.

'Can't waste my time staring at that thing, Marriott,' said Hardcastle. 'I'm for another pint, and then we'll pay a visit to number 12.'

There was the crump of a violent explosion as the two detectives returned to the pub, and its front windows were blown out, swirling the sawdust on the floor, and scattering glass across the street outside. A cloud of coarse brick dust swept in, covering the two policemen and the bar counter.

'Bit close, that one,' commented the landlord drily, as he began to wipe the top of the bar. 'That's the second time Fritz has done me bloody windows.' He seemed otherwise unperturbed, and drew two more pints for the detectives, and one for himself.

Staying only long enough to down their beer, Hardcastle and Marriott made for the door, now hanging drunkenly on its hinges. After a moment's pause, they began to make their way along Nelson Street, the rubble and glass crunching beneath their feet and becoming thicker as they neared number 12. The stench of explosive, coupled with the heavy odour of a broken gas main, filled the air.

But even before they drew level with North's temporary abode, they could see it was a smoking ruin, reduced to a pile of broken bricks, splintered beams, laths and plaster. Several houses opposite, and on either side of Fraser's dwelling, had been badly damaged, and looked like giant doll's houses that had been opened to reveal furniture hanging precariously on the upper floors.

A twisted iron bed and clothes and sheets had been sucked out of one house and spread across the mean front garden. A wedding photograph, its glass shattered, lay on the pavement alongside a smashed vase and a dead cat. As the detectives surveyed this scene of devastation, a dressing table slid across the sloping upper floor of one house and crashed into the brick-strewn front garden. It seemed unlikely that anyone in number 12 could have survived.

'It's no good you hanging around here,' said an officious policeman, moving to bar the detectives' way. 'There's nothing to see. Just move along and let us get on with the job.'

'I'm DDI Hardcastle of A.'

'May I see your warrant card, sir?' asked the policeman, clearly unconvinced that so high-ranking an officer from a division miles away should be in Nelson Street that late at night. 'Sorry, sir,' he said, having satisfied himself as to the DDI's identity, and saluted. 'We always get a few looters after there's been an incident.'

'Is that so?' Although Hardcastle was inwardly amused at the policeman's description of the devastation as 'an incident', he was at once irritated at having been mistaken for a looter. 'I'm looking for Albert North, who I'm told was staying at that house along with a Joe Fraser. Know him, do you?'

'Joe Fraser, sir? Yes, I knows him. Bit of a sharp fellow, that one. I've nicked him a couple of times.' The policeman fingered his moustache. 'I shouldn't think you'll have much luck, sir. It was a landmine that fell on number 12, fair and square. Pretty powerful them are.'

'What did you nick Fraser for?' asked Hardcastle, his eyes narrowing.

'Street betting mainly, sir, and a bit of crown-and-anchor, but he's a difficult beggar to catch at it. Mind you, he's nigh on fifty now. Time he give up.'

'D'you know if there are any survivors?' persisted Hardcastle, having dismissed Fraser's offences as beneath his interest.

'Bit early to tell yet, sir. The brigade's only just arrived.' Indeed, a fire engine had stopped in front of the wrecked house as the three police officers were conversing. The crew of an ambulance was tending a man sitting on the kerb, putting a bandage around a head wound. 'I don't doubt they'll tell us soon enough. Mind you, sir, that don't look too promising.' The policeman pointed at three shrouded bodies that had been laid out at the kerbside by the firemen. 'But I'll see what I can find out.' And with that he moved off towards the fire chief.

'Well, that's a bloody turn up and no mistake, Marriott,' said Hardcastle, as he pulled out his pipe and started to fill it. 'I reckon the bugger's escaped our clutches.' It was almost as if the DDI believed North had got himself killed just to avoid arrest.

'Good job we stopped off for a wet, sir,' said Marriott. 'If we'd been in there, talking to North, we might've copped it as well.'

'Well, they say everything turns out for the best, Marriott,' said Hardcastle enigmatically.

The policeman returned. 'It'll be some time before the brigade can tell if there's anyone underneath that lot, sir,' he said, gesturing at the mountain of rubble that had once been 12 Nelson Street. 'Could be tomorrow at the earliest, so the fire chief reckoned. But he don't give much hope, given that there's fatals in the houses on either side.' He glanced at the box of matches in Hardcastle's hand. 'I shouldn't, if I was you, sir. There's gas escaping, so the fire chief says.'

'Bugger it,' said Hardcastle, turning on his heel.

'Yes, sir,' said the policeman, and saluted.

Hardcastle arrived at his office early on Friday morning, and his first act was to summon Catto.

'Get down to Flavell Road, Catto, and see what Mrs North has to say. It's just possible she's been told that Albert North was killed in last night's raid.'

'Raid, sir?' said Catto.

Hardcastle explained about the Zeppelin raid on Nelson Street, and his regrettable conclusion that North had been killed.

'And if she hasn't heard, Catto, don't tell her what you know. Play the innocent.' Hardcastle began to fill his pipe. 'Shouldn't be too difficult for you,' he added.

'He's still not back, Jim.' Marjorie North wore the same worried expression that had been evident the last time Catto had called.

'I'm sorry to hear that, Mrs North. Have you told the police?'

'Only in manner of speaking,' said Marjorie North mysteriously,

'What d'you mean by that?' asked Catto.

But Mrs North did not answer immediately. 'I don't know what's come over me lately, Jim. I'm forgetting my manners,' she said, as she opened the door wide. 'Come in and I'll make you a cup of tea.' Waiting until they were both in the kitchen, she expanded on her cryptic statement. 'I think he's in some sort of trouble, Jim. Just after you were here on Wednesday the police turned up. Some dreadful rude inspector arrived on the doorstep, and straight off started accusing my Bert of stealing. And when he went he took that little figure you admired. Then a bit later two more plainclothes men came and started turning the place upside down, and they took some of the things he'd been collecting, including the clock.' She waved vaguely at the empty place on the mantelpiece where once the ormolu clock had stood. 'Honestly, Jim, I don't know which way to turn.'

'What did they say about Bert being missing?'

'Nothing. They just took the things and said to be sure to let them know if he turned up. I can't help thinking something dreadful's happened to him.' Marjorie paused. 'I hope I haven't got you into trouble, Jim,' she said thoughtfully, 'but I told them you'd been here earlier, and had been interested in that ivory statue. They wanted to know about you and where you lived, and I'm afraid I told them. I'm sorry, but I'm afraid I let slip about your uncle as well.'

'My uncle?' said Catto, having forgotten the story he had made up.

'The one who sells antiques. In Islington, I think you said.'

'Oh, him.' Catto laughed, more from relief at having recalled what he had said before. 'Don't worry about him, Mrs North. He's big enough and ugly enough to take care of himself.'

Later that morning Hardcastle received a call from the police at Woolwich.

'I understand you were enquiring about the occupants of 12 Nelson Street, sir,' said the station officer.

'Yes. What about them?'

'Two bodies were found under the debris, sir. They've been identified as Joseph Fraser, and his wife Maud.'

'Is that all there were?' demanded Hardcastle.

'Were you expecting more, sir?' asked the sergeant.

'I was led to believe that a man called Albert North was living there. He's wanted on warrant.'

'I'm sorry, sir, but the fire brigade were sure there was only the two bodies found. They're in the mortuary at the local hospital if you want to see them.'

'It might come to that,' said Hardcastle. 'Who identified them, Sergeant?'

'One moment, sir.' There was a rustling of paper as the station officer turned a page in the occurrence book. 'Identified by nearby neighbours who knew them well, sir.'

'Sod it, Marriott!' said Hardcastle, after he had finished his conversation with the Woolwich police. 'It looks like the bugger's escaped. Now we'll have to start all over again.'

But the mystery deepened with the publication of the evening newspapers, the first edition of which came out at midday. The *Star* published a report of the Zeppelin raid on Woolwich, and announced that three people had been killed in Nelson Street: Joseph and Maud Fraser . . . and a lodger called Albert North.

'There's something funny going on here, Marriott,' said Hardcastle, as usual understating the case. 'I think we'll go up to Bouverie Street and find out where this reporter got his information from.'

*   *   *

Becoming increasingly irritated by his inability to find Albert North, Hardcastle was in no mood to be balked by petty officialdom.

'I want to see the reporter who wrote this,' said Hardcastle, waving his copy of the *Star* under the commissionaire's nose.

'Oh, and who might you be?'

'Divisional Detective Inspector Hardcastle of the Whitehall Division, and I'm in no mood to have my time wasted, so find him.'

'Does it say who wrote it, then?' asked the commissionaire, rapidly becoming more conciliatory in the face of the DDI's wrath.

'It says, "By our own correspondent".' Hardcastle flourished the newspaper yet again.

'If you hold on, sir, I'll see what I can do.' The commissionaire disappeared through a door at the back of the entrance hall.

A few minutes later, a young man appeared. 'I'm Charlie Froggett,' he announced, fingering the lapels of a suit that Hardcastle regarded as too flamboyant.

'Did you write this?' asked Hardcastle, pointing at the offending article.

'Yes, I did.'

'Where did you get this information about Albert North, lad?' demanded Hardcastle.

'It's not our custom to reveal our sources, Inspector. It's called privileged information.'

'Is that a fact?' said Hardcastle. Someone more familiar with the DDI's moods would have sensed that his temper was shortening quite dramatically. 'Well, Mr Froggett, unless you tell me who told you that Albert North was dead, I'll arrest you and charge you with obstructing police in a murder enquiry. And that information won't be privileged because I'll happily tell the *Evening News* all about it,' he added, deliberately naming a rival newspaper.

The young reporter blanched, and capitulated immediately. 'It was the landlord of the Goose and Duck, on the corner of Nelson Street, Inspector,' he said, licking his lips.

'Was it indeed? And when did he impart this valuable titbit to you?'

'Late last night. About midnight, it was.'

'And I suppose you paid him for it, did you?'

'Well, yes, it's the practice of the newspaper to pay for information.'

Hardcastle laughed, and stuffed the newspaper into his pocket. 'Well, you've been sold a pup, my lad,' he said.

Sixteen

Determined to get to the bottom of the mystery surrounding Albert North, the tireless Hardcastle journeyed once again to Woolwich. The much younger Marriott, for his part, was beginning to feel quite fatigued with all the travelling. As for the Marriott family, they were wondering when they would see husband and father again.

The windows of the Goose and Duck had been boarded up, but otherwise it was business as usual, and the pub was crowded with drinkers whose main topic of conversation was the previous night's Zeppelin raid.

Hardcastle heard one toper proposing a toast to the memory of Joe Fraser and, in the next breath, cursing the Kaiser.

'Hello, Inspector, I'm surprised to see you again.' Without waiting, the landlord drew two pints of bitter and placed them on the bar.

'Seen this, have you?' asked Hardcastle, producing his copy of the *Star*.

'Can't say as I have, guv'nor,' said the landlord, donning a pair of wire-framed spectacles, and pulling the newspaper towards him. 'Something interesting in it, is there?'

'You could say that. There's a piece about the raid last night. It was written by a young whippersnapper called Charlie Froggett, a stringer on the paper.'

'Oh yeah?' The landlord showed the first signs of nervousness.

'Seems he got hold of some cock-and-bull story about Albert North having been killed when a landmine hit 12 Nelson Street last night.'

'Is that a fact?'

'And he got the information from someone in this pub,' said Hardcastle, retrieving his copy of the newspaper. He was playing with the landlord now.

'Now you come to mention it, I do recall some reporter coming in here.' The landlord spoke nervously. 'Late last night it was.'

'Oh, I see, Mr, er . . . I don't think I know your name.' That was not true; it was painted over the door, and Hardcastle had noted it.

'Sid Fowler, guv'nor.'

'Well, Mr Fowler, Froggett is adamant that it was you who told him North had snuffed it.'

'But I thought he had,' said the landlord defensively.

'Did you really?' said Hardcastle, at his sarcastic best, and leaning a little closer to Fowler. 'Well, it's not true, is it?' He stared accusingly at the licensee.

The landlord licked his lips. 'But . . .'

'But nothing,' said Hardcastle angrily. 'You see, Mr Fowler, I've got enough on my plate without having people obstructing me in the execution of my duty. And when I'm investigating a murder, I'm likely to run in anyone who gets in my way. Now, matey, I'd better be having the truth, or we'll carry on this little chat down at Woolwich nick.'

'Murder!' Fowler crumpled. 'I don't know nothing about no murder, guv'nor, and that's straight. Whose murder are you talking about?'

'That needn't concern you, but what I don't believe is that when the beat-duty copper called round the back of your boozer for his usual pint of free beer, you didn't ask him a few questions about the bombing in general and Albert North in particular.'

That Hardcastle was so knowledgable about the practices of constables and their relationship with pub landlords further unnerved Fowler. He licked his lips again. 'Well, he did happen to mention it, like.'

'And he told you it was only Joe Fraser and his missus who'd copped it, didn't he? He never said anything about Albert North. So who put you up to telling this tale, eh?' But Hardcastle had already guessed the answer to that.

Realizing that he was in a defenceless position, Fowler capitulated. 'It was Bert North, guv'nor,' he said.

'Ah, now we're getting to the bottom of it,' said Hardcastle.

'When did this happen, Mr Fowler?' asked Marriott, alarming the landlord even more by taking out his pocket-book and resting it on the bar.

'Not long after you gents left, guv'nor. He come in about half eleven, I s'pose. Said he'd been up the West End with a mate of his, and when he got back the house was wrecked.'

'And what else did he say?' persisted Marriott.

'He said he'd have to find somewhere else to kip down, and asked if I'd got any rooms to spare here.'

'And what did you say to that?'

'I said I was full up. Well, I am. The wife's sister's place in Lowestoft got shelled by the German Navy a few nights ago, and I'm putting her and her brood up for the time being. Her old man's across the water in France somewhere. Grenadier Guards, he is.'

'And North told you to tell any interested party that he'd copped it in the raid, I suppose,' put in Hardcastle. 'Particularly if it was the police asking the questions.'

'Yeah. He said you lot was after him, but that he could sort it all out if he had a bit more time. He reckoned you'd got the wrong end of the stick.'

'And how much did he give you to spread that little tale?'

'Nothing, guv'nor,' protested Fowler. 'On my mother's grave.'

Hardcastle nodded slowly. 'Well, Fowler, you're not out of the woods yet. If the Director of Public Prosecutions decides to institute proceedings against you for aiding an offender, you'll likely be standing in the dock alongside him at the Old Bailey.' And with that fallacious threat, the DDI turned and left the anguished landlord wringing his hands in despair. Marriott stared briefly at Fowler, scribbled a few lines in his pocketbook as if noting his description, and followed.

* * *

'Bugger the Kaiser,' said an exasperated Hardcastle, once he and Marriott were back at Cannon Row police station. 'If it hadn't been for that bloody Zeppelin, we'd've had North locked up here.'

'He could be anywhere now, I suppose, sir,' said Marriott, declining to point out that he and Hardcastle had left by half past eleven, and would have missed North anyway. 'D'you think he'll have risked going back to Flavell Road?'

'Not in a million years, Marriott. He'll lie low until he thinks the heat's off. Well, I've got news for him. The heat ain't going to be off until I've felt the bugger's collar. Not if it takes every man jack of the Metropolitan Police to find him.'

And that, Marriott knew to be true. 'He's been circulated in the *Police Gazette*, sir.'

'And he might even get arrested if some of these idle detectives ever bother to read the bloody thing and get off their arses,' muttered Hardcastle. He glanced at the calendar on his desk. 'We'll wait and see, Marriott. There's no point in running about if North's looking for somewhere to rest his head.' He laughed. 'Must've been a bit of a setback having his lodgings blown to smithereens by old Fritz. Oh, to hell with it. We'll go down to Kingston on Monday and put Beach the butler through the mangle. I'm sure he knows more than he's telling, and it's time we had a go at the precious Lady Rivers, too. If her old man's short of somewhere to kip, he might just have asked her for a bed.'

On the morning of Saturday the first of July, Hardcastle was eating breakfast at home, a copy of the *Daily Mail* propped against a sauce bottle in front of him.

But on the other side of the English Channel, in trenches facing the battleground of the Somme, soldiers were waiting apprehensively.

The sergeants had dispensed liberal measures of rum to their men. The assault ladders were in place. Subalterns were at the centre of their platoons, men spaced evenly on either side of them, waiting. At exactly seven thirty the officers blew long whistle blasts and led the unwilling infantrymen, laden with sixty pounds of encumbering equipment, impeded by bayonet scabbards, helves of entrenching tools banging their legs, out of the trenches.

It was then that the Maxims started their deathly chatter. Men froze; men screamed; men fell, pitching forward on to their knees, faces against the mud, dead, and ludicrous even in the posture of death.

The soldiers stumbled forward, mud clawing at their feet, flashes blinding them, smoke choking them, noise deafening them. Some were caught on the uncut wire, helplessly trapped until a merciful death came for them. The shells above them travelled so fast they created a vacuum in their wake, sucking the air back with terrifying inhuman gasps.

A running figure came out of the gloom, a lad of eighteen, rifle abandoned, arms waving, white face working with terror. His mouth was open as if he were screaming, but it was unheard against the noise of the attack. The boy's officer pointed his revolver at the crazed, running figure. Then it fell.

The advancing men were falling like corn before a scythe. Explosions covered them in mud, throwing them sideways. The assault faltered and the lines of soldiers broke. First in ones and twos, then in tens and twenties, the few survivors retreated to the trenches they had so recently left.

On Monday morning, the nation learned of the disastrous attack at the Somme. By nightfall, the British had suffered 58,000 casualties, of which 19,000 men lay dead.

On the previous Saturday evening, General Sir Henry Rawlinson, commanding Fourth Army, had stared unbelieving at the statistics that staff officers were constantly bringing up to date.

'You sent for me, sir?' Brigadier General Ewart Rivers entered Rawlinson's office in the chateau that was his headquarters, and saluted.

Rawlinson looked up, an exhausted expression on his face. 'Sit down, Ewart.' He crossed to a table and poured a substantial measure of the fine cognac with which the chateau was provided. Handing it to his subordinate, he sat down opposite him. 'I'm afraid I've bad news, Ewart.'

A young staff captain entered the room, clutching a sheaf of papers.

Rawlinson looked at him with an expression of annoyance on his face. 'Leave those and get out,' he snapped.

'If you're going to tell me we've as good as been pushed back to the start line, sir, I know,' said Rivers.

'That's bad enough, Ewart, but it's personal.'

Rivers tensed, guessing the worst. He took a sip of brandy, but remained silent.

'I'm afraid your brother Gerard's been killed,' said Rawlinson. 'He was leading his battalion, and was cut down by machine-gun fire. I'm told he didn't suffer.' The GOC hurried on in an attempt to stem any response from his staff officer. 'There's hardly any of his chaps left. According to the latest figures,' he continued, waving a hand at the pile of signal forms on the map table, 'only seven officers and thirty-seven other ranks of the Third Surrey Rifles survived. The battalion was decimated.' The general paused. 'Along with a hell of a lot of other units,' he added gloomily.

Hardcastle was unaware of Gerard Rivers's death until he arrived at The Grange on Kingston Hill at eleven o'clock on the Monday morning.

A sombre Beach opened the door. 'Good morning, sir.'

'Morning, Beach.' Hardcastle noticed, but did not comment upon, the fact that the butler was wearing a black armband, hardly visible against the black vicuña of his formal tailcoat. He also noted that it was not a sign of mourning that Beach had worn following the death of Sir Adrian Rivers.

'You'll be wishing to see her ladyship, I presume, sir.'

'Not at the moment, Beach. It's you I want to talk to.'

'Just as well, sir. Her ladyship has retired to her boudoir on account of having received some distressing news.'

'Really? What news is that, exactly?'

'Colonel Gerard has been killed on the Somme, sir. He was in action with his battalion on the first of July – last Saturday, sir – and died very soon after the attack began.'

'I'm sorry to hear that,' said Hardcastle, but his real concern was to wonder how, if at all, the death of Gerard Rivers would affect his enquiries into the murder of Gerard's father.

'General Ewart sent a telegram yesterday, sir,' continued Beach. 'Apparently the losses have been quite dreadful. They thought the German defences had been completely destroyed, but it wasn't the case.'

'Yes, I read about it in the paper,' commented Hardcastle.

'However, sir, you said you wanted to speak to me,' said Beach. 'Perhaps you'd find the morning room convenient.' And without questioning the suitability of such an arrangement, he led the way.

'When did you last see Albert North, Beach?' asked Hardcastle, once he, Marriott and the butler were seated.

Beach gazed pensively at the far wall of the morning room. 'About three days ago, sir. Yes, it was Friday. He called here to see his daughter, her ladyship, sir.'

'Did he say why he'd come?'

'No, sir.'

'Does he often call on Lady Rivers?'

'Not to my knowledge, sir. In fact, I don't recall him ever having visited before.'

'Have you any idea where he is now?' asked Hardcastle, convinced, for no good reason, that the butler was lying.

'At his home, I presume, sir. Flavell Road, Wandsworth, I believe. Were you wishing to speak to him?'

'No, Beach, I was wishing to arrest him,' said Hardcastle.

Beach raised his eyebrows in surprise. 'Arrest him, sir? Whatever for?'

'Because we found certain items of property at Flavell Road that had been stolen from here when the burglary took place.' Hardcastle had decided it was time to push Beach in the hope that he might implicate himself.

'I find that hard to believe, sir.' Beach shook his head.

'There must be some mistake. I'm sure her ladyship will be dreadfully upset at the prospect of her father being wanted by the police.'

'Probably,' said Hardcastle, but he was not convinced she would be distressed by anything that did not impinge on her own well-being. He had already concluded that Muriel, Lady Rivers, was a selfish woman whose only concern was to make life as easy as possible for herself, regardless of the feelings of others. 'In that case, I shall see her now. In her boudoir, I think you said.'

'Er, I don't think that's a very good idea, sir. Might I suggest another day perhaps? I'm not sure she's up to being interviewed right now, not with the news of Colonel Gerard's death.'

'If that's the case, Beach, she can tell me herself.' Hardcastle did not intend to brook any further obstruction from a mere servant and, accompanied by Marriott, he swept upstairs and knocked loudly on the door of Lady Rivers's bedroom.

'Come in,' came a firm voice.

'Good morning, Lady Rivers. I was sorry to hear about Colonel Gerard.' It was clumsy, but it was the best that Hardcastle, hopeless at expressing condolence, could do.

Lady Rivers ignored his words of sympathy. 'Inspector! What a surprise to see you again. Do you have some news?' She was barefooted, and wearing a loose, slipper-satin peignoir that Mrs Hardcastle, had she seen it, would undoubtedly have described as risqué. But the woman herself did not appear in the least embarrassed by her flimsy attire.

'In a manner of speaking, Lady Rivers,' said Hardcastle as he followed her through her bedroom to the sitting room on the far side. 'I'm seeking the whereabouts of your father, Albert North.'

'My father?' Lady Rivers stopped suddenly, and turned to face the two detectives. 'What on earth d'you want to speak to him for?'

'Perhaps you should sit down, Lady Rivers.' Hardcastle was going to have to tell her the whole story.

Muriel Rivers, far from being distressed, as Beach had suggested, was clearly well in control of herself, and showed no signs of grief. That, of course, was not surprising; Gerard was her stepson; one she had known for only two years, and seen only rarely. She spread herself on the chaise longue in what could only be described as a seductive pose, her legs crossed at the ankles.

'Well?' Sir Adrian's widow stared imperiously at Hardcastle.

'Police officers searched your parents' house in Wandsworth on Wednesday of last week.'

'Oh? What the hell for?' This time there was an edge of hostility in the woman's voice.

Hardcastle struggled on. 'And they found your late husband's medals, and an ivory figurine.' He turned to Marriott. 'Show that thing to Lady Rivers, Marriott.'

Marriott took the ivory statuette from his briefcase and stood it on the small table near Lady Rivers's left hand. 'Do you recognize that, ma'am?' he asked.

'Of course I do. But what's the mystery?'

'It was one of the items stolen from here during the burglary when your husband was murdered, Lady Rivers.'

'What nonsense this all is.' Muriel Rivers reached across for her fan, flicked it open and waved it vigorously in front of her face. 'They were given to my father.'

'By you, Lady Rivers?' asked Hardcastle.

'No, by Beach. On my instructions.'

'How was it, then, that Beach told me that the medals had been stolen during the burglary?'

'I really have no idea, Inspector. Perhaps you should ask him. He's not very intelligent, you know, and not at all reliable. I can only assume that it was some misplaced sense of loyalty that made Adrian take him on.' It seemed that in an instant, Muriel Rivers had decided to abandon her erstwhile lover Beach, although Hardcastle only had the cook's word that Beach had enjoyed her ladyship's favours.

'That, however, does not explain why your father was in possession of several valuable items that our enquiries have shown to be the proceeds of other burglaries, Lady Rivers.' Hardcastle sat back and waited to see what she had to say about that.

'Did you ask him how he came to have them?'

'He wasn't there.'

'Then he was probably working, Inspector. As a turf accountant, he travels quite widely. But I think you must be mistaken. If you ask me, I think you'll find that Beach is at the back of all this. If anyone has been carrying out burglaries it's that wretched ex-soldier. I can assure you that my father would never get involved in anything criminal.'

'Nevertheless, Lady Rivers, it is necessary for the police to interview him, if only to clear his name.' Not that Hardcastle thought Albert North was as innocent as his daughter seemed to think. The most likely explanation was that she was shielding him. But if that were true, the reason was not immediately apparent.

'Then I suggest you go back to Wandsworth – you obviously know the address – and speak to him.'

'As I said, Lady Rivers, your father's not there. What's more, your mother has no idea where he's gone. She hasn't seen him for days. But Beach tells me he called on you here last Friday.'

'He never did no such thing,' protested Muriel Rivers, her affected accent and grammar lost in her distress. 'In fact, my father's never been here. But, as I said before, Beach is not to be trusted.'

'Very well, Lady Rivers, I shall go back downstairs now, and interview him.'

'I should hope so an' all. If you question him sufficiently, Inspector, I think you'll find that he's lying. And when you do see him, perhaps you'd be so good as to tell him he's dismissed.'

Lady Rivers's abandonment of Beach came as no surprise. Despite her carapace of pseudo-gentility, it was apparent that she possessed a self-protective core of steel.

But when Hardcastle and Marriott returned to the front hall, a shock awaited them.

Daniel Good, the chauffeur, was standing at the open front door, peering down the drive. Standing behind him was John Digby, the footman.

'Where's Beach?' demanded Hardcastle.

'He's gone, sir,' said Good, turning to face the inspector.

'Gone? Gone where?'

'I don't know, sir, but a few minutes ago, I heard the Royce being started up. The next thing I knew was that it was going down the drive at a fair gallop.'

'And was Beach driving it?'

'I think he must've been, sir,' said Good. 'He ain't anywhere in the house.'

'That's right, sir,' said Digby. 'As soon as Daniel here shouted that someone had stolen the car, I had a look for Mr Beach, to tell him, like, but there was no sign of him.'

'Get the index number from Good, Marriott, and telephone Kingston nick. Tell 'em what's happened, and get them to send out patrols. And while you're at it, tell 'em to alert surrounding stations. If they sight it, they're to stop it, and arrest Beach. And you'd better tell Wandsworth, in case he turns up at Flavell Road.' Hardcastle paused. 'And it'd be as well to remind 'em it ain't the same as stopping a runaway horse, otherwise they'll likely get themselves killed.'

While Marriott was dealing with the matter of the stolen Rolls Royce, Hardcastle went downstairs to the kitchen.

'I s'pose you've heard what Tom Beach has been up to, Mr Hardcastle,' said Martha Blunden.

'Yes, I have. Have you any idea where Beach's people live, Mrs Blunden?'

'I don't think he's got any family, Inspector. I never heard mention of any. If he has, he likely lost touch with them, being an army man.'

'Well, I'm not running after Lady Rivers's Rolls Royce, that's for sure,' said Hardcastle. 'If you've got any tea in the pot, Mrs Blunden, a cup wouldn't go amiss.'

'Of course, Mr Hardcastle. You just sit yourself down and light your pipe, and I'll get the tea mashed.'

'Kingston police are sending out a telegraph to all

stations, sir,' said Marriott, appearing in the doorway of the kitchen.

'I suppose we'll just have to wait now, then,' said Hardcastle. 'Sit down, Marriott, and have one of Mrs Blunden's splendid cups of tea.'

Seventeen

Thomas Beach's escape from Hardcastle was short-lived, due in no small part to his inability to operate the complex controls of Lady Rivers's Rolls Royce Silver Ghost. Several times he was forced to a stop while he tried to work out what to do with each of the levers and pedals.

But he did manage to reach Esher in Surrey before he was brought to an enforced standstill by a flock of sheep that was completely blocking the road.

A Surrey Constabulary policeman, PC Gaze, was standing nearby, fretting about the obstruction the shepherd and his charges were causing. But then he glanced at the expensive car, his interest aroused by its superb coachwork. Beach, however, was convinced that the constable knew the car to be stolen, and that Beach was the one who had stolen it.

Abandoning the Rolls Royce, Beach ran, and it was that foolhardy act that alerted the officer.

'Oi! Where d'you think you're going?' shouted Gaze, sprinting after Beach. 'You can't leave that there.'

As Lady Rivers's butler attempted to distance himself from the policeman, he quickly found he was no match for the much younger man. Added to which, PC Gaze was a keen rugby player, and very fit. Within seconds it was all over, with Beach hitting the ground as Gaze brought him down with the sort of classic tackle that would have merited a standing ovation from the crowds at Twickenham rugby ground.

'And what d'you think you're up to, cully?' asked Gaze as he dragged the winded Beach to his feet. Still holding his captive in a firm armlock, he probed further. 'Is that your car?'

'Not exactly, Constable. I'm chauffeur to Lady Rivers.' At once, Beach realized that that was the wrong thing to have said, but on reflection he also realized that there was no alternative.

'Is that a fact?' asked Gaze suspiciously. 'D'you always drive about in a tailcoat and striped trousers, then? Can't her ladyship afford to kit you out with the proper livery like every other chauffeur round here?'

'I can explain, constable,' gasped Beach, still attempting to regain his breath.

'You're going to have to, cully. At the police station.'

At this point, Gaze was joined by another constable. 'What you got, Ted?'

'This bloke jumped out of that Rolls there, and ran,' said Gaze. 'Do us a favour and take him into the nick while I push it to the side of the road.'

As Beach was escorted away, PC Gaze enlisted the aid of a couple of idling members of the public who had gathered to see what was happening, and together they manhandled the heavy motor car out of the way of other traffic.

It was natural enough that the apparent theft of an expensive motor car should arouse the interest of a detective at Esher police station – now joined by Gaze – and he decided to involve himself in the investigation.

'So, you reckon you're chauffeur to Lady Rivers, eh? D'you expect me to believe that?'

'It's the truth, officer. She'll vouch for me. You get in touch with her.'

'Oh, we shall, cully, don't you worry about that. Where does this Lady Rivers live?'

Reluctantly, Beach provided Lady Rivers's address, regretting that he had to do so; but not to tell the police would only make matters worse. The detective departed to make what he ominously described as 'further enquiries'.

A quarter of an hour later, the detective returned, a triumphant grin on his face. 'Lady Rivers has laid complaint that you stole her Rolls Royce, Beach, and she ain't too happy about it. But I also spoke to the Metropolitan Police at Kingston, and they told me an interesting tale.'

'They did?' said Beach lamely.

'Apparently there's a DDI Hardcastle who's very keen to have a word with you about something much more serious than nicking a Rolls Royce.'

'Oh!' muttered Beach, slumping in his chair.

'And that's a weight off my shoulders, I can tell you,' continued the detective. 'I can do without charging you with stealing a motor car, so we'll be keeping you here until an escort arrives to take you back.' He turned to PC Gaze. 'You can lock him up until the Met boys arrive, Ted,' he said.

Having been alerted to the news of Beach's arrest, Hardcastle and Marriott made their way from The Grange to Kingston police station to await his arrival.

As they walked through the town, they noticed how many people – women mainly – were attired in black mourning clothes. The losses at the Somme the previous Saturday had touched almost every family in the nation. And the East Surreys, Kingston's own regiment, had been particularly hard hit.

It was four o'clock that afternoon before two Metropolitan Police officers arrived in a van at Esher to escort Beach back to Kingston police station. And it was close to five o'clock by the time they got there.

'I can explain everything, Inspector,' pleaded Beach when Hardcastle and Marriott entered the cramped interview room.

Hardcastle laughed scornfully as he gestured to the uniformed constable to leave them alone with the prisoner. 'The first thing I have to tell you, Beach, is that Lady Rivers has given you the boot. She didn't take kindly to you nicking her Rolls. Apparently, she was about to go out for coffee with her mates,' he added, fabricating the last statement.

'She always had it in for me,' complained Beach.

'Why? Didn't you come up to snuff as a lover?'

'How did you know about ...?' spluttered Beach, but then lapsed into silence.

'I know a lot about you, Beach. For a start, what was the arrangement between you and Albert North regarding the property stolen from The Grange?'

'I don't know anything about that, and if you think you can prove I had anything to do with it, try,' sneered Beach, his butleresque servility at last abandoned.

'Where is North now?'

'No idea.' Beach had belatedly decided that there would be little profit in admitting anything.

'That's a pity,' said Hardcastle, 'because it means that I shall charge you with receiving stolen property, and you'll stand trial on your own.'

'It was Muriel,' Beach blurted out.

'Oh, so it's Muriel now, is it?' Hardcastle took out his pipe and began slowly to fill it, all the time gazing at the discomfited ex-butler. 'And what was it that Muriel did?'

'She killed Sir Adrian.'

Hardcastle burst out laughing. 'Did you hear that, Marriott?' he asked, making no secret of what he thought of that allegation. 'Make a note in your pocketbook, quickly before you forget. Beach here has solved the crime for us. Lady Rivers murdered her husband.'

'It's true,' protested Beach.

'Really?' Hardcastle leaned forward menacingly. 'Are you seriously suggesting that Lady Rivers calmly walked across the landing to Sir Adrian's room in the middle of the night, and shot him? And where did she get the revolver, eh?'

'From Daniel Good,' said Beach, a little too quickly.

'She told you that, did she? And how did she know Good had a revolver? Was she in the habit of bedding him as well as you? No, you'll have to think again, Beach, because I ain't buying it.'

'It's true,' said Beach again, but his statement lacked conviction.

'I don't believe a word of it, Beach, but now that you've raised the suggestion, I'll have no option but to question her ladyship about it. However, I'm interested to know how Sir Adrian's medals and the ivory statuette managed to get from The Grange to 22 Flavell Road, Wandsworth, which, as you well know, is where Honest Albert North lives. And how some of the other gear fetched up with a couple of shady pawnbrokers called Joseph and Benjamin Levy.' Hardcastle held up a hand as Beach was about to speak. 'But I'm sure North will tell us when we find him. On the other hand, Lady Rivers now says that she instructed you to hand those items of property to her father, the selfsame Albert North, so it seems they weren't nicked at all.'

'That's a lie,' protested Beach. 'She never said any such thing. I don't know how they got to her father's place. I reckon she gave them to him after she'd killed Sir Adrian.'

Hardcastle shook his head wearily. 'You'll have to do better than that, Beach,' he said, 'because the evidence indicates otherwise. Put him down, Marriott. We'll resume our little chat after we've had a word with Lady Rivers.'

John Digby opened the door. 'Good evening, sir.'

'Evening, Digby. Have you been appointed butler now that Beach has got his marching orders?'

'Yes, sir. Her ladyship very kindly offered me the post.'

'No more than you deserve, Digby. Where is Lady Rivers?'

'This way, sir.' Digby crossed the hall and opened the door of the drawing room. 'Inspector Hardcastle, m'lady,' he announced.

'Do come in, Inspector.' Muriel Rivers glanced at her newly promoted butler. 'Thank you, John.' Now that Digby had been promoted, he was apparently entitled to have her ladyship use his Christian name.

'Beach has been arrested, Lady Rivers,' said Hardcastle.

'What about the car?' Muriel Rivers seemed more concerned about her precious Rolls Royce than she did about the fate of her former butler, which, in Hardcastle's view, was in character.

'It's at Esher police station, safe and undamaged, ma'am. Perhaps you could arrange for Good to go down there and collect it.'

'I shall certainly do that, Inspector. I must say the police was very prompt in finding it. Tell me, is there a police charity what I can make some contribution to?' Once again, Lady Rivers's grammar was less than perfect. Hardcastle attributed it to nervousness, and wondered whether there was any truth in Beach's assertion that she had killed her husband.

'It was a Surrey Constabulary officer who arrested Beach, and took the motor car to the station, ma'am. I'll make some enquiries to see if they have some suitable fund. Usually there's something established for the welfare of the widows and orphans of policemen.'

'I'm most grateful, Inspector.'

'There is, however, another matter that I have to put to you, Lady Rivers.'

'And what is that, Inspector?' Again there was that imperious lift of the chin. Since becoming Lady Rivers, the bookmaker's daughter had obviously picked up a few mannerisms from the more refined of her newly acquired friends.

'I questioned the man Beach earlier today, and he alleges that it was you who murdered your husband.' It was a bald statement, but Hardcastle had made it intentionally so, in order to see what sort of reaction it would produce. And it produced the one he expected.

Muriel Rivers threw back her head and laughed. 'I've never heard anything so ridiculous in my life, Inspector.'

'Nevertheless, ma'am, in a serious case I am duty-bound to follow up any allegation, however unlikely it might sound.'

'Well, Inspector, I can assure you I did not murder my husband.' Muriel Rivers paused while she picked a minute piece of fluff from the front of her crêpe de Chine skirt. 'I think you will find that Beach was responsible.'

'What makes you say that, Lady Rivers?'

There was a further pause while Muriel Rivers gathered her thoughts. 'I really can't believe he would have done it, but some time ago – shortly after Adrian and I were married – Beach came to me with a proposition that he should murder my husband. Actually, the phrase he used was "get rid of him". I dismissed it as fantasy, but he said that if he

did so, we could then share the proceeds of Adrian's legacy.'
She laughed. 'The audacity of the man.'

'Why didn't you mention this before, Lady Rivers?' asked
Marriott. 'It might have saved us a lot of time.'

'As I said, Sergeant, I dismissed it as fantasy, and I didn't
want to waste your time. I really thought he was making a
rather crude joke.'

'Perhaps you didn't mention it, Lady Rivers, because you
were having an affair with Beach,' said Hardcastle, and
waited for the spirited denial that he was certain his allegation would bring.

But Muriel Rivers merely smiled. 'Perfectly true,
Inspector. I'm a healthy young woman, and I have normal
appetites. I'm afraid that Adrian – who was nearly twice
my age – just wasn't up to it. Beach was available, and I
took advantage of him.' She laughed again. 'Don't look so
shocked, Inspector. It happens all the time. Even among the
aristocracy,' she added, somewhat presumptuously.

Hardcastle stood up. 'I think that'll be all for the time
being, Lady Rivers. I will have to see you again, of course.'

'Of course, Inspector,' said Muriel Rivers, smiling at
Hardcastle's obvious discomfiture.

'And should your father contact you, I'd be grateful if
you would advise me, ma'am.'

'I doubt he will, Inspector. My father doesn't exactly
approve of me.'

That came as no surprise to Hardcastle.

At nine o'clock, Hardcastle and Marriott returned to
Kingston police station.

'Get Beach brought up,' snapped the DDI at the sergeant
on duty.

When Beach was escorted into the interview room, he
appeared tired and dishevelled, and looked rather ridiculous in the morning dress that he was, perforce, still wearing.
'What now?' he demanded truculently.

'I'm sick and tired of being jigged around by the likes
of you, Beach. Sit down. I've been to see Lady Rivers and
she denies absolutely having anything to do with the death

of her husband. In fact, she told me that you'd offered to kill him in exchange for a share in the old man's legacy.'

'Nonsense,' said Beach, forcing an unconvincing laugh.

'She said she didn't tell me about it because she was sharing her bed with you.'

'So what?'

'It's true then.'

'Of course it is. It started not long after she was wed to Sir Adrian. Quite blatant about it, she was. It was one evening, just after I'd served her dinner. She was dining alone as she usually did, on account of Sir Adrian taking his meals in his room, and she said she wanted to see me in her bedroom at midnight. She said I was to be discreet because she didn't want any of the other servants to know what was going on.'

'So, like the good butler you were, you did as you were told.'

'Of course I did,' replied Beach smugly. 'I'd've been mad to refuse an offer like that. Her ladyship's a lively young filly when she gets between the sheets, I can assure you.'

'So there's no truth in her allegation that you suggested murdering Sir Adrian and splitting the proceeds of his will with her.'

Beach scoffed at the idea. 'No, there isn't. But she did sort of hint at it herself. She said everyone would be better off if Sir Adrian snuffed it. So it came as no surprise when he was found murdered. It's obvious it was her ladyship who did it.'

'Right!' Hardcastle smote the tabletop with the flat of his hand, and stood up. 'I've had enough of this. Tomorrow morning, I'm charging you with the murder of Sir Adrian Rivers. Along with Lady Rivers who I'm about to take into custody. The pair of you can fight it out at Surrey Assizes.'

John Digby was alarmed at the police calling at gone ten o'clock. 'Her ladyship's retired for the night, sir,' he said.

'Has she really? Well, you can tell her ladyship that Divisional Detective Inspector Hardcastle is here and needs to see her immediately.'

'Well, I don't know, sir.' Caught between a clearly enraged police officer on the one hand, and a fickle, demanding mistress on the other, Digby dithered.

'Just do it, Digby,' ordered Hardcastle. 'I'm in no mood to be buggered about. I'll be in the drawing room. You can tell Lady Rivers to join me there.'

'Very good, sir.' The unhappy Digby mounted the stairs, and Hardcastle and Marriott adjourned to the morning room.

'Is this wise, sir?' asked Marriott, caution evident in his voice.

'Is what wise?' demanded Hardcastle.

'Taking the widow of a baronet into custody, sir, especially at this time of night. I'm sure she'll have powerful friends.'

'I don't give a fig what time it is, Marriott, or who her friends are, and as far as I'm concerned arrests for murder don't take account of a ticking clock.'

Five minutes later, Lady Rivers swept into the room, wearing the same slipper-satin peignoir that she had worn that morning.

'This is outrageous,' she exclaimed. 'What the bloody hell's the meaning of this? Surely it can't be anything that couldn't have waited until tomorrow.'

Hardcastle was not in the least cowed by Muriel Rivers's outburst, but was inclined to proceed with caution nonetheless. 'I have it in mind to charge you with the murder of your late husband, Lady Rivers,' he said.

Muriel Rivers sat down on a sofa, and crossed her legs, displaying a trim ankle as she did so. 'I'm afraid you'd be making a terrible mistake, Inspector,' she said with a smile. 'I've already told you it's nonsense.'

'Is that so? Well, I've already decided to charge Beach, and like I told him, the pair of you can fight it out in court.'

'Oh dear!' The baronet's widow extended an elegant forefinger in the direction of a silver box on a side table. 'Sergeant Marriott, I wonder if you'd be so good as to pass me that cigarette box.'

Marriott opened the box and offered it to the woman, at the same time producing a box of matches.

'Thank you. I don't often indulge, but it seems to me that this could be a fairly long conversation. Do sit yourselves down, gentlemen. May I send for a drink for you?'

'No thank you, ma'am.' Even Hardcastle was taken aback by the woman's composed reaction to his intention of charging her with a felony that could result in her being hanged.

Muriel Rivers exhaled a puff of smoke. 'I didn't think I'd have to say this, Inspector, and even now it pains me to have to do so, but I was with a man for the whole of the night that Adrian was murdered.'

'Were you indeed?' said Hardcastle sceptically. 'Where, might I ask?'

Muriel Rivers laughed, a gay deprecating laugh. 'Here, of course. In my bed. Where else would you expect me to be?'

'And who was this man?'

'I was afraid you were going to ask that.' Muriel Rivers leaned across and stubbed out her half-smoked cigarette in a pewter ashtray. 'He's a married man, Inspector. In fact, he's married to a very good friend of mine, and it would be awfully embarrassing were he to be brought into this sordid business.'

'In that case, I'll put it to you like this, Lady Rivers,' said Hardcastle, now on firmer ground. 'Either you tell me who he is, so that I can interview him discreetly, or you'll be obliged to reveal your alibi to the assize judge. If you want to save your neck, that is.'

'Oh, what a bloody nuisance!' exclaimed Lady Rivers, surprising Hardcastle yet again with her coarse language. In his experience, ladies, particularly titled ones, did not swear. But then he recalled that Mrs Blunden had said that her ladyship was no lady. 'His name's Ralph Barker.'

'And where does he live?'

Even then it appeared that Muriel Rivers was reluctant to reveal the whereabouts of her lover, but then she relented. 'Not far from here. It's a house called Fir Tree Cottage – although it's quite a large house – just down Kingston Hill. But perhaps you would use your discretion and interview him at his place of work. I'm not quite sure what he does, but I know he makes a lot of money doing it. Something to do with aeroplanes, I believe. He works at an office on the edge of town, but I'm not sure where.'

'I'll find it,' said Hardcastle, almost certain it was the aircraft factory that he had heard mentioned before. He realized this was a delicate situation, and did not want to become embroiled in some matrimonial dispute by blundering into the man's house when his wife would most certainly be there.

'Who let this Mr Barker into the house, Lady Rivers?' asked Marriott. 'Not Beach, surely?'

'I did, Sergeant. I had told him to wait until after the servants had gone to bed, and to arrive at exactly midnight, and not under any circumstances to ring the doorbell.' Muriel Rivers smiled at her little deception. 'I was waiting in the hall for him, and took him straight upstairs to my bedroom.'

'And what time did he leave?' asked Hardcastle.

'At five o'clock the following morning. I let him out. You see, Inspector, servants do tend to gossip, and the last thing Ralph and I wanted was to be at the centre of some terrible scandal.'

'How did he explain his absence to his wife, then?' Hardcastle was sceptical about the whole story.

'He travels a lot in his business, Inspector, and often has to spend the night away from home. It's surprising how the war effort can be made an excuse for all manner of things.' Muriel Rivers smiled at the DDI, apparently willing him to see nothing wrong in her sexual adventures.

'Very well, Lady Rivers, I'll check your story, but be sure that unless Mr Barker confirms that this meeting took place, I shall be back to arrest you.'

'Oh, he'll confirm it all right, Inspector.' Lady Rivers gave a gay little laugh. 'Ralph enjoys our little trysts too much for them to cease. And if he denies spending the night with me, cease they will. And now, gentlemen, if you have nothing further, I'll bid you good night.' With that, she stood up and floated gracefully from the room. 'John will see you out,' she said, over her shoulder.

'I don't know, Marriott,' said Hardcastle. 'This is a right dog's dinner.' And giving up all hope of finding a taxi at that time of night, the two detectives set off to walk through Wolverton Avenue to the railway station.

Eighteen

Despite having arrived home in Kennington at gone midnight, Hardcastle still managed to get to Kingston police station by half past eight the following morning. But Marriott, ever chary of accusations of lateness, was there before him, even though his wife Lorna had complained bitterly at having to prepare breakfast at such an unearthly hour.

By a quarter past nine, the two detectives were being shown into Ralph Barker's workmanlike office at the aircraft factory in Canbury Park Road.

Barker – at forty years of age, a senior executive – was a tall, elegant man, attired in a well-cut three-piece suit, with a gold Albert stretched between his waistcoat pockets. His moustache was neatly trimmed, and his hair, greying slightly at the temples, was pomaded flat to his head.

'I'm Divisional Detective Inspector Hardcastle of the Whitehall Division, sir, and this is Detective Sergeant Marriott.'

'And to what do I owe the pleasure, Inspector?' asked Barker, exuding confidence as he crossed the room with an outstretched hand.

'A delicate matter, sir,' said Hardcastle, as he and Marriott accepted Barker's invitation to sit down.

'It'll concern national security, you being from Whitehall, I suppose?' Barker offered cigarettes, which the two officers refused. 'We pride ourselves here that we keep our secrets secret.'

'Do you, sir?' commented Hardcastle drily. 'No, this is not a matter of national security; it concerns Lady Rivers.'

'Oh!' Barker fitted a cigarette to an amber holder, and

sat down behind his desk. 'How can I assist you? I know she's suffered a grievous loss. You see, Inspector, Lady Rivers and my wife Barbara are very good friends.'

'And you're quite friendly with Lady Rivers yourself, sir, so she told me.'

'Oh, she told you that, did she?' Barker's initial confidence began to ebb, and he played briefly with a letter opener.

'She also told us that you spent the night of Monday the fifth of June with her.'

'I don't really see that that is any of your business, Inspector.'

Hardcastle chose to ignore Barker's warning. 'That, of course, was the night Sir Adrian Rivers was murdered in his bed, as I'm sure you know.'

Barker took a gold watch from his waistcoat pocket and glanced at it; a hint perhaps that he had another appointment, and was more than anxious to close this interview. 'I hope you're not suggesting that I had anything to do with that dreadful affair, Inspector,' he said, as he returned the watch to his pocket.

'Did you?' asked Hardcastle, just to see what the man's reaction would be.

'Certainly not. I hope that Muriel – er, Lady Rivers – is not suggesting otherwise.'

'Not at all, sir, but an allegation has been made that it was Lady Rivers herself who murdered her husband. She, of course, denies it, but I'm obliged to investigate that charge.'

'I don't know who told you that, Inspector, but it's a preposterous allegation. Quite without foundation.'

'How can you be so sure, Mr Barker?'

Barker sighed deeply. 'Because, as you said, I was in bed with her from midnight until about five o'clock the following morning.' He made the admission quietly, and with an obvious and embarrassed reluctance.

Although Hardcastle had been told this by Muriel Rivers, he was bound to verify what she had claimed. 'But how did that come about, sir?' he asked, with feigned innocence. 'Lady Rivers has a house full of servants. How did you manage to gain entry, and then leave again some five hours later without being seen? I'm presuming you weren't seen.'

Barker shook his head wearily, as it obviously began to dawn upon him that his pleasurable night of adultery had resulted in unforeseen complications; complications that could prove costly if his wife ever got to hear of them. 'Lady Rivers told me to arrive at precisely midnight, and was waiting in the hall to admit me. And then at five o'clock, she escorted me downstairs and let me out. I'm sure we weren't seen by the servants.'

Hardcastle did not much care whether the servants had seen them or not. 'I presume you walked to and from Fir Tree Cottage, then.'

Barker raised his eyebrows in surprise. 'How d'you know where I live, Inspector?'

'Lady Rivers told me.'

'Did she, be damned.' Barker seemed to be rapidly coming to the conclusion that it had been a mistake to embroil himself with the amorous Lady Rivers. He was, after all, a married man, whereas Muriel was a widow – although she had not been at the time – and could take whomsoever she wished to her bed. At that moment, he decided that Muriel Rivers was a dangerous woman to know, and it would perhaps be better if he were not to risk seeing her again. And given the careful arrangements she had made to admit him to The Grange, he wondered how many other men had been let into the house with similar precautions. 'Have you discovered who killed Sir Adrian, Inspector?' he asked, in an attempt to divert the DDI's incisive questioning.

'Not yet, sir.' Hardcastle chose not to reveal that Beach was his principal suspect. 'But I shall.' He reached across for Marriott's pocketbook and flicked it open, more to check his sergeant's notes than to verify what Barker had said. 'So, Mr Barker, you were in bed with Lady Rivers from just after midnight until about five.'

'Correct.'

'Did Lady Rivers leave you at any time between your arrival and departure?'

'No, she didn't.'

'And would you be prepared to swear to that in court, sir?' Hardcastle returned Marriott's pocketbook, and gazed intently at the man opposite him.

Barker started back in alarm. 'Good God, I hope there'll be no need for me to give evidence.' He paused. 'Will there?'

'That depends,' said Hardcastle.

'Upon what?' Barker could already visualize his marriage, and his standing in the community, in tatters.

'Did you perhaps hear anything untoward during the night, sir?' asked Marriott, glancing up from his pocket-book.

'Untoward? What d'you mean exactly?'

'Like the sound of a gunshot.'

'No, Sergeant, I didn't. I was rather distracted at the time.' Barker had the good grace to smile, albeit weakly.

'Very well, Mr Barker,' said Hardcastle. 'My sergeant will now take a statement from you setting out what you've just told me about spending the night of the fifth of June last with Lady Rivers.'

'Out of the question,' protested Barker, having no desire to commit an account of his indiscretion to paper.

'Failing that,' said Hardcastle, as if Barker had not spoken, 'I shall arrange to have you subpoenaed if I decide to charge Lady Rivers with her husband's murder.'

Ralph Barker could obviously see the sense in not having to submit the sordid details of his liaison to the public glare of a murder trial – particularly as it would be held here in Kingston – and capitulated. The *Surrey Comet*, Kingston's local paper, in particular would make a meal of it, and he could visualize the headlines already. 'If you insist, Inspector, but I hope you'll use your discretion. If this were to get out, my wife would undoubtedly divorce me.'

'I've no doubt she would, sir,' murmured Hardcastle. 'No doubt at all. But you can rely on me.'

* * *

Still chuckling at the embarrassment he had caused Ralph Barker, Hardcastle returned to Kingston police station.

'Sir.' Alerted to Hardcastle's arrival, Detective Sergeant Atkins met him in the front office.

'I thought you'd retired, Atkins,' said Hardcastle.

'No, sir.' In the face of Hardcastle's sarcasm, to which, unlike the Cannon Row men, he was unaccustomed, Atkins confined himself to a simple negative. 'There's a telegraph from the police at Wandsworth, sir.'

'Oh? And what do they have to say?'

'They've arrested an Albert North, sir,' said Atkins, glancing at the message form in his hand. 'I'm told you have an interest in the man.'

'Yes, I do. How did they manage to capture him, then?'

'According to DS Grimes – who sent this message, sir – they set up an observation on North's house. He returned home at six o'clock this morning. He's now in custody at Wandsworth nick, sir, charged with receiving stolen property.'

'Excellent,' said Hardcastle, rubbing his hands together.

Hardcastle and Marriott mounted the steps of the police station in Wandsworth High Street, and made their presence and their business known to the station officer.

'I'll show you to the interview room, and have North brought up from the cells, sir,' said the sergeant.

'What's that bloody awful smell?' asked Hardcastle, sniffing noisily.

The sergeant smiled. 'It's the horses, sir. We've got a Mounted Branch section here. Their stables is out the back. Not that there's many of 'em left. When the war started, the army took most of the mounts.' He scoffed. 'Still thinking about having cavalry charges across the trenches, I wouldn't wonder.'

When North was brought into the interview room, wearing the same loud, checked suit in which Hardcastle had first seen him, he stared at the DDI.

'We've met before, guv'nor,' he said.

'Yes, we have. At Hurst Park about three weeks ago. But, as a matter of interest, where have you been since then?

You see, we went down to Woolwich to have a word with you, but we found your mate Joe Fraser and his missus had got killed when a bomb wiped out their house at 12 Nelson Street.'

'Yeah, I heard. Dreadful business. But I want to know why I've been arrested,' complained North. 'The rozzers who nabbed me said something about stolen property.'

'If you've done nothing wrong, why did you tip off Sid Fowler at the Goose and Duck to tell everyone, including a reporter, that you'd got your come-uppance in that raid?'

'Thought it might keep the heat off while I got things sorted,' said North lamely.

Hardcastle laughed. 'Yes, well, whatever. But I'm not much interested in that,' he said. 'Except for your late son-in-law's medals, and an ivory statuette that went missing at the time of his murder, and which we found at your house.'

'Muriel give 'em me,' said North without hesitation. 'Leastways, she sent Tom Beach down with 'em, and said I was to have 'em.'

'When?' asked Hardcastle.

North leaned back and stared at the ceiling. 'Must have been a couple of days after the old boy was done in, I reckon,' he said, leaning forward again. 'Tom said as how she had no further use for 'em, and would I like 'em.'

'Did you ever ask your daughter if she'd sent them?'

'Well, no. Why should I?'

'Because I don't think she did, North. General Ewart Rivers was Sir Adrian's son and heir. If anyone should've had his medals, it should have been him.'

'Ah, I never thought of that,' said North, running a hand round his chin. 'Yeah, you're right, guv'nor.'

'I am about most things,' commented Hardcastle, a statement that drew a nod of agreement from Marriott. 'Last time we spoke, you said you knew Beach before your daughter got wed to Sir Adrian.'

'S'right, I did. Great one for the horses, was Tom Beach.'

'Now listen carefully to what I'm going to say next, North, because your neck might depend on it.'

Albert North obviously did not much care for the sound of that, and leaned forward, devoting all his attention to the abrasive detective opposite him.

'Sir Adrian, who'd been widowed for ten years, was a great racing man, so you said, and was often at Epsom. Isn't that so, North?'

'That's right, he was.'

'And Beach told you one day that Sir Adrian was going a bit doolally-tap. He then went on to suggest that if your daughter, who, I have to say, is a handsome woman, was to make his acquaintance, the old boy might be tempted to marry her. From what I've heard, Sir Adrian always had an eye for a pretty woman. Once he'd snuffed it, Muriel, Beach and you would share his legacy, provided Sir Adrian's two sons could somehow be cut out of the will. And, of course, they were. But now we come to the murder. Sir Adrian Rivers didn't die quickly enough, and so you, your daughter and Beach decided to speed things up, so to speak.'

'Now hang on, guv'nor . . .'

'And that, North, amounts to conspiracy to commit murder. Which means that all three of you could be taking the eight o'clock walk.' Hardcastle sat back and gazed at North. 'Not all together, of course. You and Beach would likely have your necks stretched at Wandsworth or Wormwood Scrubs, but your darling daughter'd be topped at Holloway.' None of that was true, of course; conspiracy to murder carried a maximum of ten years penal servitude. But Hardcastle deemed it unnecessary to mention it.

Sweat broke out on North's face, his chest heaved, and he began to suck in air so violently that he was showing signs of a heart attack.

'Loosen his collar, Marriott, and give him a drink of water,' said Hardcastle mildly, half convinced that North was play-acting. 'Although it won't hurt for him to get used to having something tight round his neck.'

Marriott skirted the table and pulled off North's tie and tore his collar away from its stud, before pouring a mug of water from the jug that was kept on a shelf in the interview room.

'You've got it all wrong, guv'nor,' muttered North, once he had begun to recover. 'It wasn't like that at all.'

'Then perhaps you'd better tell me how it really was.'

'See, Tom Beach was into me for quite a few quid, and . . .'

'How much?'

North did some quick mental arithmetic. 'About two hundred, guv'nor.'

'*You let him run up gambling debts of two hundred pounds?*' asked Hardcastle incredulously. He had never before come across a bookmaker as generous as this one.

'Yeah, well, stupid of me really, I s'pose, but he was a mate, after all. Any road, I knew he often come down Epsom along with the family – Sir Adrian's family, I mean – and I told him it would be very handy if he could sort of fix for the old boy to meet our Muriel. If he could pull that off, Muriel'd be able to persuade her husband to part with enough cash to settle Tom's debt. And that's how it happened. They come down Epsom just before the war started, and Tom told Muriel to sit on the grass next to 'em. Well, I never thought it'd work out, but the minute old Sir Adrian set eyes on my girl, she romped home, as we say in the racing game. The next thing I knew was that Tom coughed up all he owed me.'

'You expect me to believe that?' asked Hardcastle, although he was sure it was the truth.

'On my life, guv'nor, that's all there was to it. Like you said, it was well known that Sir Adrian had an eye for a bit of fluff. Never could resist a pretty woman.' North lowered his voice. 'I shouldn't never say this about me own daughter, but Muriel was always one to lie back and think of England if the geezer on top of her was worth it, so to speak.'

Hardcastle stood up. 'Get the gaoler in here, Marriott. He can take the prisoner away. You'll be charged with receiving stolen property, North, but as I said that's a matter for the local police. Meantime, I have to work out which of you three to charge with murder . . . and which with conspiracy. Not that it makes much difference.'

North stood up too. 'If it's any help, guv'nor, I reckon it's down to Tom Beach.'

Hardcastle sat down again, and gestured at North to do the same. 'Why d'you say that?'

'He told me once that he knew the chauffeur had got a gun – Dan Good, his name was – and reckoned it'd be a simple thing to do poor old Sir Adrian one night. He said he'd take a few things to make it look like a burglary. Not that I thought he meant it.'

'But he did,' commented Hardcastle. 'And you were mug enough to take some of the proceeds from him when he came down to your place and pretended your daughter had sent them.'

'Yeah, wasn't too clever that, was it? And I should've known, because a few days after the murder, Tom Beach told me he'd done it. And he said he'd fixed up with Muriel to share out the old man's legacy. But that's when it all went wrong.'

'How?'

'Poor old Tom didn't know my girl as well as I do. He come to see me and said she wasn't going to play along. She told him she didn't know what he was talking about, and she wasn't sharing her fortune with him or anyone else.'

'Marriott, take a statement from North setting out all he's just said.' Hardcastle faced the bookmaker again. 'And you'll be giving evidence to that effect at Surrey Assizes when I charge Beach with the murder of Sir Adrian Rivers, North.'

Having abandoned his tailcoat, the pitiful figure of Thomas Beach shuffled into the interview room at Kingston police station in his shirtsleeves and an unbuttoned waistcoat. The gaoler had wisely confiscated Beach's tie, bootlaces, and braces, and he was obliged to hold up his trousers.

'How much longer am I going to be kept here?' he demanded.

'Until you appear before the magistrates, Beach. After that you'll be remanded in custody to Brixton prison charged with murder.'

Beach collapsed into the chair. 'What are you talking about? I never murdered anyone.'

'Oh, but you did, and I have evidence to prove it,' said Hardcastle, although he was far from certain that he had enough.

'I told you before, it was Muriel that killed him.'

'That's not what your friend Albert North said.'

'Have you found him?' Beach seemed disconcerted that the police had discovered someone he thought was well out of the way.

'Oh yes,' said Hardcastle, 'and I couldn't stop him talking.'

'What's he been saying then?' Beach began to pick nervously at a waistcoat button.

'You'll find out soon enough, Beach,' said Hardcastle. 'Once your trial starts. But I can tell you this much: Lady Rivers has a cast-iron alibi for the night of the murder. So you're going to cop it on your own.'

'It's all up, then,' said Beach miserably. 'I might've pulled the trigger, but it was Muriel who persuaded me to do it.' At once, he must have wished to God he had never said it, but Hardcastle's wry smile, and Marriott's feverish writing, told him it was too late. There was now no alternative but to finish what he was saying. 'She promised me a third of Sir Adrian's fortune. Albert was going to get another third, and Muriel'd have the rest.' He let out a long sigh. 'But once Sir Adrian was dead she said she wasn't going to give me anything.'

'You've been had, my lad,' said Hardcastle. 'But there's something else to cheer you up. According to the pathologist, Sir Adrian would only have lived another month or so at the most. He was at death's door already when you topped him.'

Beach said nothing, but just stared glumly at the table.

'I shall now charge you with the murder of Sir Adrian Rivers,' said Hardcastle, standing up.

At half past six that evening John Digby admitted Hardcastle and Marriott to The Grange.

'Is Lady Rivers at home, Digby?'

'Yes, sir. Her ladyship's in the drawing room.'

Muriel Rivers smiled at the two detectives as they were ushered in. 'Inspector, you're becoming quite a regular visitor.'

'Yes, ma'am. I have one or two questions I wish to put to you.'

'Please sit down and ask away.' Muriel Rivers lit a cigarette, and leaned back against the cushions of the settee, quite relaxed.

'But before I start, ma'am, I have to tell you that I've just charged Thomas Beach with the murder of your late husband.'

'Oh dear, how sad,' said Muriel Rivers, but she did not look sad. 'I've already made John my butler, you know. But now I shall have to find a footman to replace him. How very tiresome. It will be awfully difficult, Inspector, with so many men away at the war. You just can't get servants these days.'

Hardcastle was not surprised at the woman's casual approach to the fate of her former butler. 'I also have to tell you that your father, Albert North, is in custody at Wandsworth police station charged with receiving stolen property.'

'I find it hard to believe that he would have done such a thing, Inspector,' said Muriel Rivers, but otherwise did not seem too upset that her father was probably facing a spell in prison.

'I can assure you there's no doubt about it,' said Hardcastle.

'You said you had some questions, Inspector.' The baronet's widow dismissed the fate of her father in much the same way as she had that of Beach.

'Mr North told me, and Beach corroborated it, that the three of you were going to share the proceeds of Sir Adrian's will once Sir Adrian was dead, and that you had agreed to this arrangement.'

'What a silly thing to say. I can't imagine why either of them should have thought that.'

'Beach also told your father that he knew Daniel Good had a revolver, and knew where he kept it. He implied that Beach intended to use it to murder your husband in further-ance of this plan to share the legacy.'

Muriel Rivers laughed. 'What a funny thing to have said. I never credited Thomas with a sense of humour, Inspector. How on earth could he have imagined that I would be a party to such a frightful plan?'

'It's untrue then?'

'I'm surprised you find it necessary to ask that question, Inspector. Of course it's untrue. I would never have condoned such a thing, and neither would my father. Anyway, as I'm sure you will have confirmed by now, I was in bed with Ralph Barker practically all night.' Muriel Rivers smiled dreamily at the recollection, little knowing that Barker had already decided their occasional intimate trysts would not be repeated.

'I just wanted to clear that up,' said Hardcastle. 'In fact, Beach eventually confessed to the murder.'

The trial of Thomas Beach for the murder of Sir Adrian Rivers opened before a 'red' judge at Surrey Assizes, held in Clattern House, in High Street, Kingston, on Thursday the third of August. It was for him perhaps an unhappy coincidence that this was also the day that Roger Casement, now stripped of his knighthood, was hanged for treason at Holloway prison.

Beach pleaded not guilty, but there was little that his counsel, eloquent though he was, could do for him in the face of his client's admission to Hardcastle, and the damning evidence of Albert North.

When Muriel Rivers appeared in the witness box, she was dressed in the same black ensemble she had worn for Sir Adrian's funeral. Deploying all her feminine wiles, she immediately captivated the judge, as so many men before him had been captivated, by lifting her veil and smiling fetchingly at him. From that moment on, his lordship defended her against the more savage of the defence counsel's attacks upon her integrity.

But she needed no defending; Lady Rivers was well able to take care of herself. And Beach's barrister's suggestion that she had been party to a conspiracy to murder Sir Adrian, and had promised to share the legacy, was met with scornful dismissal.

Within an hour the jury returned a verdict of guilty. In a solemn and hushed courtroom, the judge donned his black cap and passed sentence of death, and the chaplain intoned the customary plea that the Lord should have mercy on Beach's soul.

Beach's appeal was dismissed, and the Home Secretary, Sir Herbert Samuel, saw no reason to interfere with the sentence. Three weeks later the former butler was executed at Wandsworth prison.

Before that, at the Inner London Sessions, Albert North was sentenced to twelve months imprisonment with hard labour for receiving stolen property, but he did not finish his sentence. Two months later, he died of a stroke.

On Monday, the sixth of November, Marriott entered Hardcastle's office flourishing a copy of the *Daily Telegraph*. Spreading it on the DDI's desk, he pointed to the announcement that had caught his eye:

Major General Sir Ewart Rivers, DSO, MC, Bart and Muriel, Lady Rivers
The marriage took place on Saturday, November 4, 1916 at St Stephen's Church, Tolney Reach, Wiltshire, between Ewart, elder son of the late Colonel Sir Adrian and Lady Lavinia Rivers, of Kingston upon Thames and Wiltshire, and Muriel, Lady Rivers, elder daughter of the late Albert North and of Marjorie North of Wandsworth.

'Well I'm buggered,' said Hardcastle. 'She didn't waste much time. I suppose Ewart being promoted helped. And if he eventually gets to be a field marshal, he'll likely get a peerage. Muriel will love that.'

'I suppose he had to marry her to get his hands on the

money, sir,' said Marriott. 'Isn't there something in the law that says all a woman's fortune goes to her husband on marriage?'

'I thought that had been done away with,' said Hardcastle. 'I'll tell you this much though, Marriott. I'm bloody certain that what North and Beach said about her being a party to the murder, and sharing the legacy, is probably the truth. But we'll never be able to prove it now. She's a cunning little vixen is our Lady Rivers.'